THE CLIENT

A ZORIC WORLD STANDALONE

paige press

THE CLIENT

A ZORIC WORLD STANDALONE

STELLA GRAY

Paige Press
Leander, TX 78641

Ebook:
ISBN: 978-1-957647-50-0

Print:
ISBN: 978-1-957647-51-7

Editing: Erica Russikoff at Erica Edits
Proofing: Michele Ficht

ALSO BY STELLA GRAY

The Zoric Series

The Client: A Zoric World Standalone

Arranged Series

The Deal

The Secret

The Choice

The Arranged Series: Books 1-3

Convenience Series

The Sham

The Contract

The Ruin

The Convenience Series: Books 1-3

Charade Series

The Lie

The Act

The Truth

The Charade Series: Books 1-3

The Bellanti Brothers

Unwilling Bride: A Bellanti Brothers Novella

Dante - Broken Series

Broken Bride

Broken Vow

Broken Trust

Marco - Forbidden Series

Forbidden Bride

Forbidden War

Forbidden Love

Armani - Captive Series

Captive Bride

Captive Rival

Captive Heart

ABOUT THIS BOOK

When I won the modeling contest, I lost my freedom.

KZ Modeling owns my body.

But they're willing to rent it out.

The first time I learn my fate and I'm auctioned off changes everything.

Because it's also *my* first time.

And the gorgeous, haunted billionaire who now wants exclusive rights to me for the next six months?

He has no idea I can't say no.

But the real shock is discovering I don't want to.

PROLOGUE

RHYS

Tonight, my father has spared no expense showcasing what a self-important asshole he is.

The private ballroom appears to have been decorated for the purpose of welcoming foreign royalty, rather than for celebrating the 55th birthday of Rupert McConnell, a middle-aged businessman with an ego problem.

There's gold and crystal everywhere, extravagant ice sculptures, champagne fountains that sport a roulette of changing colors, truffle towers on each table. There's even a literal red carpet rolled out from the entry doors to a center table, where the man himself sits like a fucking king on a throne, pretending to be engrossed in something one of his illustrious guests is saying.

But I know better.

The saccharine laughter, the meticulously groomed

charm, and the stage-worthy smile: these are the building blocks of the man my father becomes whenever he's front and center. He'll go to any length to draw attention to himself and keep it there. It's an act he's perfected over the decades, and one that people are all too quick to fall for. Why shouldn't they? He's the best bullshitter I've ever met.

Smoothing my tuxedo jacket, I pause as my palm glides over the bulge in my left pocket. Reaching inside, I touch the square box and allow myself a brief smile as I scan the sea of guests. The room is packed with gorgeous women, but there's only one I came here to see.

Celine.

If not for her, I would have stayed home tonight. She's been in her native Paris for two weeks visiting family, the longest we've been apart in the year that we've been dating. I'm itching to run my fingers over her supple skin and feel the delicate arch of her hip in my palm as I pull her against me and show her off. She's the perfect glitter to my darkness and I've missed her. More than anything.

There had been little for me to cherish in my life until I met her. And if all goes well, she'll be wearing my ring before the night is over.

Fuck my father and his party. I'm not afraid to upstage him at his own shindig by proposing to my girlfriend and drawing everyone's attention to the five-carat behemoth that I'm going to slip on her finger, engraved with tonight's date. The old man can stand to share the spotlight for once in his life.

This is going to be a night to remember for me, too.

"Rhys!"

My father stands from his chair and waves me over. I turn my back to him, pretending I didn't hear his shout. As I do, a smirk springs to my face. He knows that my grandfather—his father, and the CEO of McConnell Enterprises—asked to meet with me today. There's no doubt in my mind that Dad has been stewing for hours, filled with rabid curiosity about the meeting.

If only he knew. But he won't hear a word about it. Not for another five years, when my grandfather's decree has been carried out and I take over as the new CEO, effectively skipping right over my father. Until then, Dad and I will work as equals while I'm groomed for my new role. Then I'll be in charge. Just as it should be.

The truth is, I've always served the company's best interests, while Dad has always served his own. I work hard, I maintain strong relationships with our clients, I incentivize our employees...I don't take the company jet to Vegas every other weekend to play golf and impress call girls. Apparently, this has not escaped my grandfather's notice. The fact that Dad will be getting the shaft brings me almost as much satisfaction as making Celine my wife.

Which is why I'm more than happy to put a smile on my face tonight for this party.

"*Mon chéri.*"

A shiver courses down my spine as Celine speaks softly beside me, her slender hand moving over my shoulder to rest behind my neck. My tense muscles relax with the relief only her presence can give me. I turn and our eyes lock, her ice blue meeting my own hazel brown.

Drinking her in like a man dying of thirst, I cast my greedy gaze over her statuesque body, sheathed in a silvery gray dress that fits her like a glove. Below a diamond choker, the plunging neckline shows off the inner rise of her breasts, the edge of the fabric skimming dangerously close to her nipples, which perk enticingly against the silk.

Fuck, I've missed her. Even the scent of her gardenia perfume is enough to make my cock twitch.

"Celine," I breathe as I move in to kiss her.

Her smile falters. She turns her head so my lips land on her cheek instead of her pillowy lips, then turns the other way so I can kiss her opposite cheek. How easily she's fallen back into the social etiquette of her home country.

Cupping her chin, I study her as she produces another brilliant smile, but it's her modeling smile, the exact same one I've seen on so many billboards and in magazine ads. Gleaming, beautiful, but empty, as if her thoughts are a million miles away.

Something is off.

"I've missed you, goddess," I tell her.

Stepping back, Celine bites her lip, then lowers her lashes. Is she playing coy now? My fingers clench as I refrain from driving her against the wall and crushing my lips to hers. I'd love nothing more than to drag her off right now for a quick reunion fuck in the coat closet.

"*Il faut qu'on parle*," she says. "Can we take a moment together, please?"

We need to talk.

"Yes," I agree. We certainly have a lot to discuss.

Not only do I need to know what's bothering her, but I also need to tell her that my grandfather is handing the company over to me. In five years I'll be running a multi-billion-dollar empire. I can already see us there, holding court in a party to shame this one, accepting congratulations. All my dreams are coming true. With her at my side, I'll be unbeatable.

"*Rhys!*" my father bellows over the din.

A sigh of irritation escapes me, and Celine lets out a little laugh.

"Best do as the birthday boy asks." Running her fingers lightly over my cheek, she says, "And happy birthday yourself, *mon chéri*. He didn't forget; don't worry."

Grabbing her wrist, I turn her hand over and kiss her palm. I'm not worried that my father "forgot" that we share a birthday. I'm not worried at all, in fact. I've had a lifetime of this.

5

And now that Celine is back, I have plenty of my own ideas about how to celebrate.

Before I can share any of them with her, however, she tilts her head to tell me that my father is approaching. Then she saunters away to mingle, grabbing a glass of champagne from a passing server as she goes. God, the way she moves. Like water, like wind, like a dancer.

A harsh slap on the back rudely pulls me from my thoughts.

"Son. You made it!"

"Looks like I did," I say dryly.

He grips my shoulder tightly, steering me to the edge of the crowd.

"Is there something you want to tell me?" he asks. "Some news your grandfather may have passed along this afternoon?"

Some things about my father are predictable: an iron-clad belief in himself, for one. He thinks his father was prepping me to become his right-hand man. Luckily for the company, my grandfather isn't an idiot. Another predictable thing: good drinks, and plenty of them.

I grab a glass of scotch off a tray and take a sip. "It was a confidential meeting, so no. Is there something you want to tell *me*?" I shoot back at him. "Maybe, happy birthday, son? I couldn't help noticing my name isn't on the cake."

The light in his eyes darkens. His jaw works back

and forth while he watches me sip my drink rather than roll over and show him my belly.

"Fine," he says tersely. "I suppose we both have our secrets, don't we?"

It's a cryptic thing to say, but I don't have time to ponder it because suddenly the lights dim and a spotlight shines down onto a stage at the end of the room. Without another word, my father trots over there like a celebrity about to host a live game show, grabs a microphone that someone tosses him from the wings, and makes a grand "ta-da" gesture.

"Would you just look at this turn out tonight! I will be damned. Here I was, thinking I had no friends but the devil himself, and then you all came out to celebrate me."

He gets a round of good-natured laughter and some applause from the crowd.

"Honestly, though, from the bottom of my heart. I am so grateful for each and every one of you," he says, laying it on thick. "This is what life really is all about."

More applause, and all the while I'm cringing inside.

He yammers on some more, thanking the caterers, the live string quartet, the people who put the party together, and then takes a bow.

I roll my eyes and toss back the rest of my drink. Replacing it with a fresh flute of champagne, I search for Celine as the crowd compresses around the stage. Time for us to find a quiet corner. I want to ask her to marry me, and then get out of here. My bed has been cold for two weeks and I can't wait one more minute to see her beneath me, wearing nothing but my ring.

Spying her in a corner, I start to make my way over.

Dad's voice drones on, but I barely bother to listen. Celine grabs a fresh drink and begins moving closer to the stage...the crowd parting to either side as she moves toward the stairs and climbs up to stand next to my father.

What the fuck is she doing? I have a brief vision of her disrupting my father's speech to do a Marilyn-esque birthday song for me, but of course I haven't told her yet that I'll soon be president and CEO.

My dad looks over at Celine. The lights fall on her, making her glow, from her halo of white blonde hair to the diamond choker to the soft sheen of her silver dress.

"It may be my birthday, but there's another reason I'll never forget this night," he says.

She slips her hand into my father's.

My vision tunnels.

He pulls her in a graceful spin, so she ends up leaning back over his arm.

There's a ringing in my ears now, so loud I can barely hear anything else.

And then my father leans down and kisses Celine, full on the mouth.

I'm about to rush the stage, pull him off her, and slug him across the face, but then I see her arm wrapping around his neck, the way her eyes are closed, the way she's *kissing him back.*

Bile rises in my throat, fury scalding through my veins. My whole body goes numb. It's like I'm watching a movie of my own life.

A horror movie.

My father is speaking into the mic again, Celine's arm looped through his, her head on his shoulder, and my stomach is clenching, the room is spinning.

"There's another reason I wanted to gather all my friends and family here tonight," he's saying. "Which is to introduce you all..."

He takes a dramatic breath.

"To my new wife, as of this very morning: Celine Lefevre McConnell."

The flute falls from my hand and hits the floor, splattering glass and champagne all around me. Nobody seems to notice. Their eyes are all glued to the stage, where Celine smiles radiantly, though not quite as radiantly as the massive diamond ring that has somehow magically appeared on her left hand.

I stumble back just as my father's eyes land on mine. The glare of the lights stunts the pleasure on his face, but I see it. I feel it.

I can't even wrap my head around what just happened. The woman I've spent the last year giving myself to, the woman I was about to propose to, and he just...swooped in like a fucking monster out of a nightmare and carried her off for himself.

He's taken her from me. Taken exactly what he wants, when he wants it, without a single thought of the consequences to anyone else. Just like he always does.

Spinning on my heel, my footsteps crunching on glass and sliding on spilled champagne, I measure my steps until I'm outside, encased in cool night air. Doubling over with my hands on my thighs, I pull in hard breaths as I try to center myself. I need to calm down and get the hell out of here. I need to put this entire night behind me. Put Celine behind me.

The last year we spent together clearly meant nothing to her. How could I have been so stupid? This was a lesson I learned over and over again in my childhood.

This time, I won't let myself forget.

If I never care about anything, it won't hurt when it's taken away from me.

1

IZABELA

"You better not tell him you're a virgin, Iza."

I don't give my roommate, Diya, a response as I pull my hair into a slicked-back ponytail and double-check my makeup. She's standing close enough that I'm overwhelmed by the heavy vanilla scent of her perfume. Her worried frown is reflected at me in the mirror.

There are four of us crammed into this one-bedroom apartment, and while I'm used to cramped living spaces, the constant togetherness is stifling. Sometimes it's hard to breathe with the other girls constantly in my face with their endless chatter and gossip. It's been almost three months since I arrived in the United States, but acclimating has been difficult.

I miss my uncle's small, tidy, *quiet* farmhouse. The smell of strong, dark coffee and fresh *naleśniki* crepes filling the house every morning, the warmth of the woodstove making us sweat no matter the time of year. Pulling an old pair of my uncle's overalls over my pajamas to go out and feed the chickens, collect their eggs. A simpler life. That house was a sanctuary that I thought was stifling me, seemingly too small to hold my dreams.

And then my sister got sick. Her cries of pain and the sounds of her body constantly rejecting food and medications changed everything. My aunt and uncle were saints for taking us in after our parents died. But they hadn't signed up for the helplessness that came with my sister's sudden and devastating illness, or the cost of work lost while trying to fight the disease.

Then my dreams changed.

That's why I'm in Chicago, and I'll tolerate any amount of chaos or gossip and a true lack of personal space if it means sending them the money they need to send her here. Her doctors are doing everything they can, but everyone knows the best care in the world happens in the US.

"I'm serious," Diya prods.

She gives my shoulder a gentle but firm shake. Catching her striking green eyes in the mirror, I reapply my lip gloss and blot my lips together.

"Why would it even matter?" I ask. "I'm sure this meeting is just to check in. And it's been three months with the agency now, so maybe I'm getting a rate increase."

"Yeah, three months. That's exactly why you should be worried! Come on, Iza. Do I need to spell it out for you? Konstantin Zoric isn't calling you in himself to give you a pat on the back. Think about it. He likes Russian girls the best. *Especially* virgins. You need to be careful."

My makeup bag clanks loudly as I set it down a little too hard on the dresser. "I really don't see how my...personal situation...has anything to do with my job. All I do is stand there and look pretty. And for the last time—I'm Polish, not Russian."

She gives me a sympathetic smile. "Same thing to them, right? You're tall, beautiful, blonde, and you have an accent. That's all that matters to them."

Ever since I won an international modeling contest hosted by KZ Modeling three months ago, it seems people have been warning me about one thing or another. Don't eat too much. Don't work out too much. Never show up late for a shoot. And the one most often on repeat: you're going to have to sleep your way to the top, because that's how the industry works. But that hasn't been my experience at all.

When it comes to my roommates, the warnings are even more dire. The things they tell me are so genuinely shocking, I can't even believe them.

Take Diya, for example. She insists that she and several other girls were tricked into sleeping with men to get their first modeling jobs. Her harrowing tale involved being locked in a hotel suite with ten other immigrant modeling contest winners for two days with no way of communicating with the outside world while they were forced to have nude photos taken and undergo virginity exams. Those who passed as virgins were carted off, never to be seen again.

Except for Diya. She said she was auctioned off in a dim room full of older men, and that the highest bidder took her to a penthouse where he kept her tied to a bed, forcing himself on her repeatedly before having his driver drop her off here, as though returning her from a date.

The very next day, she was booked on a shoot with a fifty-thousand-dollar price tag. She netted ten grand after KZ Modeling took their cut, more money than she had ever dared to dream about in her native New Delhi. Which is exactly where she sent the money. To her mom.

I think it's all bullshit to scare me, like some kind of hazing or rite of passage. Maybe they hope I'll get scared and go back to Poland. There is a lot of competition in modeling, more than I ever could have guessed. But I signed a contract and I'm glad that I did. I've already been given over a dozen modeling assignments; no sex required.

I'm not going back. Not ever. This city is bigger than my entire world had been back home. I want to show it to my sister. I want her to get well so we can be like the tourists I watch every day out the window, laughing and taking pictures of each other, pain-free. And that only happens if I do what I'm supposed to. Keeping my head down and my eyes forward.

"What time are you supposed to meet him?" Diya asks.

I check the time. "Half an hour. I better go." It's a fifteen minute walk, and I want to be early. It shows initiative.

She sighs. "Okay. Just remember what I said, yeah?"

Assessing my appearance one last time, I begin to doubt the outfit I put together from the apartment's shared wardrobe—stylish black trousers with a matching blazer, a low-cut silk tank, and heels—but shut it down. I look professional, with just a hint of sexy. I don't need to dress for the club. This is a business meeting. Although Konstantin Zoric's assistant didn't tell me exactly why his boss wanted to meet with me. And sure, it's a little odd that the owner of the agency wants to have a one-on-one, considering I've only ever dealt with agents. But I figure it must be a good sign. Like I told Diya, it might mean a rate hike. Or a travel assignment, which pays higher and offers more exposure.

I'm not full of myself, but I know I've done a good job at the gigs I've been sent on—I take instructions well, I'm easygoing, and I've been told that the camera loves me. I'm also kind to the photographers, lighting crew, hair and makeup, the wardrobe people, and anyone else on the crew, because the reality is that taking pretty photographs is hard work, and it's a group effort that I appreciate. Surely I've made a good impression so far. Made the agency money.

A thrill goes through me at the prospect of being rewarded with something bigger.

The other girls look up from their phones as I enter the living room to grab my purse, Diya at my heels. Jackie snags my wrist from her place on the couch.

"Don't go, Iz. Call out sick. Say you have the stomach flu."

I roll my eyes. "Not you, too."

Her attention shifts to something on the TV. I look over and see footage of a man getting out of a town car and smoothing his tie with a very attractive, strong hand. The back of his dark head is turned to the camera, and then he turns and looks directly into the lens for a split second before pulling away. His golden hazel eyes smolder. He has a strong, masculine face with a square jaw. My heart flips at the sight.

"Jesus, if the guys who bought virgins looked like that guy, I'd pretend to be one again," Jackie blurts, collecting a few laughs.

"Yeah right," Diya says. "They're never hot like this guy."

"Nobody's hot like this guy," I point out.

He's exactly the kind of man that I used to think you could meet on any street corner in America...until I got here. Movies and magazines imply that all American men are handsome, successful, ambitious. That definitely hasn't been the case. Not yet.

One day I'll meet the successful, kind, honest man of my dreams.

Still staring at the screen, I read the ticker along the bottom of the image. Something about a billion-dollar acquisition and the company's young VP, rumored to be next in line for CEO. *Rhys McConnell.* A name that fits his handsome face.

"Anyway, I'm off. See you all later," I say, edging away from the couch.

Suddenly, all eyes are on me.

"You should lie," Cat says, not unkindly. "Virgins always get the most toxic men. The sick-in-the-head ones, or the violent ones. The power trip they get off on is ten times worse."

"She can't lie," Jackie cuts in. "They'll know."

"They're not going to know," Cat insists. "They only check you if you say you *are* a virgin. Why would they bother checking otherwise? Iza, just don't tell anyone you're a virgin and you'll have a much better experience. Trust me. And remember, it'll be over soon."

"What about that girl Anja?" Jackie says. "She wasn't—"

"Shut up, Jackie," Diya says, shutting her down. "We don't talk about that."

The room goes silent, the tension thickening.

Slinging the strap of my purse over my shoulder, I stride to the door and duck out before anyone can stop me. I can't be late for this meeting. My whole career might depend on it.

As I power walk to the KZM building, I can feel the anxiety racing through me. Normally, my roommates' chatter rolls off my back, but something about their parting words and the dark mood is clinging to me this time.

I'm lost in my own head as I enter the lobby, and I'm about to present myself to the guard at the security desk when a man in a suit appears at my elbow, as if he's been waiting for me.

"No need to check in, Miss Jasinski," he says. "This way, please."

"And you are?" I ask.

"Mr. Zoric's assistant," he says, without offering his name.

We get into an elevator and ride silently to the top floor, which is so high up that my ears pop on the way. The door opens into an extravagant hallway with gleaming marble floors, fussy antique furniture, and gold-framed art on the walls. I catch the faintest hint of cigar smoke.

The assistant leads me to a vast room with an impressive, hulking mahogany desk in the center and three walls of floor-to-ceiling windows with a panoramic view of the city.

"Mr. Zoric, your three o'clock is here," the assistant says.

I take in the man behind the desk. Wide, powerful shoulders. Gray hair slicked back. One hand furiously writing on a notepad in front of him. Unsure if I should approach the desk or stay where I am, I look to the assistant, but he's already walking away. Leaving us alone.

I clear my throat. "It's so nice to meet you, Mr. Zoric. May I say how—"

"Sit down, Izabela."

At the sound of his voice, my stomach drops. I walk over to the leather chairs in front of his desk and lower myself into one. That's when I notice a white department store bag sitting on the floor next to his desk. There is so much tissue paper spilling out of the top that I can't see what's inside.

"Take the bag," he commands. "It's for you."

He still hasn't looked up.

Scooting a bit on the seat, I reach over and pull the bag closer. "Thank you."

"Answer me this, Izabela. Are you a virgin?"

Electric zaps race from the base of my spine to the back of my neck and grow like a predatory weed, curling and twisting. The room seems smaller suddenly, my focus hazy, as if I'm in a dream. I've misunderstood him.

That's what's happening. I didn't hear him correctly.

"I'm sorry?"

"Is that a yes or a no?"

My lower lip twitches. "Um... could you repeat the question, pl—"

His head snaps up and his impatient glare nails me to my seat. Displeasure and irritation color his features and for a slip of a moment, I fear that I'm going to be fired. My contract ripped up.

"Have you fucked before or not? That's the question."

Oh, God. Diya wasn't joking. None of them were joking. There warnings were... real.

I feel like I'm floating outside of my body as I struggle to answer. "Is this...relevant to a modeling job, Mr. Zoric?"

He smiles like I'm the tenderest of idiots who must be spoon-fed. "You didn't read the fine print on your contract before signing. Ah, well, that's your fault, not mine. It clearly states that you are legally bound to provide any and all relevant information about your body, including height, weight, medical history, and health status, and therefore you are required to answer the question. Are you a virgin or not? Because the men who are going to bid on you at the auction tomorrow night will want to know. So. Yes or no?"

The *auction*?

Diya said she was auctioned off.

Tied to a bed.

Trafficked.

The edges of my vision turn gray as the reality of the situation sinks in and a wave of nausea rolls through me.

It's my turn now.

2

IZABELA

I'm standing, though I don't recall getting to my feet. The illusion that the room is getting smaller and smaller grows tenfold. As my fight or flight response kicks in, sweat beads at my hairline. My mind is still desperately trying to reject what my boss is saying.

At the same time, my first impression of him shatters. I thought he was handsome for his age, his steel gray hair streaked with silver, the lines on his face giving him a distinguished air. His confident, powerful presence was going to usher in a new era for me. It wasn't supposed to be like this.

"This isn't appropriate, Mr. Zoric," I say, my voice coming out much higher than usual.

All I can do is stand there frozen, staring at him across the desk. He looks bigger than before, his body taking up more space. Maybe it's because of the way he's resting his elbows on the desk, steepling his fingers while cutting me down with that self-satisfied look. As if he's already won this game, and I merely need to accept my fate.

His eyes take on a predatory glaze, and for the first time, I'm afraid for my life.

"Sit. Down. Miss Jasinski," he says, laying out each word as if it's a weapon.

He's about to eat me alive, a lynx in the henhouse, and he's going to enjoy it.

I've seen this look before, from men back home. It never mattered that I was an excellent student or a hard worker. Males gravitated to me with hunger in their eyes regardless of my accomplishments, assuming, I think, that I would be easy to manipulate because pretty girls are never supposed to be smart, too. Pretty or smart, you can't be both. And if you're pretty, every man feels entitled to catcall or make a pass at you, and it's your job to smile and bear it, as if it's some kind of penance for the face or the body you were born with. I'm not naïve.

Surviving in rural Poland was one thing. The world I'm trapped in at this moment is something else entirely.

Mr. Zoric won't let me walk away from his desires the way I did from men back home. He's my boss. I signed a contract. There is no escaping him.

"I said, *sit*."

I can't do as he asks. My legs are stiff and locked at the knee. Every nerve in my body resists his order.

"I...can't," I tell him.

He arches one brow. "You can't what? Cooperate with the auction, or sit?"

"Either."

He makes a saddened sound and glances down at something on his desk. "I'm sorry to hear that. This auction would be the gateway to your future. Jobs, money, networking opportunities that can change your life. Don't you want that for yourself?"

As he speaks, his demeanor gradually morphs from domineering to...kind? Fatherly, almost? Yet despite the gentleness of his tone, the softening of his expression, the way he leans back in his chair with his arms spread wide, I feel no comfort. He's not convincing me, and he knows it.

"I am not a prostitute, Mr. Zoric," I say firmly.

He leans forward so fast, the back of his chair makes a popping sound. A divot forms between his brows as he shakes his head. "No, of course you're not. But you are a beautiful, ambitious woman who wants to work her way to the top, aren't you? And you're going to spread your legs for a man eventually. So why not do it for one with power and money?"

The muscles in my chest tighten as he stares at me. Seconds die to the drum of my pulse, one after another after another, until the silence becomes impossibly uncomfortable. He's trying to break my resolve with this disgusting logic, to break me down.

Lifting my chin, I drop into the chair again,

crossing my legs. Thank God I wore pants today. There may not be a way out of this, but I won't let him take my dignity in the process.

His gaze drops to my breasts as I lengthen my spine, a reminder of the only worth I have to him. Separating one of the folders from the rest of the stack on his desk, he leans back in his chair again and brings it front and center.

"Juvenile rheumatoid arthritis is a terrible disease, isn't it?" He clicks his tongue and shakes his head. "So much pain. And nausea. Fatigue and sleeping for days, just... wasting away."

My eyes sting.

He flips over a paper and slides it toward me. It's a full-page photograph of my sister, Eva. "I heard the medication she took early on shut down her pancreas and now she's on insulin? If only she'd had the correct medication from the start, right?"

A tear falls.

He sits back with a disdained sigh. "It would be a shame if your modeling jobs dried up and the money stopped coming in, and she couldn't afford the excellent American medications she's taking now, wouldn't it?"

I can't breathe.

"Who knows how bad things might get then? The mortgage on your uncle's farm might skyrocket. People might get sick from eating the lamb he sells and then what? No one will buy what he butchers. How will he pay triple the mortgage?"

Grappling for the arm of the chair, I sit just as my legs give out. My thoughts fracture in different directions and for the quickest moment, I consider my options. But there aren't any, are there? There's only one choice that I can make, or he'll ruin my family. Silence yawns in the room. He's letting me stew in the poison of being trapped, patiently waiting until it fully sinks in that I have no choices, no voice. No free will.

Pulling breath through my nose, I look at the edge of his desk. It comes into focus as his body blurs in the background. When I was young, my father used to sit me on a one-legged milking stool in the barn for a time-out. The single leg allows the stool to be manipulated as you move forward and back to draw milk from the cow's udders, but if you're not perfectly balanced, you'll crash to the ground before you even realize the seat wasn't balanced.

The chair below me now spins and wobbles as if I'm back on that stool, trying so hard to control it so I don't fall and scrape my hands trying to catch myself. I have to keep it upright, on center, balanced or it won't be me getting battered and bruised.

It'll be my family.

His face is a mask of concern, but inside, this man is laughing at me—I can sense it. No doubt he's amused by the fact that I'm trying to fight him on this, because it's obvious that he's the one holding all the cards.

Tears blur my vision, but I keep my voice steady. "What would you like me to do, sir?"

"I'd like you to answer my question."

Remembering what my roommates told me, I blink back my tears, lift my chin, and force myself to meet his eyes. "No, I am not a virgin. I was popular in my hometown."

My accent gets thicker when I lie. Will he notice?

He scowls and leans back in his chair. "That is unfortunate. You would have sold for a small fortune." He thinks for a moment. "There will be Arab royalty in attendance tomorrow night, and you're just his type. Perhaps we'll see a decent bidding war for you regardless."

Rifling through my file again, he finds a small booklet with a burgundy cover and holds it up. I instantly recognize the gold eagle emblem on the front, and even though I'm too far away to read the words stamped on it, I know exactly what they say: RZECZ-POSPOLITA POLSKA PASZPORT. My stomach bottoms out and little bells go off in my head. It's my passport, the one I kept in my room at the apartment. How...?

"You won't think about running home now, will you?" He smiles and slides the passport back into his file. "Of course not. You're a good girl, Izabela."

Bile rises in my throat, burning and sour. I say nothing.

"Tomorrow evening, a car will arrive for you at

eight. Do not dress for the event ahead of time." He gestures to the shopping bag. "Bring the bag with you. Remember, this is a job. Your hair and makeup will be done at the venue, just as it would for a photo shoot. You'll change afterward. You'll also need to be nice and bare, but we'll take care of that now."

"Przepraszam?" I say, accidentally slipping back into Polish. "Excuse me?"

Ignoring me, he presses a button on his desk phone. "She's ready."

Panic flutters in my chest.

"After you've been waxed, you can go," he says. "Oh, and Izabela."

Zoric stands and offers me a hand. Unsure if my legs will hold me, I push to my feet and accept his handshake like a dead fish. Dread rolls up my arm from his touch. The men who will bid on me tomorrow will be just like him. Rich. Arrogant. Cruel. With greedy hands and triumph in their eyes as they defile me. My first time won't be with someone I love, but with a man who paid for the opportunity to keep me for a night, touch me, and violate me.

"I'm so glad you won our eastern European contest. Welcome to the VIP division of KZ Modeling. I think you'll be very successful."

Pressing a hand over my thumping heart, I turn away and squeeze my eyes shut. When I open them, Zoric's assistant is standing in front of me with a glimmer of sympathy in his eyes.

"Are you ready, Miss Jasinski?"

He asks as if *he* isn't quite ready, as if he hates what he's about to do.

Wordlessly, I nod.

"I'll escort you to the in-house spa," he says. "This way."

He picks up the shopping bag. We're back in the elevator. The floor feels like it's bottoming out, unbalancing me like the damn milking stool. It takes all my will not to crumple into a ball in the corner.

There's no sense in asking the assistant for help. I know better than that. Besides, why would he risk his job trying to help me? I'm one of many, hundreds—maybe thousands—to take this exact same ride.

The doors open and spill me out into the bright white hallway of the spa, where a woman in a black button-up smock and white palazzo pants waits. She doesn't smile or greet me, just leads me to a small room with a padded table covered in white paper. A pink robe is folded on the foot, waiting for me to slip into it.

She doesn't leave the room as expected, so I undress with my back to her, feeling the weight of her eyes on my naked back before I slip on the plush, velvety robe, and for one blissful moment, I feel shielded from what my life is about to turn into.

And then comes the pain.

3

IZABELA

THE CAR ARRIVES AT EXACTLY eight p.m.

My roommates don't ask where I'm headed. I haven't said a word to any of them since I got back from my meeting at KZM yesterday, but the looks they exchange suggest they already know what's happening tonight.

The black sedan at the curb below our living room window confirms it. Or maybe the three times I threw up in the bathroom in the past hour, not quietly, gave it away. They've all been in my shoes before, haven't they? They know what it feels like, waiting for that black car.

Wondering what's going to happen when it delivers them to their final destination.

I'd stashed the white department store bag inside my slouchy, oversized duffel so no one would see it. I still haven't looked inside, so I have no idea what type of outfit Konstantin Zoric chose for me. I'm afraid to find out. Since he forbade me from getting ready ahead of time, he could have given me the bag this evening, but I think he wanted me to cart it around as a cruel reminder that I'm not a free woman.

He owns me, and my body, and starting this evening, I'm going to be nothing more than a toy for the pleasure of paying men. A toy to be manipulated, played with, used and discarded. Over and over again.

Nausea bites the back of my throat as I turn away from the window and head to the door.

Diya gives me a hug in the hallway. I cling to her like she's a life raft.

"Don't let it break you, Iza. Just close your eyes and pretend you're in Spain, on the beach, with the sun on your face."

Her words follow me out, cut off by the closing click of the door. My knees tremble as I descend three flights of stairs to the lobby. My fingers feel numb as I push the heavy glass door open and step into the balmy night air. Glancing up at the window of my apartment, I see three faces staring down at me. Watching.

Diya waves slightly. I don't wave back.

The driver gets out, nods, and opens the back passenger door. He doesn't make eye contact, doesn't confirm my identity, doesn't say a word. As I slide onto the seat, it hits me that my name doesn't matter. Any woman who lives here, in a KZM apartment, is just another commodity.

On the drive over to the auction venue, I do my best to gather myself, but my nerves are too chaotic. Closing my eyes and imagining my sister's face is the only thing that keeps me from flinging open the door and throwing myself out into traffic.

About twenty minutes later, the car comes to a stop in a dark alley, the brick walls of the adjacent buildings only visible by the headlights.

Panic courses through me. I think I might be sick again.

My cousin gave birth when I was fourteen. It happened fast, catching both of us off guard as we worked in her mother's vegetable garden. Lena lay down in the grass after the pains started suddenly, and before I could run for help, she started pushing. Her breaths came fast and gasping. Fear sparked in her eyes as she struggled against it, panting, bracing herself, crying when she realized that what was happening was out of her control. There was no way to protect herself from the unknown that lay moments ahead.

That's how I feel right now. I'm caught in an ominous swell, but without any sweetness on the other side to make it worth it.

I nearly jump out of my skin when the driver opens my door and offers me his hand. I'm trembling too hard to take it, so he waits for me to slide out of the car and then ushers me to a nondescript black door. He knocks three times. It opens a few inches before catching on a chain.

"Another Zoric girl," the driver says. "Izabela something."

The chain grates against its holder, the sound reverberating in my bones. The door opens and then a beefy hand reaches out for me.

"Get in here," a deep male voice says. "Hurry up."

He pulls me in.

The door slams behind me and I get a full breath of sour cigar smoke. Before I can get my bearings, an older woman with short, dark hair and deep red lipstick appears through the cloud, puffing on a slim brown cigar as she assesses me. She's in a sheath dress and pearls, looking more like a professional businesswoman than a madame. Then again, I suppose the two are one and the same.

"Good. Very good," she says, nodding to herself. "What's in the bag?"

I tighten my grip on the duffel straps and say, "Nothing. It's just my keys and—"

But then the guard grabs the bag off my shoulder and searches it, ripping the department store bag in the process.

"Clothes," he tells the woman in pearls, shoving the bag back at me.

"That's fine, you can take it in," she says. "This way, darling."

Sauntering off, she cuts through the dimness, and I

nearly lose her. Something inside says I need to keep up. I don't want to get lost in a place like this. Still I hesitate, looking back over my shoulder at the guard who stands there blocking the exit. His hard gaze practically dares me to try escaping this place. I don't. I follow the woman in pearls.

"Don't start crying," she warns. "You're here now and there's no turning back, so just keep your chin up and get it over with. And do it with a smile. Smiling makes everything better."

Her words, meant to comfort, horrify me instead. I can't believe I was so stupid, thinking there wasn't a dark side to this amazing opportunity with KZM. It takes all my willpower to control the panic fluttering inside my chest like an angry shrike. If I lose my tenuous grip even a little, it will overwhelm me.

But the woman in pearls is right about one thing: there is no turning back. I have to do this. For Eva. Thinking of my little sister, and how much she needs me, is the only thing that keeps me on my feet.

The woman stops at a door on the left that's guarded by another heavyset man, this one with tattooed biceps the size of my thighs. He unlocks the door and throws it open. Bright light and the overpowering scent of perfume spill out. Soft, feminine voices sound from within.

"Get ready," she tells me. "Girls, you have twenty minutes until showtime. Chop chop."

I'm shoved inside and the door slams. Immediately,

nine or ten pairs of eyes land on me. Without making eye contact with any of the other young women, all of them dressed in white bathrobes, I glance around the room. It's long and narrow. Mirrors have been hung along one wall, above long counters with stools. There's no changing area.

Trembling, I clutch my duffel to my chest.

"Jesus, another one?" A scoff. "Why not just pack us in here like rats in a trap?"

"Hurry up, honey," a middle-aged woman says, coming forward to lead me to a free stool in front of a mirror. "I'll help you. Then you can change. They'll auction you naked if you're not dressed in time."

She's kind, almost motherly, but I don't let my guard down. This must be the "professional" hair and makeup artist that Zoric mentioned.

Admittedly, she's good. Within fifteen minutes, she's brushed my long blonde hair out and lightly tousled it with some texturizing cream. My makeup is so subtle, so minimal—just a touch of lip gloss, a little blush, and lots of mascara—that I'm a little confused, until I realize that all the girls have been given the exact same treatment. It's meant to make us look younger.

My stomach turns.

"You have about five minutes," the makeup artist says. "Why don't you go ahead and get dressed? The corner offers a bit of privacy. That's where the girls keep their personal items."

The others chatter behind me as I unzip my duffel

and pull out the outfit Zoric gave me. "Outfit" is a stretch, however. It's nothing more than a white lace bra and matching thong with little satin bows at the hips. Once I'm changed, I shove my bag into the corner and stand there awkwardly, my hands clasped in front of my chest. I'm cold, scared, and humiliated.

"Hey. Here's an extra," a redheaded girl says, handing me a robe.

"Thanks."

I slip into it, wondering what she's wearing under hers. Are we all in lingerie?

"The first time's the worst. Once you've been through it, it's not so scary after that," she says quietly.

She gives me a shy smile. Is she another foreigner, like me? Her voice was so soft, I couldn't detect an accent. Did she sign with Zoric to support her family, too?

"Here. Be bold, so you stand out and rack up the bids."

She fishes out a tube of red MAC lipstick from her bag, gently grips my chin to turn me to her and slicks it on my lips.

A pang of tenderness hits the center of my heart. Her touch is light and tender, like Eva's when we'd play dress up and pretend to be movie stars. This isn't her first auction. Far from it, it sounds like. She shouldn't even be here. None of us should be here.

"What am I supposed to do when it's my turn?" I hear myself ask her.

Assessing her work, she wipes a little bit of lipstick from my lower lip. "You stand on a stage, all alone. You're supposed to smile. Force yourself to have the biggest, most radiant smile that you can. If you look scared, you might get a certain kind of man. A man who..." Her voice trails off, and she drops her gaze.

"I understand," I say. A predator. Someone looking for a victim. Someone like Zoric.

""I pretend that I'm gutting them all when I'm in the spotlight. Like pigs at the harvest. Just pray you get one who's nice," she adds.

Her accent is pronounced now. Czech.

"*To mi je líto*," I tell her. *I'm sorry*, one of the few Czech phrases that I know.

She doesn't react to it, and I think maybe I've gotten it wrong. Then she puts a hand on my shoulder, squeezes, and I know I've gotten it right. She walks away, leaving me to look at myself again in the mirror.

I look scared. And I am. Remembering her warning, I force a smile. It doesn't help much.

The door suddenly bangs open and the brawny guard comes in. There's a pistol strapped to his hip that I hadn't noticed before. Is that to keep the men in line, or us? We're hustled out of the room to navigate the dim hallway, all of us lining up like obedient children, about to perform on a stage that none of us wants to be on.

We're told to stop, and then a different man comes down the line, stripping off our robes and tossing them over his arm. Someone behind me begins to sob quietly. My ribs ache from constantly controlling my breathing. My abdominal muscles are a vice, holding back the anxiety that threatens to drown me. We're rearranged in a different order, and I'm moved from near the front to almost the very back.

The voice of an announcer—the auctioneer?—sounds from behind the black velvet curtains at the end of the hall, and the first girl is pushed through. A crack between the curtain panels and the stage gives me a glimpse of bright lights and then suddenly the announcer's voice becomes fast and jumbled, like a real auctioneer showcasing prime livestock for sale.

My mind sinks in on itself, my heart jackhammering in my chest as the young women ahead of me disappear one by one. I don't want to do this. There has to be a way out.

When there's nobody left in front of me, my body starts to tense up. I have to run. I have to hide. I have to—

"Go."

A hand pushes me between the shoulder blades, shoving me through the curtain, and I stumble onto the stage, washed in blinding white lights.

Everything beyond the lights is dark, so dark that I can't tell how large the room is or how many bidders are here. Ten? Fifty? A hundred? I have no idea. The air conditioning is cranked up in here, and I start to tremble. I lift my arms to cover my chest, but the auctioneer barks "Arms down!" and I drop them at my sides and freeze.

"Twenty years old. Polish. Speaks English. Five foot nine," the auctioneer drones, ticking off my hair color, eye color, bra size, weight. "Natural breasts, no augmentations, no scars. A new girl, so we'll start the bidding at three thousand."

My brain latches onto the number, playing it over and over as I scan the crowd. My vision adjusts to the low light, the old, lecherous faces leering at me like I'm a prize horse. One of these men is going to be the person I remember for the rest of my life as my first. And who knows how many more I'll be forced to remember after him? My breathing starts to speed up, and I realize I'm not smiling. But I can't do it. I can't. It's all I can do not to burst into tears.

The bidding quickly begins to climb, from three thousand, four thousand, five thousand. The auctioneer occasionally commands me to turn my body or lift my chin, and I obey each time, a perfect puppet. Each bidder's dimly-lit, shadowy face is more terrifying than the last. I've gone numb. I feel like I'm floating outside my body.

"Five thousand going once—"

This is it. I'm about to be sold for five thousand dollars.

"Twice—"

And then a man in the second row from the stage raises his paddle. He's middle aged, in his forties or fifties maybe, lean and dressed in a suit that looks like it was cut to his exact measurements. He's...handsome, actually.

"Six thousand dollars," he declares confidently, making eye contact with a few of the other bidders before he sits back down.

The men he stared down were also bidding on me, but they look reticent now. The auctioneer raises the bid, but no one raises their number, as if they'd been intimidated out of it.

Which is how I know that the man who bought me is the worst one of all. Because every other man in this room is afraid of him. He's a wolf.

"Sold to number 1 1 0 for six thousand dollars!"

I'm ushered off stage, into a holding area, before I can wrap my head around what just happened.

"Hello, beautiful."

My head snaps up. It's him.

The wolf.

My heart lurches as he steps closer and takes my chin in his hand.

"Look at those perky little tits," he murmurs appreciatively. "Too bad you're a gift. But I don't mind playing with someone else's toys. I'll have my turn when he's done with you."

When who's done with me?

He leans in before I can register what he's doing, his moist lips covering mine aggressively, trapping my cry. Then he bites my lower lip, hard enough that I gasp.

My flight instinct kicks in too late. He pulls away, his eyes heated.

"Get her things and put her in my car," he barks to an attendant. Then, to me, "See you soon, beautiful."

4

IZABELA

I'M GOING to spend the rest of my life trying to forget this night.

The bidding itself had happened so fast, but now that I'm in the back of this chauffeured car with the man who bought me—the man who bit me—time slows to an agonizing crawl.

We're sitting thigh to thigh, and I'm suffocating in the musky fog of his cologne as his damp palm cups my knee. I was allowed five minutes to pull my clothes over the white lingerie before being ushered to the car, but even though I'm fully clothed, I feel vulnerable and naked. And I know it's only going to get worse from here.

I try to tell myself that I should feel fortunate that the man who bought me is good-looking, but it isn't helping. He might be cruel or creepy; I don't know. This man's face will be burned in my memory as my first sexual experience. The placation of his handsomeness isn't working. He could be the most beautiful man in the world and it wouldn't matter. I don't want to be in his bed or anyone else's as the result of being sold to the highest bidder. My palms are clammy, but I don't dare dry them on my pants. I don't want him to know how nervous and dread filled I am.

It's not right to focus on my sister's treatments right now. It feels wrong to think about her when I'm about to do... what I'm about to do. Nothing else comes to mind to help hold the panic back. It starts to break through, leaching into my brain and raising all the alarms.

I could open the door and bail. No one will want to explain why a woman jumped from a moving vehicle and I might be able to get away. But Zoric has my passport. I'd have to approach him about getting it back... if I survive jumping from a speeding car. I could use it as blackmail, though, tell him I'll keep my mouth shut if he lets me out of the contract and returns my passport.

But what about my family?

He could easily hurt them before I returned to Poland. Take my uncle's farm or spread lies that tarnish his butchering business. He could use his power and influence to stop my sister's medications. Or worse. Because there *will* be some kind of retaliation. Konstantin Zoric is a dangerous man, and I am entirely disposable.

Pressing a hand to my middle, I clench my eyes and

hold back the urge to rage against the confines of this car and the feel of a stranger's hand on me.

The buyer said I was a gift for someone else, and that he'd take his own turn with me afterward. What does that mean? Is this man going to watch his friend or associate use me first, and then have me for himself? Are they going to be passing me back and forth? Exactly how long am I obligated to be rented out for? Zoric told me nothing about the terms, and he definitely didn't mention that I could be "shared" by multiple clients. I think of Diya's story about getting tied up for days, and I pray that I won't experience a similar fate.

I side-eye the buyer and try to get a read on him. Is he going to be violent? The way he bit my lip says he's unpredictable, but that doesn't necessarily mean the whips and chains are coming out. Maybe he won't be awful. Or maybe I'm just lying to myself because I'm terrified of how bad this could get. And who's to say his associate won't be a monster in his own right?

Either way, it doesn't seem like I'm going to have much luck gleaning any clues right now. The buyer hasn't said a word since he slid into the back seat with me. Instead, he's been on his cellphone, tapping out texts or emails at a rapid pace. I'd like to say that being ignored is giving me a chance to collect myself, but I can't really take a deep breath with his hand on me like this. He's been slowly working it higher and higher up my leggings with each passing mile.

I turn my head to look out the window, willing the tears in my eyes to dry up before they fall. The city lights are nothing but blurs of white and yellow and red, the stars obscured by clouds overhead. I can't believe this is happening. I can't believe I—

"They say everyone has a doppelganger," the buyer says suddenly. "Look at me."

Startled from my thoughts, I look over, trying not to look scared. He reaches his hand out, lifting my chin and turning my face one way and then the other, inspecting me like livestock. I can feel my pulse kick harder, my face going hot.

Avoiding his gaze is the only way I can keep myself together.

"Come on. You're not a virgin so don't act so shy."

His fingers creep all the way to my inner thigh and crawl higher.

Higher.

Suddenly, he grabs the back of my neck and pulls me to him. His lips slam onto mine for the second time. A startled gasp gets stuck in my throat as he wedges his tongue into my mouth. He pulls back with a lecherous grin.

"You know," he says, "you're very—"

But he doesn't finish the sentence, because the car suddenly pulls to a stop. Dropping his hand, he straightens his jacket and waits for the driver to open his door. Once he steps out of the car, I slide out after him, my trembling hands clenching the straps of my duffel.

I'm startled by what I see. We're not at a hotel or a high-rise apartment building like I'd expected. We're parked in front of a beautiful townhouse. This place looks like something out of an architectural magazine. It's a mansion. It's four stories tall, made of light-colored stone, with arched windows and ornate black iron rails on the balconies. The front door is flanked by white pillars and painted high-gloss black. I hope that isn't a sign.

Taking my arm, the buyer leads me through the front gate, down a paved pathway, and up to the door, where he punches in a code on a keypad before going inside.

Were the circumstances different, I might really be able to appreciate this entrance, with its marble floors and massive chandelier hanging above my head. A maid appears at the end of the short entry hallway.

"Mr. McConnell, I didn't know you were...oh."

She clasps her hands together and twists them, pausing for a beat, and then scurries away without another word. But I didn't miss the fear in the older woman's eyes. My throat tightens. The buyer—Mr. McConnell—is probably a horrible boss. He must be for her to react like that. Maybe he yells at his staff, or worse, beats them for doing something wrong.

And his hands are going to be on me next?

Something worse occurs to me—does he put his lips, unwanted, on *her*, too?

Heaviness weighs on my shoulders. I wish I could sink into the floor.

McConnell loosens his tie, working it back and forth, back and forth. "Go upstairs to the first bedroom on the right," he tells me. "Take off your clothes and wait on the bed. Naked."

I give a quick nod and then hurry up the elegant staircase with its wrought iron railing. As soon as I get inside the bedroom, I drop my bag on the floor and sink down to the carpet, resting my back against the closed door. As if I can stop him or anyone else from coming inside and doing whatever they want to me.

My mind starts racing with panic, images of my fate flashing before my eyes. He'd said something about me being a present. Is he gifting me to someone who is going to join in? My insides flutter. What if there's more than one other person? Sobbing into my hands, I take a few deep breaths and remind myself that I have to hurry and do as he said but I can't seem to move. It's my first time. What if he invites an entire party up here to share me? I'll never survive that.

Considering the dark gleam in the man's eyes on the ride here, I'm not sure I'll get through this at all. There will be consequences if I don't. Word will get back to Zoric that I tried to get out of it, or didn't perform, and he'll do something to my family. I know it in my bones. He didn't have to spell out every threat for me to understand that I have to do what's expected of me or there will be retribution.

Slowly pushing to my feet, I don't look around the bedroom as I go into the ensuite bathroom and dab beneath my eyes with a tissue. Despite my raging emotions, my makeup still looks good. The lipstick left a nice stain on my lips, giving me a demure, just kissed look. Of course my own makeup would betray me. I wish I could mess it up and give myself mascara streaks and a blotchy complexion. Anything to make me unattractive so they'll let me go.

Consequences, Izabela. Consequences.

Zoric's voice whispers through my mind and I cringe.

"Be strong for Eva," I tell myself in the mirror.

Pulling myself away from my reflection I turn away from the sink.

Turn off the bathroom light.

Hesitate in the dark before going into the bedroom.

It's a yawning room, done in white and gray with a modern feel. The bed is massive and adorned with a thick white comforter and a black throw blanket at the foot. Matching side tables hold a lamp, each of them lit with a soft white glow. There's matching overstuffed gray chairs by the peaked window, and an alcove holding a desk and chair. Everything is perfectly neat, as if this room is more of a showcase than a sanctuary.

It should soothe me, this neatness, but it doesn't.

Again, I consider if there's a way to escape. I'm only

on the second floor, so maybe I can jump out the window, or find the maid I saw downstairs and beg for help...but no. There's no one in this country who can keep me safe. No one I can turn to and let them know what's happening to me and the other women who fall for the Zoric Agency's promise. It can get worse for me after this and there's nothing I can do about it. The police will dismiss me as a desperate immigrant turning to prostitution to get by. They'll accuse me of trying to blackmail a powerful man.

Not to mention the consequences that my family and I will face if I don't go through with this.

As long as he holds my contract, I'm locked into doing anything Zoric—and implicitly, the buyer—says.

With no more reason to stall, I strip off my clothes, one article at a time, setting my bag on one of the armchairs. Even more anxious once I'm bare, I dart over to the massive bed, hesitating for a moment before climbing under the covers and pulling them up to my chin. The sheets are icy. Goosebumps rise on my skin.

Breathing shallowly, I listen for any sound outside the door. Will I hear footsteps on the stairs, or will the door burst open all of a sudden, leaving me helpless as strange men flood the room? I start to shiver.

I've never been so vulnerable.

All I can do is pray for strength, pray to survive this night, and then figure out how to survive the rest of my contract once this is over.

Turning on my side, I reach for the lamp on the

bedside table and turn it off, plunging the room into darkness.

I was right in the car. My only choice right now really is to spend the rest of my life trying to forget this night.

And possibly everything that comes after it.

5

RHYS

"Get the fuck out of my house."

I wasn't surprised to find my father's limo waiting outside my front door. I was enraged. And doubly so to walk into my own house and find him milling around in my living room, two fingers of scotch in one hand. He'd clearly made himself at home while waiting for me.

The back of my neck prickles when I see him. He's looking out the side window, his back to me, but he turns as I fully enter the room. He smiles like we have a dinner date to get to. But this isn't a social call. It never is with him.

"You were not invited into my home," I say, my voice steely. "And you are most assuredly not welcome. So put that drink down and get. *The fuck*. Out of my house."

"Oh, Rhys. That's not how you speak to your

father," he scolds casually, then sips his drink while eyeing me over the rim of the tumbler.

"What are you doing here?"

He spreads his arms wide as if it should be obvious. "I came to see my favorite son."

"You can leave, now."

All I wanted was a hard drink or five in front of my fireplace. My father's intrusion into my home has me all riled up inside now and I won't be able to relax anytime soon. Damn him.

Tossing back the rest of his scotch, he moves to the sideboard for a refill but I skirt in front of him and block his path to the alcohol. "No. Leave. Now."

He arches one thick brow, and the ensuing silence only pisses me off more. I don't want to be having a standoff with my father right now. He's wasting my time and will likely draw out whatever this is until I have no choice but to physically toss him off my front steps. It wouldn't be the first time.

And it won't be the last.

I reach into my jacket for my phone, but he stands and spreads his arms wide, the picture of childlike innocence.

"Let's all just calm down, son. I really think you'll change your tune when you see the present I left you upstairs."

He gives me a shit-eating grin that says he's incredibly pleased with himself, and my stomach drops.

"Whatever it is, I don't want it. I don't want anything from you except your exit from my home."

Sidestepping me, he slams his glass down on the sideboard. "You know, kid, it's been years now, and you're still walking around with a chip on your shoulder. Playing into that victim mentality, when the truth is, I didn't 'steal' Celine from you. She *chose* me!"

"Get. Out. Now."

"You know what I say? Be a man, grow a pair, and get over it. So you got dumped. Big deal. There's plenty of other pussy out there. Besides, I'm trying to make things right with you. Can't you see that?"

"Just so we're clear, you could bring me a goddamn pyramid from Luxor, and I'd still not forgive you. So whatever idiotic thing you've brought me, you're going to need to take it back."

He throws his hands up in mock surrender and backs away until he's aligned with the exit. "Nope, can't do that. I'm not one to let good money go to waste, so go on. Have fun with it." He strides off and leaves me standing there, grinding my jaw to get my emotions under control. God only knows what's waiting for me upstairs.

Phone still clutched in my fist, I walk out and head up to the second floor, taking the stairs two at a time. My adrenaline is pumping, my anger sticking to the inside of my chest like dull knives. I have no idea what my father has blown his money on, but I know it sure as hell won't fix the bridge he burned between us.

When I shove my bedroom door open, a gasp sounds from inside the room. The lamps are off, but I hit the light switch to illuminate the overheads.

And find a woman in the center of my bed, holding the covers to her chest, arms bare. Her wide eyes clash with mine before she drops her gaze and grips the sheets in handfuls. The combination of disgust and fury makes my skin itch. Ripping off my tie, I throw it across the room. She jerks but doesn't look at me.

My father put a terrified, naked woman in my bed.

"Get out of my bed and get dressed," I bark, stalking out of the room.

Slamming the door closed behind me, I race back down the steps, hoping to catch my dad, but he's nowhere to be found. Checking outside, I see his car is gone. That mother—

I call and he answers on the second ring.

"NO. You are taking it back," I tell him.

"Oh, come on. Don't be like that. I picked her out just for you. Isn't she a dead ringer for someone we both know?"

That's when it hits me. Jesus. She did look a little like Celine.

"You can't replace a woman like a bottle of scotch," I grind out.

"Sure you can. Now go on and enjoy! The taste I had was extra sweet. You can thank me later."

"I—"

But the line has already gone dead, and he doesn't answer when I immediately call back.

What the hell was he thinking? Ever since he eloped with Celine, he's gone to idiotic lengths to try to win back my favor—apparently not realizing that he was never in my favor to begin with. I've never labored under the delusion that my father is a good, decent man. The only emotions he has ever stirred in me are anger, disappointment, and frustration.

My grandfather, on the other hand, was always there for me. Unlike my father, Grandpa would show up to my baseball games to cheer me on alongside my mom, have me over for dinner on the nights Mom had to work late. He'd constantly ask me about school and my plans for the future, and he kept tabs on my report cards. He even wrote me a recommendation letter for business school. Looking back, I can't help but think he was preparing me to take over McConnell Enterprises all along—if not because he saw something exceptional in me, then because he saw something deficient in my father.

Thankfully, I won the mom lottery. My mother knows what it means to show up, and she was always there for me with a comforting word or a helping hand. She tried to shield me from my father's lies and self-indulgences when I was young, but as I grew older, she stopped making up excuses for him. By the time they divorced, I was already firmly rooted on her side. She was the only sense of stability, of home, that I had ever known.

Which is precisely why I have no plans to let my father into my good graces so he can try to take control of the family business. He's not trying to win me over because he wants a father-son relationship. He's after my rung on the corporate ladder. The position that he was passed over for because he's not the right man for the job.

And now he's dragged some poor woman into his manipulations.

Pinching the bridge of my nose, I take a breath before going back upstairs. The door swings open to reveal her standing there, fully dressed now. Dark leggings, a tight black T-shirt. The plainness of her clothes only seems to highlight her extraordinary features. I have to admit, now that the anger is no longer clouding my vision: she really is beautiful.

"Look at me." Walking closer to her, I slip my hands into my front pockets. "I want to see your face."

She does as I ask but doesn't quite meet my eyes. Although her jaw is more delicate, her nose less upturned, her chin shaped differently, she does have Celine's look. The long blonde hair, silky and fine; the wide blue eyes under arched, natural brows; the high cheekbones, the wide mouth, the plush lips that are damn near identical. Dad certainly knows how to pick them.

Where did he find her? My cock twitches but I

shove the instinct away. I don't need my father or anyone else delivering a fuck toy to my door.

Making a slow circle around her, I feel her nervous energy as I assess her tight, lean body. She's a bit fuller in the hip than Celine, and her breasts are bigger. The longer that I look at her, the angrier I become. As if I would want a woman to remind me of the one who committed the ultimate betrayal?

After my father married my girlfriend, I spent many nights, many months' worth of nights, lying awake at three a.m. thinking of how I'd get revenge, of how I'd make him pay. Make both of them pay. Not physical harm, of course. No. I merely wanted to impact their lives the way they'd impacted mine. Blindside them. Devastate them. Pull the figurative rug out from under their feet and leave them on their asses, blinking and shattered and confused.

The thing about time, though, is that it really does heal all wounds. Not perfectly, not completely, but enough to cure my burning need for vengeance.

I won't forgive them, and I'll never forget, but I've put the events of that year behind me. He and Celine are welcome to live happily ever after. Ideally as far away as possible.

Unfortunately, my father just can't stop ripping open those old wounds and dragging me down, as if he never wants me to forget that the only woman I've ever loved is now his wife.

My cock jerks again, making my pants uncomfortably tight. God, am I fourteen again? What is it about this girl that's turning me on so much? That she's a fresh, young stranger, or that she looks so similar to the woman I almost proposed to? Maybe I should have left her naked in my bed. I could be fucking her right now.

I step back and study her again. The height. The full, soft lips. Those sky-high cheekbones and her perfect bone structure. Of course. She's another model that my father plucked from some afterparty somewhere. The man has a type.

Her throat moves as she swallows. I can imagine the feel of the skin there, so delicate and vulnerable under my grip. Tempted to palm her neck and curl my fingers around the smooth column, I look away and shake my head, smiling humorlessly. Ah, the darkness that bastard of a father brings out in me. But I can't touch her. Because I don't fuck for mutual pleasure. I fuck for myself. I'd probably break her in half.

There's something equally timid, yet strong about her. Her body might be soft and pliable, but what about her mind?

Her will?

Would she break easily, or would she fight me to keep control of herself?

Huffing a breath through my nose, I look back at her. She's the one watching me now, quietly assessing, measuring me up. Wouldn't she love to know what I'm like deep inside? The part of me no one sees unless I unleash it?

"Did my father use you and drop you off here like trash?" I ask dispassionately.

Her eyes widen but she quickly schools them.

"Answer me. He fucked you in the back of his car on the way over here, didn't he? Picked you up on a street corner, probably."

I'm not trying to be cruel; I'm trying to get a rise out of her. Insult her enough that she'll let some information slip. If she's an accomplice to his games, I'm not playing. I just want to tip the board over.

Gripping her chin, I turn her face from side to side. "Nah. You're too classy for a street corner. You're a high-class whore then, aren't you? Let me guess; you're an aspiring model."

She blinks but doesn't respond, betraying no emotion. It surprises me, this stoicism. She's tougher than I would have guessed. And I'm too tired to sit here grilling her all night.

"I don't fuck gold-diggers. So whatever scheme you're involved in, it won't work."

Her scent fills my nose and does something to the rage trying to unfurl like a fucking hurricane. Coconuts. It's the light, fluffy scent of tropical coconut. Her lips are stained as if her lipstick has been kissed off. My father? Or another man?

Releasing her, I notice red imprints from my fingertips on her skin. I could mark her entire body, inch by inch, but I'd only be enjoying my father's leftovers. Hard pass.

Beautiful or not, I'm sending her back.

"I'm calling you a ride," I say, pulling out my phone. "You can tell my driver where to drop you off. Go downstairs and wait on the steps. We're done here."

I start composing a text, telling my driver to pull the car around front, when a light flutter lands on my wrist. Looking up, I see the girl's face inches from mine, her eyes pleading.

"Please don't send me back," she says, her voice just barely tinged with an Eastern European accent. "I'll do whatever you want."

6

IZABELA

It's the man from the news. The hot one from the billion-dollar merger I watched yesterday.

He's an asshole.

Yet here I am, begging him to let me stay. It's surreal to realize this is the same man I saw on the television and had a small fantasy about. My perfect American dream man. Handsome, wealthy, ambitious. But he's cold as ice, indifferent, and dismissive of me like I'm garbage and not a living, breathing person.

A socialite whore. Isn't that what he called me? The insult stung, even if it's not far from the truth. That's what I'm here to become after all; it's what Konstantine Zoric is trying to make me. And I'm failing. Miserably.

If I don't make good on the expectation, though, there's no telling what he might do to my family. This man could say I didn't follow through, that I refused, or denied him. He could say any lie he wanted about me, and I'll be screwed.

I need to see this through. Make sure my client gets his money's worth. Or...I guess it's his dad's money's worth.

I wonder if this is an American thing, rich men buying sex for their sons.

Desperation makes me curl my fingers more insistently around his wrist. Lifting my chin, I say, "I'm not a gold-digger. This is a business transaction. I was paid for a service. I will provide that service."

He must be stunned by my forwardness, because he nearly drops his phone.

Then a flash of anger blazes in his eyes.

Pulling away from me, he gives me a scathing look, as if I'm a misbehaving servant. I think of the maid from earlier. No wonder she's timid.

"Do *not* touch me," he says coldly.

I'm so startled by the bitterness in his voice that I stumble back a step. He comes toward me and I step back again, and again, my breath hitching, pulse racing, until I hit the wall.

Now I'm panting, nailed in place by the intensity of the fury radiating off him. One big hand slams the wall beside my head, his arm a barrier between me and the door.

The scent of his cologne reaches me then, musky and warm. It's like leather and sandalwood, but with something smoky mixed in, and it's intoxicating. His body slides closer, only an inch or two of separation between us. I'm not bold enough to hold his gaze, so I drop my eyes and find myself staring at the undone buttons of his dress shirt, the exposed patch of skin at the base of his throat. The urge to lick him there hits me so suddenly, I get chills.

Disconcerted by my physical attraction to him, I look up again. His hazel eyes are studying me so intensely, it makes my nipples tug inside the thin bra I'm wearing. I recall his fingertips on my chin only moments ago, the possessive, dominating grip that held me in place.

"It's time for you to go now," he says, his voice throaty.

"Please, Mr. McConnell—"

"Whatever my father paid, I'll pay you double to leave."

He's willing to give me twelve thousand dollars just to go away? That money could change my family's life in Poland. Pay off my aunt and uncle's debts and pay for Eva to come here. Buoyed by the possibility, I can't keep the smile off my face.

"Really?"

Sighing, he leans back. "It's always about money, isn't it?"

Reality crashes my fantasy. What the hell am I even thinking? I don't have a bank account to transfer to. Zoric still has my passport. Even if I had cash in my hand, I can't leave the country. Certainly not before he could get to Eva. I'll lose everything if I don't finish this job.

Besides...

This man isn't at all what I was expecting.

He may be scornful, entitled, and cruel. He might even hurt me for his own pleasure, take me so roughly that it takes days to recover. Yet something about him is drawing me in. I'm still buzzing from his touch, from the scent of him. So, in some perverse way, maybe this client is a blessing. There are far worse men I could be trapped with right now.

"This isn't about money," I say, dropping to my knees in front of him.

This is it. I have to secure my family's future, and I have to do it now.

Even if I have no earthly idea what I'm doing.

Finding boldness, I reach for his belt. He breathes hard through his nose, his hips pushing forward automatically even as he looks down with surprise. He doesn't stop me as I fumble with his belt buckle, struggling to get his pants undone. There are metal hooks, a button, a zipper, all of these fasteners seem so foreign to me at this moment that I can barely manage to work my way through them.

As my fingers tremble over his zipper, my mind scrambles to recall the details of any sex scenes I've read in romance novels. God, I thought I'd be more prepared when my first time came. I definitely didn't envision...this.

I can feel the heat coming off his body as I finally get his pants down, revealing a sizable bulge in the front of his black trunks. And wow. He's built like a model himself, a vein popping against his tight abs and trailing down the front of his underwear. *Focus*, I remind myself.

With a deep breath, I reach down past his waistband and touch him for the first time. My hand jerks back the second my palm brushes against the hard, hot thickness of him. Forcing myself to wrap my hand around the shaft, I swallow hard and close my eyes.

Take it out. Just take it out and suck it into your mouth. It's not that complicated.

A sound like a chuckle comes from deep in his throat. My eyes pop open, my face burning with embarrassment, but he doesn't stop me, so I keep going. The tip of his cock juts out from the top of his briefs, plump and glistening. I close my eyes again and tug the waistband of his underwear down.

His cock springs free, tapping me on the side of the mouth and startling me into opening my eyes.

Fascinated and a little scared, I lean forward and give his head one slow, tentative lick with the flat of my tongue. He hisses. In a good way or a bad way, I don't know. Sliding my grip down toward the base, I stare at the impossibly huge thing, licking my lips in preparation.

My thighs clench together completely involuntarily, drawing my attention to the deep pulse that's throbbing between my legs.

"Are you just going to look at it, or are you going to make yourself useful?" he says.

I look up at him as my cheeks heat again, and though I intend to look away—try to look away—I hold his gaze as I sink my mouth over the tip of his cock. Determined to see this through, I look up at him and hold his gaze as I slowly bob my head forward. My jaw aches as I open wider, wider, trying to take all of him in.

This isn't at all what I expected. The silken, hot skin. The pulsing vein underneath the shaft. The smooth, firm feel of his fat tip, so plump as I suckle it.

Maybe it won't be so bad. Breathing out of my nose, I pause for a moment to take in his unfamiliar taste, the fullness of his length in my mouth.

There's only one problem: he's too big. I don't think I can handle any more.

But I have to.

Shifting my weight on my knees, I start sucking gently, moving my head back and forth a little, trying to please him. Am I doing this right? Is this how it works?

With a soft groan, he starts to thrust as I suck. I start to panic at not being able to breathe. He's not just well endowed, he's strong. Physically powerful, barely restrained. It would be easy for him to overwhelm me, choke me with his cock. But then I inhale through my nose, exhale, take a little more of him, inhale, and find a rhythm that seems to work for both of us. I'm shocked to feel that deep pulse throbbing harder at my center.

I think...I like this.

"Take it all. Every last inch," he commands, his thrusts getting more aggressive.

Tears prick my eyes, but it's more a visceral reaction than an emotional one. I try to relax my jaw again, bobbing my head faster to keep up with his pace. With each movement, I wet more of him with my tongue, helping him plunge deeper, harder. I can do this. I just have to let him fuck my mouth until he's finished.

But then his head hits the back of my throat, so suddenly that a violent gag drives me back. Pulling off him, I press a hand to my wet, swollen mouth and try not to cough.

"This feels like practice," he says. "I'm not your training wheels. If you can't do better than that, you need to—"

I glare up at him, equally humiliated and infuriated by his laughing, and then open up wide again to swallow him down. There's no hesitation this time. I draw him in deep, in one smooth slide, until he bottoms out at the base of my throat. Holding back the reflex, I bob back and forth, bracing my hands on his thighs. His fingers dig into my hair and he pulls it back into a ponytail, using it to hold my head steady as he pumps even faster.

After a few seconds, awareness comes slowly back to me and the fog that's swirled in my head clears. My tongue maps his anatomy, learning and testing him. The silken, hot skin. The pulsing, fat vein underneath the shaft. The feel of the mushroom tip, so plump as I suckle it.

My jaw burns, saliva dripping from the corners of my mouth. I never break eye contact.

He's panting heavily now, his thrusts getting more erratic, almost violent.

"You turned it around. Good girl."

The pulse between my legs turns sharp. Wincing, I press my thighs more tightly together. Warmth pools there and I realize that my panties are wet. My nipples are hard and a little painful, aching with the need for... more. I know what an orgasm is and how to give myself one. Right now, my body is demanding it. My pussy feels empty. Desolate. Wanting to be filled.

Shame washes over me and I nearly stop what I'm doing. But his breathing spurs me on. And it's far too late for me to run. Instead, I start to moan, hoping he'll finish faster with some encouragement.

Suddenly, he's pulling away from me, lifting me up and pressing me against the wall. My feet leave the floor, my shoulder blades hard against the wall as he holds me in place with hands around my ribs.

"My father wasn't enough for you? Fine. Apparently, I'm good at seconds."

He slides a hand down the front of my pants, squeezing me through the fabric of my leggings. I gasp in shock as my hips jerk, my pussy hungry for his touch.

He presses his thumb over the exact spot where my clit is, and the wetness in my panties turns to complete saturation.

Tilting my head back against the wall, I close my eyes and let my mouth fall open. He works me some more, squeezing hard and then releasing, until I'm a throbbing, panting mess. I've never felt like this before.

The taste of him rolls around on my tongue, my body eager to resume the position and continue the pleasure I was learning to give him. I want to do it, to taste him again and see what happens if I keep sucking.

How powerful would it feel to bring a man like this to *his* knees with just the touch of my mouth?

More than anything, I want to try.

7

RHYS

SHE SAID IT HERSELF: this is a business transaction. Money exchanged for goods and services. She obviously likes what I'm doing to her, and she's already bought and paid for, so why not take out the frustrations of my night on her?

Her dirty little mouth has me all worked up now, and there's no sense in stopping this when it feels this good.

And honestly, what's one more girl after the string I've tried (and failed) to make myself happy with by using and leaving?

"You like that?" I growl against her neck.

"Yes," she moans.

"You want more?"

Her cheeks are flushed, her eyes glazed when they flutter open. "Yes."

"Get on the bed," I command, and then give her fair warning. "It's going to hurt when I fuck you."

Her eyes flash, but not with fear. With desire. For a second she doesn't move, and then she crosses the room and lowers herself onto the bedspread. With one more glance my way, she lies flat on her back and looks up at the ceiling. She seems inexperienced, maybe a little afraid. All part of her act, I'm sure.

She's good at playing innocent. The way she fumbled through that blow job almost convinced me she didn't know what she was doing at first, but then it turned so, so good. It's been a while since a woman has made me feel good. A hard orgasm always provides relief, but true pleasure doesn't always accompany it. There's a difference, one I'd forgotten about until her mouth flamed up those hot little sparks that curl at the base of my spine, and course through my brain. The pulses of ecstasy and surges of erotic pleasure have been missing for a while, no matter how many women I go through to try and find it.

Of course it would show up from the mouth of a woman my father gifted me.

Fuck.

Running a hand over my mouth, I kick out of my pants and rip off my shirt as I approach the bed. Huge eyes watch me advance. Flushed cheeks, red lips, heaving chest—everything about her is driving me insane. Oh, I'm going to use her good, until I'm completely spent. And then I'm going to use her again.

I step out of my pants and trunks, then take off my jacket and shirt as I approach the bed, tossing them onto a chair. The girl's eyes rove my naked body as I advance. Her blue eyes are wide, her lips puffy from her oral exertions, her chest still rising and falling rapidly with excitement—even fully clothed, everything about her is driving me insane.

"Where did you learn to use your mouth like that?" I ask, leaning over her.

Digging my fingers into the waistband of her leggings, I pull down hard, panties and all, dropping the wad of clothing on the floor and leaving her bare from the waist down. Miles of legs, creamy skin, her thighs clenched together as if she can keep me from my prize.

At the foot of the bed, I cross my arms and give her a glare.

"Take your shirt off. Answer me while you do it."

I've never seen cheeks redden so fast. But she obeys. She grabs the hem of her T-shirt and slowly, almost reluctantly, peels it over her head. The lacy white bra she's wearing is so sheer, I can see her nipples through the fabric. Bright pink, like raspberries. My mouth waters.

"You haven't answered me," I say. "Do I need to repeat the question?"

"No. I just—"

Too late. I climb onto the bed and position myself

over her face, my cock just inches away from those plush lips.

"Fine. I'll give you a reason not to answer me. It's hard to talk when your mouth is full."

Reaching behind her head, I pull her toward me at the same time as I ram my dick back into her mouth. My eyelids close at the first touch of her wet, hot tongue. A choking sound escapes her but she adjusts quickly, suctioning my cock like her life depends on it. Digging my fingers into her hair, I pull until she winces, but I don't let go.

Once she's lubed me up well, I start to thrust. She matches my pace, sucking, pulling, licking like the pro that she is. I grab the headboard to steady myself, pumping back and forth, trying to forget where I am and who this is. All I want to focus on is pleasure.

"Fuck, that's good," I encourage her. The rise of her perfect ass makes a great view as I guide her head, moving her up and down on my cock exactly the way I need her to. Holding her head in place, I look down into her eyes and keep her still for a few seconds longer, reminding her who's in charge here, and then slide out of her mouth. She gasps for air but doesn't move, awaiting my next instruction.

"Move to the center of the bed."

I shift to the side so she can scoot down, then rearrange myself over her with my knees between her legs. She's still playing coy, giving me barely enough room to wedge myself between them. Placing my palms on the tops of her thighs, I run my hands down the supple length, reaching her knees and then wrapping my fingers around them.

She gasps as I push her legs apart wider, wider, opening up the sweet pussy that I own for the night. She's breathing more heavily now, looking up at me wantonly with her hair splayed across the bedspread like pale silk. But I barely have time to register the lust in her expression, because I'm far more distracted by the prize at the apex of her thighs.

She's waxed bare, the insides of her lips pink and glistening, her cunt juicy and ripe. The sight of her so vulnerable like this drives an almost mad desire inside me. My balls ache. Yet I've always been a sucker for self-torment, so I delay my gratification.

I press a knuckle against her soft pussy lips and stroke up and down, swirling her wetness from her opening to her clit. She pulls a ragged breath in every time I circle that tender nub. Eyes falling shut, she goes completely still except for the force of her breathing, as if she's so focused on what I'm doing to her that she can't respond to anything else.

I've barely touched her and she's already primed to orgasm. Satisfaction washes over me. She's so responsive, so easy.

"Look at me."

Her eyes open.

"Is this what you want? You want me to touch your greedy little pussy until you come?"

I can see her weighing her response, her brows drawing together, trying to figure out what I want to hear. Trying to play the part for me, but unable to think of anything but what I'm doing to her.

"Answer me," I growl, slapping her vulva.

"Ah," she cries, another gasp rushing out of her.

Goosebumps rise on her arms. She likes it rough, then. I slap her again.

"Yes!" she moans.

Slap.

"Yes what?" I demand.

"Yes I want you to...touch my pussy until I come."

God, that accent is a turn-on. I toy with her some more, massaging and squeezing, alternating between soft and hard, fast and slow, stroking around her hole with my thumb but never dipping inside. Clenching my jaw, I work her until she's in a frenzy, her hips jerking desperately as she tries to grind against my hand. Passion colors her features. Her fists clench the bedspread. She's so close I can almost taste it.

But I'm not going to let her finish.

"Not so fast," I scold, a grin tugging at my lips as I pull my hand away.

"You're not going to come until I can feel it on my cock. I want to feel it all—your pain, your pleasure, because it makes it better for me."

I rip open the front of her flimsy white bra. I've ruined it in the process of exposing her breasts, but I don't care. The straps hang loose from her shoulders, the lace torn. She looks perfect like this. The ideal combination of innocent and filthy. I can't wait to fuck her.

Palming her tits, I brush my fingers over her hard nipples, stopping each time she moans, just to tease her. Then I lean down and wrap my mouth around her left nipple, sucking it into my mouth with relish. I tug with my teeth, gently at first, then harder, before moving onto the right. My cock is raging against her smooth inner thigh, and when I feel the dribble of precum, I know it's time.

The condoms are in the bedside table. I lean onto my elbow and whip the drawer open, pulling out a foil packet and tearing it open. After rolling the condom on, I reposition myself between her thighs.

She's so wet that it's effortless to rub the tip along her slit, working my way inside a little more, a little more, until I feel her tight hole give way to my intrusion. My entire body tingles as I drive into her. She takes me so good, so tight and greedy... until she doesn't. Clamping down, she twists to the side, pushing up with her hands, a sob dropping from her lips.

"Lie down."

Panting, she does and covers her eyes with one hand.

I'm used to this kind of reaction, especially when it's the first time with a new partner. But I don't give her much time to adjust. She's clamped around me like a goddamn vise, but she's so hot and wet that I can feel it right through the latex. I use the backside of my middle finger against her clit, rubbing and rocking my knuckle there until her body relaxes.

I pull back slightly and then drive into her again, deeper this time, harder. Both of us let out a groan. Fucking Christ, she feels good. I ease back again, then pump into her again, just as deep but agonizingly slow. Trying to draw it out so I don't lose control.

But I can't hold back forever. Soon my thrusts are getting faster, shorter, drawing sharp gasps out of the woman beneath me. It sounds almost like she's in pain initially, but then all I hear coming out of her are moans of surprised pleasure, pitching higher and higher.

As I fuck her, I look down at her face. At the closed eyes, the open mouth, the pink cheeks. Her pussy must be doing something to me, because I very nearly drop my head and press my lips to hers.

I remove the temptation by rolling onto my back, taking her with me, so now she's the one on top.

"Ride me," I tell her. "Ride me until you come."

Her palms press against my chest and she takes a moment to adjust herself. Then she leans her head back, slowly finding her rhythm, until she's jerking her pussy back and forth around my dick. Her tits bounce with every thrust, her breaths getting faster and faster, punctuated by those hot little moans.

"Fuck that cock, you little whore," I murmur, urging her on. "Fuck me. Fuck me. Don't hold back."

Reaching down, I pinch her clit between my thumb

and forefinger. She starts mumbling to herself in what sounds like an Eastern European language.

"Come on my cock," I command. "I want to feel you come all over me. Now. Now."

"Oh my God," she pants. "Oh God, oh God."

"Now, I said."

A gasping cry of ecstasy spills from her lips as the storm unleashes in her body. She wails out her orgasm, clinging to my shoulders as she arches against me. I can feel her inner muscles milking my shaft in tight bursts, so good I know I can't hold back any longer.

Without warning, I push her off me, flip her onto her hands and knees, and slam into her from behind. Grabbing her hips, I pump into her hard and fast. Fucking her, fucking her, fucking her. God, I love this position. I'm in absolute control, and the view is tough to beat.

"Making you come makes it better for me, so you'll do it twice," I say. "I want that pussy soaking wet."

I slap her round, tight ass with a loud clap and she cries out. I do it again, just to hear her cry again. Then I slow my pace until her moans pick back up, holding myself steady at the speed she obviously prefers. I can feel my orgasm start to build, inevitable now, every thrust sending shocks of electricity through me.

My fingers dig into her hipbones and I grind into her, making figure-eights with my hips, taking my time, stroking every last sweet spot inside of her with my fat cock.

"Oh God," she whispers, her body starting to tense. "Yes."

I know what's about to happen. I can read this girl like a book now.

"Time for you to come again."

But my order is unnecessary. She's already there. A surge of wetness coats my dick, her whole body arching as the orgasm hits her in waves. Just what I've been waiting for.

"Good girl," I tell her, pumping into her clenching cunt, riding her so fast and hard that I know I'm bruising her inside.

But I can't stop. The pleasure radiates through me from head to toe, permeating my brain, making me see flashes of light, and I need it. I need it.

"Fuck yes. I knew you'd be good."

I push her down onto her elbows, mashing her face into the mattress so her ass is tilted higher. This angle feels even better. Instead of tapering off, her moans get louder, higher, only serving to egg me on. God, she's good. If I didn't know any better, I'd think she was actually enjoying herself. Enjoying me.

With a final groan, I empty into her, letting my climax take over. Gray shades the corners of my vision, working inward until I think I might pass out.

Once my head is clear, I pull out of her and roll the condom off, knotting it efficiently before walking to the en suite to toss it in the trash and clean up. When I go back into the bedroom, I find her lying on her side facing me. Her pleasure was pure white light, incendiary. It drove me completely and effortlessly over the edge.

"Time to go," I say, grabbing her clothes off the floor and throwing them on the bed.

The bra is in ruin, but she leaves it on anyway. I look away to pull on my own clothes and to give her a sliver of privacy, though it seems unnecessary after what we just did. When she sits up, I look back at her. She shifts beneath my scrutiny and a flash of red catches my eyes.

There's a small, pinkish-red blood stain where she'd been sitting just a second ago.

My mind tumbles over itself. She'd recoiled in pain, and her cunt was so, so tight that I had to work at that very first thrust. The sounds of discomfort she'd made...

Oh, fuck me.

Running a hand over my chin, I point to the bed. She glances down, then looks away. It's all the answer that I need, but I want to hear her say it. Christ.

I whip the sheets back farther, so she has no choice but to acknowledge it.

"Jesus Christ, you were a virgin?"

8

IZABELA

I SHOULD DENY IT, but I'm so overwhelmed—by the experience I just had, by my unexpected orgasms, by the humiliation of being found out by this man afterward, by *all of it*—that I can't even speak. I just look at him with pleading eyes, silently begging him to let the fact of my virginity go. To pretend he never found out.

"My father must have paid a fortune for you," he says.

There's something about his voice that gives me a slight chill—it's like a mixture of remorse and satisfaction.

All I can do is stand there feeling panicked and ashamed, unsure of what to do now.

"Of course he did," he says as he runs a hand through his hair. "Fuck. Just...get your shoes on. I'll get you a ride home."

For a moment, I look around the room in panic,

forgetting where I put my Adidas. But then I see the white laces peeking out from under the bed, and I kneel and grab them.

My body aches everywhere as I get the shoes on my feet, risking furtive glances at McConnell as I do. He doesn't seem panicked about what just happened, or guilty either. He seems more irritated at being tricked, at the inconvenience of having to deal with me.

Then again, it's difficult to read a man like him, who apparently requires the sight of literal blood to change his expression. I wonder how this would be playing out differently if I hadn't bled at all. Some girls don't their first time. I guess I never really gave it much thought.

The second I finish tying my laces, he says, "Let's go."

I get up, grab my duffel, and follow him to the door. Even these few steps are enough to send fresh waves of soreness through me. I feel raw and burning between my legs, my inner thighs aching like they're bruised, my lips puffy when I run my tongue over them. I'm sure I'll be fine in a day or two, but for now I feel shell-shocked and exhausted.

McConnell opens the door and gestures for me to leave first. I skirt past him and out into the hallway. That's when it finally hits me: it's over now. It's done. I'm free to go.

A wash of relief cascades over me, followed by a pang of disappointment.

There will never be another time like this one. Another client like this one. Moving forward, the men that Zoric allows to purchase me will never compare.

"Downstairs," McConnell directs me, then speaks quietly into his cellphone. "I need you to come around front. Please take my guest wherever she needs to go."

Once we're in the front entry hallway, he pulls out his wallet and digs out the wad of cash that he tried to give me earlier.

"It's twelve hundred," he reminds me, shoving it into my hand. "Take it. Please."

The money sits in my palm, a dirty reminder of what just happened. Pleasure is one thing. Being paid for it feels completely different.

Swallowing hard, I tuck the cash down the side of my waistband.

"Thank you." The words are so quiet, I'm not sure that he hears me.

Moving to the front door, he opens it wide.

"Good night, Miss—"

He looks at me, waiting for me to supply my name, but I don't. Instead I dart through the doorway, wincing as it shuts behind me. It's just as well he doesn't know who I am. That way we can both try to forget this ever happened.

A private car—McConnell's, it must be—pulls up outside the gate a second later. I slip through the gate and duck into the car hurriedly, giving the driver my address through a pane of glass that rolls down. Then I close my eyes and sink into the heated leather. My pulse is finally starting to slow.

I did it. Somehow. I survived. And I'm okay.

The night replays itself in my head, from getting picked up at my apartment by Zoric's man to the ride home now. What does it say about me that I liked it? It was the most terrifying experience of my life...until it wasn't.

His demands, his roughness... they weren't scary. They were hot. He called me a whore, and it turned me on. He used me hard, treated me like his fuck toy, and I climaxed. Twice.

One thing is certain, though: I hope I never see that man again. At least the anonymous clients in my future won't be able to remind me of how shamefully I enjoyed losing my virginity, despite the fact that it was a business transaction. Despite the fact that McConnell was so cruel. From now on, nothing that I do with the men who buy me will mean a thing.

Pulling my phone out, I power it back on and check for messages.

A breath goes out of me. Konstantin Zoric messaged me five minutes ago. It's nearly two a.m., but his text reads, *Stop at the office before you go home. I'll be waiting.*

Shit. He can't possibly have another client lined up for me already...can he? My insides still feel achy and bruised. There's no way I can go through this again.

But I'm not allowed to say no, am I? I have to do whatever Zoric says.

My stomach knots as I text him back, telling him I'm on my way.

Then I lean forward and tap on the glass partition. The driver lowers it.

"I'm sorry, but can you take me to a different address?"

"Of course. Where would you like to go?"

I give him the address, then clasp my hands tightly in my lap as I stare out the window. At this time of night, the city is quiet, the streets nearly empty. The KZM offices are in the heart of the business district, just a few more minutes away. The building is sleek, modern, the kind of gleaming skyscraper that instills a sense of glam and fame. You get the sense that you're walking into greatness when you enter, that your future will be secure once you sign on the dotted line. Because that's what they want us to believe, isn't it? And we do.

Last year, right after I had won the international modeling contest that KZM sponsored, I began receiving deceptive emails and phone calls from men claiming to be working for KZM. Excited by all the opportunities coming my way—and what they might mean for my family—I replied to a few of the messages before quickly realizing that they were not legitimate. These scammers were trying to lure me away from my hometown so they could abduct me. I found out later that this type of scam is common, and it terrified me that I almost fell for it.

Things didn't turn out much better for me here in Chicago, though. Just look at me now, taking a ride of shame from a man who paid me for sex, on my way to meet with my boss who will arrange another client, and another, and another. KZM's modeling contest turned out to be exactly the same scam I thought I had dodged, only it was delivered with a dose of glitter and opulence. This career path was nothing but an illusion all along.

The partition rolls down again and the driver says, "We're here, miss."

"Thank you."

I slide across the seat and find the driver already opening the door for me. I thank him again and walk up to the glass entrance doors, half expecting them to be locked. They aren't.

No such luck.

As I'm crossing the lobby toward the guard at the check-in desk, Zoric turns the corner from the bank of elevators and motions me toward a circle of plush leather chairs.

"She's with me," he tells the security guard.

My adrenaline kicks as I drop into a chair and set my bag at my feet. I know my hair and makeup are a fright, and my outfit of leggings and a T-shirt are hardly what I'd call business appropriate. And then a cynical laugh escapes me. What the hell am I worried about?

This isn't just my boss sitting across from me. It's my pimp. As long as I turn tricks like I'm supposed to, who cares what I look like afterward?

Zoric eyes me critically.

"He didn't keep you for the full night. Interesting."

Anger suddenly wells up inside me at the way he's sizing me up like a used car, like he's trying to figure out how many more miles he can put on me before I lose my value, but I hold my rage back. There's no sense losing my temper. It won't change anything, and it might give Zoric a reason to treat me worse. My mind and body are spent, and I just want to go home.

Not to the apartment, but home to my uncle's farmhouse where I can crawl in bed with Eva and drowse in the heat of the wood stove, one of my aunt's cotton quilts pulled over us.

"Still. You must have done well. Your buyer has already bought another date." He hands me a business card. "You'll meet him at this address tomorrow afternoon, two p.m."

My adrenaline surges as I take the card and skim the information on it. The buyer. Not the man I slept with, but his father. Who bought me at the auction for six thousand dollars. McConnell senior.

The memory of his teeth nipping my lip turns my stomach. There was something dangerous about him. Something ugly brewing underneath the handsome, haughty exterior.

"You look unhappy," Zoric says sharply. "You need

to learn to school your features. Just like when you go to a shoot, yes? Think of it as an extension of your modeling skills."

Squaring my shoulders, I sit up taller. "Yes, sir."

"That's better. You may go now."

With that, he gets up and strolls back toward the elevators. I don't watch him go. Instead, I sit here trying not to cry. I can't fall apart right now. Not here in this lobby. This prison.

I Uber back to the apartment. I'm barely holding it together, but I can't lose my shit. Not when my nightlife-loving roommates might still be up. Talking about it won't help. Nothing will help. All I want is a hot shower and eight hours of sleep. Ten, even.

Just as I suspected, Diya is on the couch playing with her phone when I walk in. Avoiding eye contact, I kick off my shoes and make a beeline for my room. She's right behind me.

"Hey."

"I'm tired, Diya," I say harshly. "I just want to go to bed."

Tears thicken my voice, and a tremble that I can't control racks my body. Diya's warm hand cups my shoulder, gently soothing me.

"Hey. I'll turn the shower on for you, okay?" she says softly.

"Thank you," I whisper.

"Do you want me to make you something? Toast, or—"

"I'm fine. Just the shower. Please."

I grab clean clothes from the bedroom and then lock myself in the tiny, steaming bathroom. After I soap myself from head to toe, I curl up at the bottom of the tub and let the hot water rain down on me. It might wash my tears away, but it can't wash away my shame.

9

RHYS

I HAVEN'T STOPPED THINKING about the girl since I closed my front door on her.

She's under my skin.

I am not a timid man and I rarely regret anything. Last night, I had sex with a beautiful woman who was more than willing to participate. It pissed me off that my father brought her and looking back, I probably should have sent her away. I'm still not entirely sure why I went through with it. I've never exchanged money for sex before, and the fact that my father paid for the girl doesn't make the deed any less unsavory.

Something struck me about her, and I didn't want to let her go. It wasn't her beauty. I can find that anywhere. It wasn't the tone of her voice considering she barely spoke to me. I'm not sure what drew me to her, but whatever it was made it impossible for me to look at my bed without feeling something strange in the pit of my stomach.

There was a fierceness to her that unsettled me.When she looked me in the eye, I saw past her youth, her eagerness to please, her fear. I saw steel.

Or maybe I'm just telling myself that to assuage the guilt I feel about taking her virginity. Someone dutifully completing a task they were paid to.

Did I destroy some purity in her, some innocence that she can never get back? Of course I did. I won't deny it. But I could have sworn that she felt something good when I was with her. And not just because she orgasmed.

Hence my relentless brooding at work. So far, no one has taken notice. I've had back-to-back calls since I got in this morning, then lunch with one of our senior board members, and now I'm preparing for an afternoon meeting with some eager new investors from Dubai.

My cell buzzes on the desk and I pick it up, inwardly cringing when I see yet another text from my father asking how my "date" went last night. I don't reply. I've been ignoring him all day. I can't hide forever, though. His office is right down the hall from mine.

"Mr. McConnell?"

There's a knock on the doorframe and my assistant, Tamara, pops her head in. I'm quite fond of her. She's a single mother who went back to school to finish her degree once her kids got to high school, and when she came in for her job interview, I was so impressed that I hired her on the spot. Unlike the younger applicants I'd seen—all slick corporate sharks in the making, only interested in working for me as a means to launch their own careers as quickly as possible—Tamara said she was interested in assisting at the executive level long term. She was also whip smart, and the ideal combination of adaptable, confident, and competent.

"I have the P&Ls you wanted for the meeting, and the company profile stats," she says. "Ten copies of each, right?"

"Yes, thank you. I'll take those."

"I made twelve, just in case," she says, passing me the folder with a melodious jangle of her bracelets.

"Nice," I tell her, snapping my laptop shut and tucking it under my arm as I stand. "Which conference room are we in?"

"Four. I assume to impress everyone with the best view of the city."

I shake my head. "Of course. Coffee and refreshments all ready to go?"

"Just set everything out. The Dubaians are waiting in reception. Is Dubaians a word?"

"It is." I check my watch. "Walk them down to four at two on the dot, please. I just need a few minutes to get set up in there. And then you can go ahead and take off early today."

"Bless your heart. You're a prince among men," she says, grinning from ear to ear.

"Hardly. But you mentioned that Jackson had a scrimmage today, and I don't want you to miss out when he makes that half-court shot. Go take care of your family."

"Thanks, boss."

A moment later I walk out of my office, pull the door shut behind me, and then immediately freeze.

Down the hall, I see the girl from last night standing off to the side of the reception desk. Except she's undergone a complete transformation, and wow. She looks like she belongs here, in a tasteful black pencil skirt, a silk blouse, and black flats. Her blonde hair is pulled up in a bun and subdued pearl studs gleam from her earlobes. She checks her watch, then glances around searchingly, like she's here for a lunch date or a social call.

My initial shock gives way to irritation. What the hell? Is she stalking me? Tracking me down at my workplace, showing up here uninvited, unannounced—is she trying to con me into one more night? God, and the timing is garbage. I have to get that conference room set up in less than five minutes.

Aware that the Dubaians are seated just a few feet away from her, I walk coolly toward the woman, take her by the elbow, and lead her back into my office. Steering her into a chair, I leave the door wide open to give the impression that this is strictly business. Which it is.

Eyes wide, she starts to say, "Sorry, I have—"

"What's your name?" I interrupt.

She hesitates and then softly answers, "Izabela."

Lowering my voice, I banish my annoyance and use a calm, coaxing tone as I tell her, "Izabela, listen, I don't know what my father or anyone else might have told you, but it is entirely inappropriate for you to be here right now, do you understand? You need to go. Now."

I expect her to get up, sashay down that hallway, and disappear. But instead she lifts her chin and gives me that same steely look I remember.

She opens her mouth to respond, but before she can get a word out, we're interrupted by my father's broad frame filling the doorway.

"There she is," he says. His gaze shifts to me. "Silly boy, did you think she was here for you? I hired her for myself."

Smugness is coming off him in waves as he moves to Izabela's side and takes her arm, pulling her up from the chair. The easy slide of his hand through the crook of her elbow makes my stomach turn.

"Thanks for being the warm-up act, son, but I'll take it from here. Show her what a real man's capable of, am I right?" He makes a finger gun at me and gives a little *click, click* sound with his tongue like we're two frat boys passing a co-ed around. "Wouldn't be the first time."

I'm literally seeing red.

Fuck this.

I home in on every part of his body that's touching her. His hand, his arm, the side of his chest, and his hip. I take one look at Izabela's face and instantly make up my mind.

There's no way in hell I'm letting my father leave with her.

"Izabela," I say, crisp and businesslike, "I need you to call your employer."

She looks uncertain for a moment, glancing at my father quickly before digging her cell out of her clutch and inching away from him. A few taps later, she raises it to her ear and waits.

"This is Izabela Jasinski," she says into the phone. "I need to speak with Mr. Zoric, please." Her cheeks turn pink from whatever the response is. "Yes, I'm aware that he's very busy. This is in regard to a...job that I'm on. No, I can't call back later—"

I grab the phone and put it to my ear. "This is Rhys McConnell. Put Mr. Zoric on *now*."

The line goes silent and then starts to ring.

"What are you doing, Rhys?" my father says impatiently, shifting his weight from one foot to the other. "She's bought and paid for. You've got no say in this."

I ignore him as someone picks up and gruffly barks, "Zoric. This better be good."

"Mr. Zoric, this is Rhys McConnell."

"Yes. My secretary informed me," he says, his voice

friendly and ingratiating. "I don't believe that you and I have yet had the pleasure of engaging in commerce."

"No, we have not."

"Which is unfortunate, Mr. McConnell. Because if we had, you would know not to call my office during business hours. This isn't how it works, I'm afraid. So you'll have to just—"

"I have a proposition for you," I interrupt, sensing he's about to give me the brush-off and hang up the phone. "I want Izabela. Exclusively. For a term of six months."

In three strides, my father is at my side, gripping my arm painfully with one hand while he tries to grab the phone with the other. Diverting, I break his grip and stop him from another attempt with a glare.

Zoric clears his throat. "Regrettably, we're not able to offer exclusivity at this time—"

"Do you know who I am?" I thunder into the phone, privately sickened at how much I sound like my father in this moment.

"Of course, Mr. McConnell," Zoric says, reverting to his false friendly tone. "You're the future CEO of McConnell Enterprises, and one of the country's richest men under thirty! But do let me arrange some complimentary entertainment for you instead. Miss Jasinski has already been paid for by another client, incidentally. She's not available. Perhaps I could find you another—"

"I would think the future CEO of this company is

worth keeping happy far more than the aging father who got passed over. This isn't personal, Zoric. It's business."

My father's face is red now. Izabela has backed up against the wall, twisting her hands in front of her as she glances nervously between my father and me. Either way, she's going to end up with a man who's going to use her. But I'll pay any price to watch my father lose.

"We have a deal, Zoric?" I say.

Zoric makes an uncertain sound, as if he's still struggling to decide. I don't have time for his hemming and hawing. I have a meeting to get to. It's time to close this deal.

"I'll pay double what he did, per day, for the duration of the six-month term, if you say yes right now," I say. "Final offer."

There's another pause. And then, "She can start tomorrow."

"Not tomorrow," I shoot back. "She starts now. I'll throw in another ten thousand."

"Done. I'll make some calls. Pleasure doing business, Mr. McConnell."

"You made the right choice," I say before I hang up.

My dad's eyes flash as I hand the phone back to Izabela. If we weren't in the office with twenty witnesses around, his hands would probably be around my throat. But he lost, and now it will be my hands around Izabela's throat.

Her phone chimes with an incoming text. A second later, my father's phone rings in his pocket.

"We're done here. Get the fuck out of my office," I tell him.

Without a word, he puts the phone to his ear as he walks out, slamming the door behind him as he leaves.

Izabela reads the message on her phone, then starts typing a response. I look her up and down appraisingly, trying to keep the triumphant grin off my face. Starting now, I have six months to find out what's hiding behind those steely blue eyes of hers. Six months to figure out why the look in them unsettles me the way that it does. Not to mention the endless nights I'll have to play with her body. To break her. To mold her.

To enjoy every last drop of her pleasure, because it means that much more of my own.

Izabela looks up at me, phone still in her hand, and says, "It appears you and I have an arrangement, Mr. McConnell."

An arrangement that could start immediately, right here in my office, with her body splayed across my desk. Too bad I have a meeting with some Dubaians.

"I have business to attend to. Stay in my office. I'll be back in an hour."

10

IZABELA

How ᴇᴀsɪʟʏ ᴏᴡɴᴇʀsʜɪᴘ of my body has transferred hands.

The last thing I want to do for the next hour is sit here and question all my life choices, though, so I take out my phone and write an email to my sister. It's not full of lies, per se, but I take care to word my sentences very carefully so it sounds like I'm having the time of my life. I say things like, "I'm meeting so many interesting new people" and "I just booked my biggest job yet." Eva doesn't need to know that the people I'm meeting are johns.

I'm so engrossed in what I'm doing that I don't realize how many minutes have passed until the door to Rhys McConnell's office swings open and my head snaps up to find him striding back into the room. His meeting must be over. His computer is tucked under his arm and he has a satisfied look on his face. I hurriedly slip my phone into my bag and straighten in the chair, heart slamming in my chest.

"There's something you need to know," he says, the look on his face daring me to lean forward. "Something you need to fully understand, because I will be reminding you every day and every night."

"What would that be, Mr. McConnell?"

"For the next six months, I own you. And I'll be damned if you forget it."

"Do you understand what it means to be owned by me, Miss Jasinski?" he asks, setting the laptop down and then turning to face me, arms crossed as he leans back against the desk.

Our gazes lock, and I feel like an antelope being appraised by a lion.

"I...I'm not sure, Mr. McConnell," I answer honestly.

"I don't think you do. In fact, I don't think you have the slightest idea what it means. But you're about to find out."

Liquid heat pools in my belly and works its way through my body. This man has no idea what the gravel in his voice and the heat in his eyes is doing to me. Or maybe he does.

Resisting the urge to bolt from the office, I force myself to hold still and wait for him to make a move. It's not that I don't want him to touch me. It's that I do. Badly. So badly.

And that scares the hell out of me.

I can feel my core start to pulse as my mind conjures up visceral memories of what we did last night. The scent of his cologne, the hot glide of his cock, the silkiness of his hair sliding through my fingers, that sound he made right when he came. A shiver goes through me, and I don't miss the predator's smile that ghosts across his face as he watches me.

"Untuck your legs," he says, running a thumb across his lower lip.

I'm sitting on the edge of the seat, back straight, legs pulled to one side, my hands folded in my lap. This is my standard position anytime I'm in a professional setting, a pose that's businesslike, modest, and demure. But right now, the way he's looking at me, I feel anything but.

I shift my legs to the front, pressing my knees together, trembling slightly. My whole body is on fire beneath the weight of his gaze, my skin prickling. Little warning signs going off in reaction to the danger radiating from him. I first felt it when he got on the phone with Zoric and demanded six months with me, refusing to take no for an answer. Rhys McConnell decided he was going to possess me, and he didn't stop until he got what he wanted. He's a powerful, relentless, and unpredictable man. And now he owns me.

"Now spread your legs. I want to take a closer look at what I just bought."

At first, I can't respond. My body is frozen. The desire and the heat are still there but they're shrouded by shame. Knowing that I have to obey him to avoid consequences, I lean back slightly in the chair and angle my hips forward until my ass rides the edge. The hem of my skirt is tight around my thighs, so I shimmy it higher. My knees fall apart, but my cheeks heat and I quickly press them back together. He drums his fingers on the desktop, loudly, pointedly.

I no longer only answer to Mr. Zoric but to Rhys McConnell, as well. There will be double the hell to pay if I don't do what's expected of me. Resigning to my lack of choice, I pushed down my need for autonomy, relax my legs and let them fall apart. I know that under the shadow of my skirt, he can see my black satin underwear. A small sound comes from deep in his throat. Appreciation, maybe? He likes what he sees. I see it in his eyes.

A small thrill ripples through me. One small adjustment of my body has completely trapped his attention. People talk of how easily men are controlled with sex and I'm beginning to see there's truth to that. He doesn't look away as he leans back in his chair, puts an elbow on the arm, and a finger beneath his chin.

"Panties off," he says.

I glance over my shoulder at the office door, which is closed but not locked.

"But—"

"*Off.*"

Oh, I want to be angry about this. I *am* angry that he's purposely embarrassing me and putting me in a vulnerable position. But at the same time I feel an odd sense of control in the way that he's responding to the view of my body.

With a gulp, I push my underwear over my hips, over my thighs, letting the panties slide all the way down to my ankles. My breath is coming faster now, and I stare up at him, wondering if he's going to fuck me in this chair right now. I'm half terrified, half dizzy with desire.

Rhys steps toward me and then drops to a crouch, right between my legs.

"Open," he says, tapping my knee.

Heart thumping in my chest, I let my legs fall apart.

"Wider."

I spread my thighs as wide as they'll go. The air is cool against the wetness between my legs, and I wonder if Rhys can see that wetness as his eyes home in on the center of me.

I await my next instruction.

But it doesn't come.

Instead he stands, walks back to his desk, and drops into the chair behind it.

"Straighten yourself," he says.

Once I'm sitting up again, underwear back in place, skirt pulled down, he nods.

"This is how it's going to work, Miss Jasinski. We will date publicly, we will fuck privately, and any feelings you develop for me you will keep to yourself. Understood?"

There's only one acceptable answer, and we both know it. "Yes."

"You'll move into my house for the duration of our arrangement and sleep in the spare room. I paid for your exclusivity, so your business is my business. You haven't paid for mine, so what I do is also my business."

"Understood," I say, but I'm still trying to wrap my head around that first part. I'm moving into his house? That beautiful mansion from last night?

"You will not come and go as you please," he goes on. "You will not leave the property without my permission. You will never invite anyone into my house. You will do nothing—nothing—without my approval. This is both for your safety and to protect my investment."

My jaw drops. "But I have to work."

"What do you do for work, besides this?" he asks, sounding skeptical.

Lifting my chin, I say, "I'm signed to KZM. I model. Professionally."

"You're not a model anymore. At least, not for the six months that you owe me. I'll be keeping you too busy to worry about photo shoots interfering with what I paid for. I'm sure Mr. Zoric would agree. Should I call him back to verify?"

A burst of panic hits me square in the chest, immediately followed by anger. He's really got my attention now. I need my career. It's my only foothold in the wider world. I have to make him understand that.

"You can't do that. This thing happening between us right now was never supposed to be part of my contract. I am a model because I have obligations and responsibilities and if you take that away from me, I won't be able to fulfill them."

"I don't give a shit about any of that."

I'll be punished for this. But I will reach out to Mr. Zorich and beg him to take it out on me and not my family. Standing, I lower the hem of my skirt and lift my chin. "Forcing me to disappear from the industry for six months is a death sentence. I'll never find work again. I can't do that. I won't do that."

His fist comes down on the top of his desk so hard and so quickly that I jump.

"You'll do anything that I fucking tell you. I thought you would understand that easily, but it seems we have some work to do."

He's going to tell my boss that I'm impertinent and uncooperative. I know I should stop talking, that I should sit down and resume the position. But I can't.

"I have a life outside of this and I need to take care of it. You will kill my career. Please, can we negotiate an agreement on this?"

He shrugs. "The way I see it, I'm paying you plenty as it is."

"You're paying *Zoric* plenty," I seethe. "I have no idea when I'll see a paycheck from this, nor what kind of percentage I'll be looking at. With modeling, I'm paid up front."

"Ah. It always comes back to money," he says bitterly. "The only thing that matters."

"Yes. Money. Have you ever noticed that only the rich can afford to be snide about it? But I can't. Unlike you, I wasn't...*nie urodziłem się w czepku!*"

For a moment, he just blinks at me. "Pardon?"

My face heats. "Nothing. It's a Polish saying."

"Tell me what it means."

"It means...born in a bonnet. Born lucky."

He leans forward and gestures around the office. "You think I got where I am because of luck? You think I haven't worked my ass off for this?"

"I'm not saying you haven't worked hard. I'm saying you were first in line. It's called McConnell Enterprises for a reason, no?"

That smirk curves his lips again. "Not first in line. But point taken."

We sit there staring each other down, and I can't tell if he's mulling over what I've just said or merely drawing out his response so he can enjoy his power over me some more.

Keeping my voice steady, I make one final plea, appealing to his ego this time.

"If I disappear for six months, I'll be out of the industry for good. I know you have a name and a reputation to maintain, and I don't think it would be nice for your image if the press were to find out you're dating an unemployed former model. Wouldn't you rather be seen dating someone successful? Someone who doesn't seem like a..." I rack my brain for the word he called me last night. "A gold digger?"

He lifts a brow, and I know I've got him thinking. How simple that was. I just had to make everything about him, not me.

"I'll take it under consideration," he finally says.

That's all I get. A maybe. Fuck.

I just have to hope he'll come around. And hope even harder that he doesn't tell Zoric I was uncooperative. Because the last thing I can do right now is ask Rhys not to rat me out to my boss. It would only give Rhys even more leverage over me, seeing how much I fear Zoric.

Checking his watch, he says, "You'll be moving in tomorrow. Go home and pack. And don't bring anything that isn't essential. Your needs will be provided for."

There's not a hint of warmth in his tone, just pure, cold dismissal. I stand up, knees weak, clutching my purse like it's a lifeline. I have to remind myself that as long as I can still take care of Eva, it doesn't matter that I'll be treated like an object instead of a person.

"Thank you, Mr. McConnell," I say, inching toward the door.

"One last thing," he says. "You'll need to be ready at eight tomorrow morning. A car will pick you up at that time and take you to your doctor's appointment."

"Doctor's appointment?"

That cruel smile pulls his lips again. "Before you

move in, you'll be thoroughly screened for sexually transmitted infections and prescribed birth control."

I feel the blush creeping across my face. "But—"

"You'll find I'm a man who plans for every contingency," he interrupts. "Now get out."

11

RHYS

THE SOUNDS of Izabela moving into my house interrupts my attempt to work.

I'm still not entirely sure if I made the right decision, but I have no regrets. My goal was to keep her as far out of my father's reach as possible. This will accomplish that goal quite tidily.

But while thwarting the man is satisfying, this is about much more than being petty or stealing his plaything right out from under him. I simply could not stomach the thought of my father annihilating the last shreds of her innocence.

I prefer to do that myself.

She's *my* plaything now.

And play with her I will. Her lack of experience makes her the ideal blank slate. I'm going to turn her into a fucking masterpiece.

Starting today, I have six full months to train her, to

shape her into exactly what I want. If amateur hour last night was any indication of what she's capable of, it won't be difficult to mold her into my own personal fantasy. She's got quite a mouth on her. Just the memory of Izabela down on her knees, choking on my cock, has my pants getting tight.

With a heavy exhale, I banish the image from my mind and get up from my desk chair, squeezing the back of my neck to release some of the tension there. I've been hunched over my laptop in my home office all morning, reviewing an endless stream of documents related to the Dubai deal, but Izabela's arrival with the moving crew just now has utterly destroyed my focus.

The scent of her coconut shampoo is all I can think about. Hearing her move around makes it worse. I become so distracted that I can't even focus on my email. Frustrated that my work time is already interrupted, reminding me why I live alone, I leave the office and watch the movers hauling things into my house. Two men cart in four medium size boxes and a shabby-looking lamp. Izabela has a laptop bag over her shoulder and a small duffle bag in her hands. They make one trip to her room, leave, and don't return.

That's it?

Despite telling her to keep her things to a minimum, I assumed she'd still cart over way more than this. Most of my past girlfriends could fit their entire shoe collection in those four boxes. Girlfriends. Izabela isn't exactly that, is she? And she's already shown me that she's not typical of the woman I tend to spend my time with. She doesn't seem interested in working her way into being a kept woman. She wants to continue modeling and making a name for herself instead of being passed from man to man. I bought her so easily and I briefly wonder why she got herself into that position in the first place. Seems she would have known what she'd gotten herself into. Not that it matters. I'm getting what I want. A woman to warm my bed and accompany me to necessary functions.

That's all this is.

But it still feels strange to have her permanently inserted into my personal space.

She opens a box and looks around the room. At first, she doesn't seem to notice that I'm watching her from the doorway where I lean against the frame. She spins slowly, her eyes full of sadness in the second before she schools her features.

My chest tightens at that shadow of emotion. I hadn't thought it would be so trying for her to live here for the next six months. My past lovers are usually trying to worm their way into a more permanent spot in my life. It's...nice that I don't have to worry about that for a while.

"Doctor gave you a clean bill of health," I tell her. "Did you take your first pill yet?"

"I took a shot before I left the doctor's office." Even better—effective immediately.

"Good. Here's a copy of the house key for you."

She takes it from me and sets it on the night table. "Thanks. Is it okay if I unpack?"

"Of course."

Izabela continues opening the box while giving me a sideways glance. Her room is perfectly styled and should suit her well while she's here. The bed sheets are Egyptian cotton, the duvet some expensive brand my designer choose. The furniture is modern and comfortable. An oversized chair is perched by the window. The bed could fit four, easily. There's a birch desk and office chair. And the walk-in closet could work as a small apartment on its own. Despite the luxury, she doesn't seem at all impressed.

Fishing clothing from the first box, she places them neatly on the bed, then does the same with the second box. The third box appears to be full of books and some framed photos. The fourth is shoes, a winter jacket and odds and ends.

She turns to the closet and begins hanging things up. Her paltry wardrobe won't touch an eighth of the space inside. I'm suddenly irritated and I'm not sure why. If she's a model, shouldn't she have more? More clothes, more makeup, more shoes and all the things models lean towards? Izabela is likely the most simplistic woman I've ever met.

"Do you have more at your apartment?" I gesture to the boxes.

She shakes her head. "No. I brought everything with me."

"Wow. I don't think I've ever met a woman who was such a minimalist."

Izabela gives me that icy stare that I'm becoming all too familiar with.

"When I moved here from Poland, I brought two suitcases with me. I don't have much. It's not like I take myself shopping with my earnings."

Working my jaw to the side, I watch for a few more minutes, knowing I should leave her to unpack. But she's mine. She can unpack later. Her high-waist jeans are sculpted to her long legs and that perfectly round derrière, making my mouth water. Her hair is in a thick braid down her back, begging to be tugged. Right now, I'm tense and on edge and she's going to help take it away.

"So, you're a professional model."

She looks over at me and a smile works its way across her face. "I'm still on my way up in the industry, but yes. It's mostly been print jobs, photos for catalogs or department store websites, but I've been getting bigger gigs recently. My agent says I'm gaining recognition."

"You good at what you do?"

There's no hesitation as she answers, simply, "Yes."

The confidence is unexpected. This woman is such a contradiction. At times she seems so young, so unworldly, so inexperienced. At others she's stubborn, fierce, self-assured. It's...interesting. Not that I'm interested in her. What I'm interested in is her capacity to please. She's a means to an end.

But there's no reason I can't be entertained by her in the process.

"Prove it," I say. "Give me a show and I'll decide if you have what it takes."

The look in her eyes says challenge accepted, even before the words are out of her mouth.

"What do you want me to do?"

Moving to the chair by the window, I sink into it. "Take off your jacket."

Izabela steps back and looks directly at me, lifting her chin and straightening her spine. Then she presses her lips together and stalks toward me. She's treating this exactly like one of her shoots, I realize. Pretending she's on an actual runway. This isn't a game to her.

Jutting one hip to the side, she shrugs out of the jacket and lets it slide down her arms. Transferring it to one hand, she slings it over her shoulder, turns, and walks away. When she reaches the closet door, she turns back around and tosses the jacket on the bed.

"What now?" she asks, still wearing that haughty model face.

I assess her blue blouse and those tight jeans, the tall boots that look scuffed enough to suggest she's had them for a while. If she's good, very good, I'll take her to buy new ones.

But first, we'll see how well she performs.

"Striptease for me, Izabela. Take it all off. Slowly."

The mask slips, and I see her emotions play out on her face. Consternation. Reluctance. A little hatred toward me. All fine, as long as she follows through.

Her hands drop to the front of her shirt and she works the first button of her blouse. Her fingers tremble slightly as she fumbles with it. The second comes apart easier. My cock starts to harden as I anticipate the blouse falling open, revealing the milky rise of her breasts, the curve of her waist, and all that silken skin. Mine. All mine.

Slowly, her hips begin to move. Just a sway, side to side. She releases the rest of the buttons, one by one. Shifting in the chair, I nearly groan as her shirt finally opens and gives me the view I was waiting for. A pink demi bra cups her breasts, round and firm, and I have to fight back the urge to go over there and dip my tongue into the narrow channel between them. I can't wait to find out if her panties match.

"Runway walk while you take off the shirt," I command.

My voice is pure gravel. My blood, so heated.

I catch another angry flash in her eyes before she saunters toward me again, strutting down the length of the room. She passes me, reaches the far wall, spins, and walks back to me. The shirt slips effortlessly down her arms. Leaning back, she grabs the shirt in her hand and sends it flying onto the bed.

"I like the attitude," I tell her. "Ditch the braid. I want that hair long and loose."

Her hips take on a motion of their own as she sways before me, pulling her hair over her shoulder so she can tug off the hair tie. Once her hair is unbound, she rakes her fingers into it along the sides of her head, biting her lower lip as she looks down at me. Damn, she's good.

She leans forward, bending low, giving me the perfect view of her breasts. Her long, silky hair falls forward and brushes against my thighs. Then she licks her lips. My cock is throbbing. With a groan, I hook my fingers into the front of her bra and pull her forward. Her hands find my knees for support, my lips an inch from hers.

"Take off your pants."

Her movements are graceful as she straightens and resumes her slow, quiet dance, reaching down to unzip her boots before she steps out of them. Her breasts strain against the bra as she works, her nipples peaking beneath the fabric. Delectable.

Sliding lower in the chair, I widen my stance and rest my chin on my knuckles. Her jeans slide down smooth, toned thighs, and now I'm the one licking my lips. She's wearing a tiny black thong, and she's wet. I can smell it, sweet and musky.

"More. The bra, now."

Reaching behind herself, she unclasps her bra. The bra falls away, her breasts spilling free. I can't wait any longer.

Grabbing her hips, I move her between my open legs and rip her black lace thong down to her ankles. I can see the wet patch in them when they hit the floor. When I look up at her, I see desire in her eyes. Fear, too, but it's the fear of the sexual amateur. She wants this.

I'll make it easy for her.

I unzip my pants and then pull her down to straddle me on the chair. Her mouth falls open, eyes going wide as I line my cock up against her slit and then thrust straight up into her. Hot, wet, tight, perfect. No kissing. No affection. Just pure, hard fucking. This is what I paid for. This is exactly what I paid for.

I have all the power, all the control. And I can't be taken advantage of. It's bliss.

"You did this," I grunt, spearing into her with relish. "You made me this hard. Now you're going to pay."

"Yes," she pants as I fill her to the hilt.

"Don't tease me, Izabela. Nobody likes a tease. Fuck me like you mean it."

Her hair sways against my chest as she begins to rock on my dick. Holding her hips, I guide her movements, my eyes glued to the way her tits shake with every thrust.

I reach down her front, dipping my finger between her pussy lips and then sliding back up to her clit. She cries out at the pressure, and I stroke her again and again, circling her swollen nub in time with her gyrations. In seconds she's soaking me, so wet that I can feel my cock slipping deeper with every stroke.

Bracing her hands on the arms of the chair, she

rides me like the good little whore she is, until both of us are breathless and I'm completely consumed by the hot glide of her pussy. Her moans fill my ears, louder, more frantic. I'm just getting started, just getting into the swing, but suddenly she comes, and the pulse of her orgasm around my cock shatters me.

"Fuck yes," I groan, tightening my hold on her hips.

Still groaning, I jackhammer into her, finishing with a brutal release that has me gasping for air. I'm tingling from head to toe, shockwaves rippling through me. Once I've spilled every last drop of my seed, I throw my head back against the chair, all my muscles relaxing.

Fuck. The last time I came that hard, I was probably eighteen years old.

Lifting her off me, I realize she's shaking. I don't know if it's from the sex or if she's just cold, but I drag the blanket off the back of the chair and hand it to her so she can wrap herself up. She stands before me, mascara raccooning her eyes, cheeks flushed. I have half a mind to carry her to the bed and take her all over again, but McConnell Enterprises doesn't run itself.

"You proved yourself," I say gruffly. "You can keep modeling. But only if I approve the jobs first. Also, I thought about what you said. About the PR. My reputation. My image."

She nods, waiting for me to continue.

"I've decided to make the most of this arrangement —get the highest return on my investment. So from now on, you'll be playing the part of my girlfriend, not just someone I'm dating casually. This will ensure I have a plus-one for events, and it'll keep other women from hounding me. It's convenient. And judging by what I just saw from you, I'm sure you'll have no trouble with the acting. When we go out, you can just pretend you're on a photo shoot."

"I can do that."

"Good."

I send her into the en-suite bathroom to shower. As I get dressed, I congratulate myself on how well I've handled things. This lease on Izabela is going to work out perfectly. No emotions, no attachments, no strings.

I can't imagine anything easier.

IZABELA

Rhys departs the townhouse before daybreak, leaving me alone in the lofty space. I lay there for a while after hearing him leave, toying the covers between my hands, and listening intently for any sound.

It was silly to be afraid considering the amount of security in the house. But after growing up in a house with only three rooms and then sharing the small apartment with my fellow models, it's overwhelming to be the only person in all this space.

Well, alone except for the staff. So far I've met Rawlings, an older gentleman who seems to manage the day-to-day goings-on of the house and the coordination of meals, as well as occasionally checking to see if Rhys needs anything; and Mrs. Dunham, who constantly bustles around cleaning things or carrying folded laundry or tea trays. They're much more at ease under the command of Rhys than they were when his father brought me here for the first time. No wonder they seemed so panicked that night—the elder Mr. McConnell just barged in with a strange woman on his arm and it's not even his place.

I finally get up and turn all the lights on to make myself feel better while taking a hasty shower.

Then I go down to the dining room in my robe and find a carafe of hot coffee waiting on the table. After pouring myself a cup, I start to wonder if I'm supposed to go to the kitchen to put in my breakfast order or make my own meal. I have no idea what the protocols are in a house of this size, especially for a long-term guest like myself.

But just as I'm about to go find out, Mrs. Dunham comes through the door with poached eggs, sliced fruit, yogurt and granola, and fresh cream for the coffee.

"Good morning, Miss Jasinski."

"Good morning. Is this all for me?"

"It is. If the selections aren't to your liking, I can have the cook prepare something else," she says. "This is what Mr. McConnell usually has during the week."

I lean back in my chair as she sets everything out on the table. It all looks wonderful, but I miss what's not there: my uncle's apple pancakes served with slices of fried kielbasa, fresh milk, hot rolls with honey and walnuts. Mealtimes are often when I miss my family most.

"This is great. Thank you, Mrs. Dunham."

With a curt nod, she sweeps from the room. I like her—I think—but I can't tell if she disapproves of me being here, or if she even knows the full extent of what my arrangement with Rhys is. Her manner is a bit cool, but I can't tell if it's borne of judgment or simply efficiency.

I dig into the food, knowing I'll need my energy for the long hours ahead. The last job I booked before Rhys took charge of my career is happening today. He agreed that I should meet this prior obligation, so I didn't have to argue with him about the merits of the assignment.

Which is good, because it's not a very prestigious gig. It's a cheesy little runway show at a bridal shop downtown. I have a feeling it's going to be a day filled with lots of tiny pearl buttons, a lot of tightly cinched corset waists, and a lot of squished boobs. And a *lot* of tulle.

Still, work is work. This is my career, and I have to take the lows with the highs. Besides, as far as "lows" go, I've recently gained a whole new perspective thanks to Konstantin Zoric.

As soon as I've eaten my fill, I go back upstairs to get ready. I don't need to worry about my hair or makeup since professionals will handle that later, but I still like to look as put together as possible. Thank God for all the free clothes I've been given on my shoots. It's easy to look fashionable when all your outfits come from next season's cream of the crop.

I pull on a pair of jeans, an embroidered cream blouse that's a little bit bohemian, and a cropped leather jacket. Eva would be proud of me. I never used to pay attention to clothes, unlike her, but now it's practically second nature for me to assemble something decent.

I hear a knock at my door and dash across the bedroom to open it.

"Your driver is here, Miss Jasinski," says Rawlings.

"Thank you. I'll be right down."

"Very good."

Rhys assigned me a personal driver and forwarded the man my schedule, along with explicit instructions that I'm not to be driven anywhere that's not listed on the daily planner. It's annoying, but I know it's all part of being a kept woman. This is what Rhys paid for, right? So I just have to suck it up. Though I admit, having my own car and driver is a lot more luxurious than taking Ubers or the L all over town.

When I arrive at the May Queen Bridal Shop, I have to put my game face on. The location is downtown, and the place looks legit enough, but it looks a little...Vegas. There's a hot pink-and-white striped awning over the front façade, and the window displays are crammed with frothy, glittery, costume-y gowns and a flashing sign that says "Brides, Brides, Brides" like some kind of strip club advertisement. It's glam, but not very classy.

I know I shouldn't judge. I should be happy that

I'm here at all, considering Rhys threatened to take my work away from me. And yes, I am glad to be working. I just wish the job was a little more upscale. More of an asset to my portfolio.

The second I step through the door, I'm whisked away to change into several gowns, one after the other, all of them straight off the rack and not my size. The wardrobe assistant is stressed out and impatient as she pins and clips the best she can, trying to make them fit me. Usually, the clothes at my shoots are exactly my size, or else they're tailored when I arrive. But that's not the case today. This fashion show seems to be flying by the seat of its pants.

People are running around, speaking frantically into their headsets, wardrobe is struggling to fit me into these gowns, and hair and makeup can't seem to agree on how to style me. The first attempt at my makeup is a disaster—the look is more overdone beauty pageant than glamorous and romantic—so it has to be done all over again.

As the tornado unfolds around me, I sit quietly like the voiceless, moldable model that I am. It's the fashion producer's job to figure out all the logistics. My job is merely to walk out there and help execute their vision. I'm having my hair pulled, and not in the good way, when another model walks in with a bewildered look on her face.

"You're an hour late!" the fashion producer yells.

Seconds later, the new model gets shoved into the

chair next to me. She looks familiar. It takes a second before I remember seeing her at another shoot. She's a KZM model, too.

She slides me a skeptical gaze and whispers, "I'm *not* late. I got called in last minute."

I flash her a sympathetic smile. "I believe you. I'm Izabela, by the way. I think we worked together last month. For a jewelry store in Wicker Park."

"The shoot with all the fake snow! I remember. I'm Stasya. What's going on around here? It's looking a little...*spustya rukava*."

I have to suppress a laugh. Stasya basically just called the show "half-assed" in Russian. The woman doing my hair gives her a sharp side-eye but doesn't say anything.

"They're still trying to figure out the right hairstyle for me," I say. "My first round of makeup wasn't right either."

Stasya frowns. "Don't they have anyone around here that knows what they're doing?"

The hair girl huffs out a sigh and turns to Stasya. "It's not my fault the stylist changed up all the models' dresses at the last minute! The hair has to match the dress!"

She coats my head in a suffocating cloud of hair-spray and then stalks away.

"Don't worry. I'm sure everything will come together soon," I tell Stasya comfortingly.

She picks at a nail and shrugs. "It's fine. We're getting paid, so. Work is work, right?"

I nod. "You said they called you in last minute? Did the other model get sick?"

"Maybe." Swiveling in her seat to face me, her voice lowers conspiratorially. "I guess that girl Vara was supposed to be here today? But, like, no one's been able to get ahold of her for a few days. Have you heard anything?"

"I haven't spoken to her since we did a shoot together about two months ago. What do you mean, no one's gotten ahold of her?"

I recall one of my roommates mentioning another girl who disappeared off the scene without a word. I can't quite recall the circumstances surrounding that. If I ever knew them.

"Does anybody know if—"

But before I can get the words out, another frazzled assistant comes rushing over, waving his arms angrily as he skids to a stop in front of Stasya. "Why are you still in your jacket? Oh my God, could they ever send a model that knows what the hell she's doing?"

"Someone put me in this chair," she points out.

He huffs. "Just follow me!"

She rolls her eyes before following him out of the room.

I'm too distracted by Vara's disappearance to worry about it. Something about it won't let me go. I've been afraid of what will happen to me if I don't cooperate with Mr. Zoric's demands. Vara's situation reinforces that my fears are very valid. I can't walk away from the contract I've been forced into. No one's going to save me. Not from Rhys. Not from the men that come after him.

Soon enough, I'm led to the curtain behind the small catwalk that has been set up on the main floor of the bridal shop. I go through the motions of the fashion show, operating on autopilot as I model several dresses that are not quite tailored to my body. There are gaps where there shouldn't be, bunching fabric in odd places, straight pins poking me and sequins falling off, but no one seems to care.

The rest of the day goes by in a blur, and I'm grateful when it's over. I don't even bother washing off my makeup before quickly getting dressed and slipping out the back door, where my car and driver are waiting to take me to Rhys's.

It's not quite seven p.m. and I'm surprised to find him waiting for me when I walk into the house. He approaches me from the front sitting room, his eyes moving over my body and then lingering on my face, as if assessing my makeup.

We make brief eye contact and I try to ignore the flutter in my stomach. "Hi."

"Dinner will be ready shortly," he says.

Is this his idea of an invitation, or am I being scolded for coming home so late?

"Okay..."

"Clean yourself up and join me in the dining room," he says. "Be prompt."

With that, he turns on his heel and walks away.

Ten minutes later I've changed, scrubbed my face of every last remnant of makeup, and done my best to brush the stiff layers of hairspray out of my hair. When I go down to the dining room, Rhys stands to pull a chair out for me at the table. Dishes of steaming risotto, steak, roasted asparagus, and green salad are set out, along with wine. Rhys serves both of us.

As I sit there watching him dish out the food, he asks, "How was the job today? You had said you were modeling gowns for a bridal shop."

"It was fine," I say vaguely.

"What was the name of the place?"

"May Queen Bridal Shop."

Frowning, he says, "Never heard of it."

He looks displeased. I wonder what I said wrong.

"How many dresses did you model?"

I shrug. "Nine or ten. I lost track. There were a lot of last-minute changes."

"*Nine or ten?* How did they have the time to fit you? No tailor works that fast."

"They weren't fitted for me. They were off the rack, pinned into place."

He scowls. "Who did your makeup and hair?"

"I don't know. I didn't get their names. Not anyone I've worked with before."

"And with whom did you walk? The other models, who were they?"

"Um. Just two other girls. One named Stormy who I've never met before—I think she was the shop owner's daughter? And then another model from KZM. Stasya Petrova."

Rhys takes a bite of risotto, so I do the same, hoping he's done grilling me about the job. The food tastes so good I have to hold back a moan. I haven't eaten since breakfast. I take another bite, then another, and then spear the biggest two pieces of steak on my plate.

When I look up, Rhys is watching me shove the steak into my mouth. Humiliation courses through me as I chew. He must think I'm a pig. I set down my fork and dab my mouth with the fancy linen napkin in my lap.

"What did they feed you today?" he asks slowly.

I drop my eyes, shame burning my cheeks. "Um. They didn't. I mean, it was so hectic..."

There's no denying the tension in the room. I'm not sure what this game of one-hundred questions is about, but it's giving me a bad feeling in the pit of my stomach. Is Rhys going to change his mind about me modeling?

"Who ran the show?" he asks.

I rattle off the name of the producer, and Rhys throws down his fork with a clatter.

"So let me get this straight," he says. "You wasted your entire day at some third-rate bridal store downtown, modeling off-the-rack dresses with a face full of pancake makeup and an updo that looks like it was done by a beauty school dropout, without a single household name on the set, and they starved you to boot. Does that about cover it?"

I clasp my hands in my lap, my eyes stinging with tears. "Yes."

"Get your boss on the phone."

My guts clench with anxiety. I don't move.

"Izabela, go get your phone and call Zoric. *Now.*"

Pushing my chair back, I bolt from the room and run upstairs. Once I'm back with my phone in my hand, I drop into my chair across from Rhys and dial the main office, knowing full well that there's no way I'm getting through.

"Put the call on speaker," Rhys says.

I do, and we both listen to the call ring and ring and ring.

"I guess no one's at the off—" I start to say, but then someone picks up.

"Miss Jasinski," comes Konstantin Zoric's voice through the speaker, sounding gruff and on edge. "Why are you calling?"

My blood runs cold. Since when does Zoric know my cell number by heart? I look over at Rhys, but he's already leaning across the table, grabbing the phone.

"Zoric," he says sharply. "This is Rhys McConnell."

Zoric's tone instantly changes. "Mr. McConnell!

137

To what do I owe the distinct pleasure of this call? I hope there's been no trouble with your...merchandise."

"Merchandise? No, Izabela is perfect. But this modeling situation isn't working for me."

My heart plummets, even as a spark shoots through me. Rhys just called me perfect?

"If you need her to step away from the modeling—" Zoric starts to say.

I direct my gaze at Rhys, pleading with my eyes.

"That's not what I said," Rhys interrupts. "I said it isn't working for me. It's not good enough. I don't date small-time models. I date Paris Fashion Week models."

Zoric sputters, "But Mr. McConnell, Izabela isn't—"

"*So make her one,*" Rhys says coldly.

With that, he hangs up the call and resumes eating as if nothing just happened. I try to follow suit, but my hands are shaking so badly that I can barely manage to hold my fork.

I feel like I've been struck by lightning.

Because Rhys McConnell has power. He has influence. He has clout. And nobody knows this more than my boss, Konstantin Zoric.

That request Rhys just made? It wasn't a casual suggestion.

It was an order.

The kind of order that could change my life.

13

RHYS

I've just gotten into the back of my private car after work on Friday when my mom calls my cell. We usually chat once or twice a week, but a friend has been staying with Mom on a visit from Florida, so we're overdue for a catch-up call.

"Hi, Mom. Did you get Helen dropped off at the airport okay this morning?"

I'd offered to send my personal car and driver to shuttle Helen, but Mom had staunchly refused. She likes to do things herself. After years of living in the gilded cage that was her marriage to my father, I don't blame her for being so stubborn about asserting her independence.

"I did. We stopped for breakfast on the way, at that café you recommended," she says.

Loosening my tie, I ask, "Which one? Three Arts?"

"That's the one! I had the loveliest truffle grilled

cheese, and they sat us right under the chandelier. But enough about me. How was your week? I've been so busy playing tour guide for Helen that I haven't had a chance to check in on you."

I give her a brief rundown, sticking to career-related things. Per usual.

"Oh, Rhys," she sighs. "You're working yourself into the ground. You're only young once, you know. Don't let life pass you by. I'd hate to see you end up like your father."

"That makes two of us. But I wouldn't be where I am if I didn't work hard. And besides, I'm not going to let myself skate by just because Grandpa owns the company."

"I understand that, sweetheart, but there's something called work-life balance."

"I have excellent work-life balance," I insist. "I'm on my way to the gym right now."

"That's another form of work," she points out.

"You go to the gym too, Mom. Is that work?"

"I go to yoga! It's different. But you need a real hobby. A diversion. Or...well, I don't know. I think a bit of female company would do you a world of good."

"*Mom*. Not this again. Please."

"You've been alone, what, three or four years now? Ever since—"

"Nope. Done talking about this. And it's only been two years and eleven months."

"See? This is exactly what I'm saying. You're still

hung up on her. Why don't you just put yourself out there and see what happens?" she says, her voice all sweet and innocent.

Inwardly, I cringe. "Look, I appreciate your concern, but I'm not dating right now."

"Because you're heartbroken, or because you're a workaholic? Honestly, I—"

"Because I'm already seeing someone!" I blurt, in a desperate attempt to quiet her.

The line goes so silent that I have to check to see if the call dropped. It didn't.

"Mom? You there?"

"Who is she? How long have you been dating? Why didn't you tell me? What's her name? Oh, Rhys, you'll have to bring her for dinner on Sunday! You will, won't you?"

I try to make up excuses for why Izabela can't make it, but I already know I'll have to bring her with me. Mom's so excited, I can't possibly disappoint her. And if I do leave Izabela at home, I know Mom will just keep on begging me to bring my new girlfriend around. Better to get it over with as quickly as possible.

Still, there is some good in this. I'll get a break from the frequent, well-meaning nagging about dating, and my mom won't be upset if news of my new relationship suddenly gets splashed across the front pages of the tabloids. Plus, Mom will be over the moon knowing that I'm not the perpetually lonely bachelor she thinks I am. Her peace of mind—even if it's only temporary, since Izabela and I need to "break up" in six months—is worth a little discomfort on my end.

The truth is, Mom is my soft spot. I indulge her at every opportunity. My father treated her terribly during their five years of marriage (he cheated, he lied, he treated her more like his personal assistant than his partner), and since she'd signed a prenup, she walked away from a very ugly divorce with nothing but the clothes on her back and joint custody of me.

Dad tried to get full custody for no reason other than to make her life hell, but she'd fought him tooth and nail in court. I ended up getting shuffled back and forth between them for the next fifteen years. It didn't matter that my father had money coming out of his ears, or a huge mansion, or that he let me run around unsupervised when I stayed with him. Mom was far and away the better parent. She worked her ass off as an international sales rep for a fragrance company to provide me with a stable, comfortable life, and we've always been close.

As soon as I started making real money at my grandpa's company, it was Mom's turn to be stable and comfortable. A lot more comfortable. I bought her a Victorian style beach house in Highland Park with a view of Lake Michigan in her own backyard, and I told her she could retire early, but so far she's refused. Still, I'm proud that I'm able to help her. It's the least I can do.

After I finish my workout and shower, I go home and eat dinner with Izabela.

As she's squeezing lemon into her iced tea, I tell her, "Sunday night we have dinner plans."

She looks up at me. "Where? What time? How should I dress?"

I hesitate, but there's no sense in keeping it from her.

"My mother's house. Six o'clock. Just wear whatever you'd wear to your own parents' house for dinner."

The way she flinches back for just a moment tells me I've hit a nerve.

"Are you not close?" I ask more gently, thinking of my dad. "There's no shame in that."

"It's not that. They, um. Passed away almost ten years ago," she says, dropping her eyes.

God, she was just a kid when it happened. How awful. Part of me wants to put an arm around her, offer some kind of comfort. But that's not the relationship we have. Not the one I paid for and not the one I want. All I can offer is a sympathetic nod.

"Besides," she goes on, "my parents weren't wealthy like your family is. I'd probably just wear a sundress and sandals, but I'm sure you'd prefer something more formal."

"No. Mom isn't like that. She's not into flashy, pretentious things like my father is. And she doesn't judge. Wear the sundress."

WE ARRIVE at Mom's house at six sharp on Sunday. Izabela's eyes are wide as she takes in the landscaped lawn that looks like a botanical garden, the stone fountain splashing merrily at the center of the circular driveway, the Queen Anne architecture with its domed turret, wraparound porch, and freshly painted wooden shingles. Mom must have been waiting for us in the entry hall, because the front door swings open before I've even finished knocking.

"Rhys!" she coos, pulling me in for a hug. Then she turns to Izabela. "And *you* must be Izabela. I've heard so much about you, and aren't you lovely? What a pretty dress. Come in."

"Your house is so beautiful," Izabela says as we head inside. "It's like a castle."

"Isn't it?" Mom preens. "I said the same thing when we came to look at it. Oh, I know it's a lot of house for one woman and a pair of senior cocker spaniels, but Rhys insisted on spoiling me, didn't you honey?"

"Happy to do it," I say.

At the sound of my voice, my mom's dogs come barreling down the hall howling.

"Orson! Violet! Enough!" Mom says, to no avail. "Should I kennel them so they don't bother everyone?"

"Oh, don't do that. They're just excited about having company," Izabela says.

Orson and Violet attack her legs with licks and

snuffles and happy barks, their tails wagging so hard that it's more of a full butt wiggle.

"*Siad*," Izabela commands, holding out her hand with her palm facedown.

Both dogs instantly drop to a sit, looking up at her adoringly.

"Was that in Polish?" I ask.

Izabela blushes and then crouches to pet the dogs. "Yes. I guess I went on autopilot."

"You're Polish? How lovely. I can't wait to hear more," Mom says, beaming. "Shall we go out onto the deck for a drink? Dinner will be ready shortly."

We walk through the hall and the kitchen and out the sliding glass doors in the back of the house. Mom sets us up with wine and a fruit tray so we can take in the lapping blue waters of Lake Michigan while she goes inside to check on the food. This is typical for her. She's not the type of person who can sit still for more than five minutes, so she's always bustling around frantically like this when I come over for dinner, prepping and sautéing and roasting until she's prepared a four-course experience with something decadent for dessert.

"This is incredible," Izabela says, resting her elbows on the railing.

I shrug. "Mom's dream house. I wanted to make sure she'd never have to move again. After she and my father divorced, we had to shuffle through quite a number of apartments."

Izabela turns her gaze to me, assessing. "You're a good son. You take care of her."

"I try," I say.

"More than try," she says.

Moving closer, I slide a hand to her lower back. She looks stunning in a white sundress with yellow roses printed on it and low-heeled sandals, her hair pulled into braid that hangs over one shoulder. The picture-perfect girl next door.

"Is the dress okay?" she asks, misinterpreting the way I'm studying her.

"The dress is perfect." I whisper the words as I lean close to her ear, then lightly take the lobe between my lips. "What are you wearing underneath?"

Keeping her focus on the lake, she replies, "Would you like to find out?"

I can feel my balls tightening. "Maybe."

Moving behind Izabela, I shift my glass to my left hand and run my right hand down the length of her thigh, then up under the hem of her dress. It's been a few days since she moved in and I've barely been able to keep my paws off her. I'm sure I'll get tired of fucking her at some point, but it doesn't seem like it's going to happen anytime soon. I love the way sex is brand-new to her. And I can't get enough of the noises that come out of her mouth when I touch her, the look in her eyes when I make her come...hell, just knowing I'm the first man to ever touch her like this drives me out of my mind.

Skimming the smooth skin of her inner thigh, I'm just about to dip my fingers between her legs when I'm interrupted by the sound of the glass door sliding open behind us.

"Rhys, I only have kalamata olives for the—"

"What, Mom?"

I lazily turn to face her. She's standing frozen in the doorway, dish towel in hand.

"The salad. Should I put in the olives or no?"

"I love olives," Izabela says.

"Okay," Mom says with a smile. "Olives it is. Dinner will be ready in about ten minutes."

Her tone is too cheery for someone who walked in on her son trying to feel up the woman he brought to dinner. Then again, I think my mother has gotten used to a few of my shenanigans, though I'm not sure how I feel about that.

"Wait. Your mother cooked dinner herself?" Izabela's voice is panicked.

"Yeah, why? She always cooks."

"I thought she had a personal chef like you. *Och nie!* This is terrible."

She hands me her full glass of wine and smooths down her skirt, then heads to the door.

"What are you doing?" I call after her.

"I have to help her! Do you know how rude this is of me to stand here and do nothing while she cooks the meal?"

With that, she disappears through the sliding door into the kitchen. I set the drinks down and follow.

"Mrs. McConnell, what can I do to assist?" Izabela is saying. "I'm so sorry; I thought you had a chef like Rhys so I didn't even think to offer...I apologize." She actually looks ashamed.

One corner of my mother's mouth goes up.

"Don't be silly. You're a guest, darling. I'd never expect you to help."

"Yes, but I'm here as your son's—" She looks at me, clearly not knowing how to define herself. "Um, as your son's guest, and it's only right that I lend a hand."

Cardinal rule number one is never set foot in Delia McConnell's kitchen unless it's time to eat. Rule number two is never criticize her cooking, though I've never known anyone to do so. Ever.

After a beat, my mother slides a tray of garlic bread onto the island and hands Izabela a brush and a small bowl of melted butter.

"Brush them well. Use all the butter." She watches to be sure her instructions are followed. "You have a lovely accent, Izabela. Where in Poland are you from?"

"Zamość. It's a small town in the southeast, near the Ukraine border. My family has a farm there."

"How lovely. You helped your mother with the cooking when you lived at home?"

My stomach drops at the question, but Izabela just smiles as she carefully spreads the butter on each piece of bread.

"My aunt, yes. My sister and I learned to cook very young with her help."

"Your sister? Do you just have the one?" Mom asks.

Izabela nods. "Eva. She's fourteen. She'd rather read fashion magazines than chop an onion, but she knows her way around a kitchen regardless. My aunt made sure of that."

"That's wonderful," Mom says. "I never learned to cook until I got divorced, but I'm so glad I took it up. There's something so soothing about all the slicing and dicing and measuring and stirring, isn't there?"

"Yes," Izabela agrees.

Glancing at my mother, I realize she's practically glowing. She's pleased. Really pleased. So pleased that she passes Izabela the salad next and has her finish putting it together.

Moving back to the deck, I sip my wine and leave the women to it. Within minutes, they come out with the food and I set the table as they arrange all the dishes.

Pulling out Izabela's chair for her, I can't resist touching the bare skin at the back of her shoulder. After she's seated, I pour her a fresh glass of wine, realizing that I've drank all of hers, and then shift my chair closer. She notices. So does my mother. Both of them smile at me.

But I don't care. I can't believe I was anxious about this dinner. Everything is going perfectly. The sun begins to set in pastel streaks of orange and pink, casting a warm glow over the table. My mother makes small talk with Izabela, but I'm barely paying attention.

Under the table, I've got my hand on Izabela's thigh. Running the tips of my fingers up her mid-thigh and back down to her knee again, making slow, lazy circles. I can feel the heat radiating from between her legs, and it takes all my willpower not to touch her there.

"You're a model? How...interesting," Mom is saying.

My hand freezes on Izabela's thigh.

"We don't need to talk about that," I say, suddenly desperate to change the subject.

Mom sets her fork down and catches my eye across the table. "You know I never thought you were going to end up with—"

"There's no need to discuss her," I interrupt gently but firmly.

"I wasn't going to. I'm just so pleased to see you happy, is what I was going to say."

Izabela sits completely still, listening, absorbing. I lean over and kiss her temple.

"I am happy, thank you. Izabela is an amazing woman. Ambitious. Accomplished. Beautiful, obviously, but I'm much more impressed by her...work ethic," I say, giving her thigh another firm, suggestive squeeze.

"And handy in the kitchen, too," Mom adds.

The praise has Izabela ducking her head shyly, but

I notice that it doesn't seem to help her relax. I've never outright complimented her before. Maybe she's suspicious of me.

The meal concludes and Izabela helps clean up. She smiles and chats with my mom, but I can tell by her body language that she's still wary. I join the women in the kitchen and help with the dishes, then I make Izabela a decaf coffee to go with the cheesecake she barely picks at.

She and my mother talk about the Polish countryside and Izabela's most recent trip to Ukraine to visit relatives. The more they laugh and engage, the more uneasy I get. Because the next six months will go by fast, and when they're over, Izabela will be passed on to another man. She won't belong to me anymore, and I don't want my mother to be disappointed. She never responded to Celine the way she has to Izabela. Never asked about Celine's past or welcomed her into the kitchen. If I'm not careful, my mother is going to get attached.

And dammit, so might I.

14

IZABELA

Rhys's mother liked me. Really liked me. I could tell.

I can't keep the smile from my face as we bid her goodbye and get into the back of the car. I feel a little sorry for our driver, who has been waiting for us this whole time. He must have been bored out of his mind. I should have brought him a slice of cheesecake to pass the time.

Rhys has been oddly quiet since dessert. I hope he's not upset with me. I behaved perfectly, I'm sure of it. Does he think I crossed a line? He must not understand how important it was for me to be helpful to his mother.

The thing is, I wasn't raised to just stand by and let my host do all the work. Where I'm from, everybody pitches in whenever they can, even if they're guests—the men, too. It's old fashioned, I suppose, but it really gives a sense of community and togetherness...the kind that I haven't felt since moving to America. Tonight, helping Delia McConnell with a delicious meal helped me feel connected. It reminded me of home, and I dearly needed that.

"Dinner was wonderful," I tell Rhys.

"Glad you enjoyed it."

"Your mother is wonderful, too. Thank you for inviting me."

"You played your part well," he says coolly.

Instantly, I deflate. Of course this entire evening was all an act. I can't believe I let myself get so caught up in the charade.

I look out the window so Rhys won't see the hurt on my face, but I can tell he's brooding beside me as he scrolls on his phone. His whole demeanor is cold and rigid. My mood sours.

What if I really did overstep with his mother? Americans are so different. I'm still learning what's appropriate and what's not.

But he was so tender and attentive to me during dinner. Pulling out my chair, getting me drinks. And all the compliments! He was so completely unlike the man I've come to know over the last week. Kinder, softer, more patient. More...human. His mother seemed smitten with the two of us. And I have to admit, I was smitten with him. What a game Rhys McConnell plays. Of course tonight was all a lie. Nothing more than an act for his mother's benefit.

Because of course he'd want his mother to think we're in love and not that he bought me to keep as a toy for six months. What mother would be approving of something like that? Rhys was warm and loving toward her and it's obvious they are very close. He wouldn't want to disappoint her.

Still, I'm bothered by his behavior. And I don't want to sit here second-guessing myself for the entire thirty-minute drive back to Rhys's place.

Looking back at him, I straighten my spine and ask, "Have I done something wrong?"

"No." He tucks his phone away and looks me in the eye. "I just want to make sure you don't have any misconceptions about fiction and reality."

"I don't," I say as evenly as possible.

Meanwhile, any lingering good feelings I had turn to dust.

He's right. We were pretending. I need to focus on doing the job that I'm getting paid to do and not let Rhys get under my skin.

I was looking forward to seeing Delia again, but now I'm not so sure it's a good idea. I don't want to lie to her, or allow our bond to continue growing under false pretenses. Not that it's up to me. If Rhys says we're seeing her again, I'll have no choice but to go along with him.

"You sure about that?" he prods. "You looked very comfortable with my mother."

I can play this game, too. "I didn't want her to question the relationship. A good girlfriend helps her partner's mother. At least, that's how it works where I'm from."

He looks away, nodding to himself. "I suppose it's fine, then."

God, I hate the way he's so appealing to me, even when he acts like a jerk. That jawline, his fine nose, the broad expanse of his shoulders, his cologne. Why am I so attracted to him when he acts so indifferent toward me?

Rhys presses a button to lower the glass partition between the rear seat and the driver.

"We'll take the lakefront route home," Rhys says.

"You got it, boss," the driver responds.

The glass slides back up.

"Where are we going?" I ask.

"Don't worry about it. Just enjoy the detour."

My skin heats and a rush of adrenaline hits me, singing in my veins. He brings out this side of me so easily—the one that craves him.

Maybe it's because the sex is still so new to me, and because every time we're together, it's a brand-new experience. I'll probably get over it at some point. Get used to the way he feels inside, get used to the shock of the sudden, deep orgasms he gives me, the shivers that run down my spine when he whispers *whore* in my ear. I'm probably only so turned on by him because I've never been with anyone else. That has to be how it works.

He pops the top two buttons of his shirt, and the second I see the flash of his bare chest, a dull ache starts to thud between my legs. I know what else is waiting for me underneath the linen fabric. Smooth pecs, rock-hard abs, those shoulders that make my knees go weak.

I never knew it could be like this, where just the sight of a shirtless man has me halfway to an orgasm before he's even laid a finger on me. I've seen other men with their shirts off before. But with Rhys, it's different. Something inside me constantly hungers for him.

"Take off your dress."

The command pulls me from the fog of lust settling over my brain. I glance at the glass partition between us and the driver. It's dark outside, but I'm sure the driver can still see us back here. And is the glass soundproof?

"I *said*, take off your dress, Izabela."

"Can he hear us?" I ask, nodding at the driver.

Rhys grabs my chin, turning my face so I have to look at him.

"That's not your business. I decide who sees you and hears you."

There's no point in arguing. He owns me. The terms of our agreement demand that I shut my mouth and do as he says.

Glancing at the driver one last time, I slip the spaghetti straps of my dress down my shoulders. Then I work the top down over my breasts, down to my waist. I'm not wearing a bra and the air conditioning feels icy on my exposed skin, instantly making my nipples tighten. With a low groan, Rhys pulls me toward him, tugging the dress over my hips and then positioning me on his lap in nothing but my white cotton thong.

My back rests against his chest, and when he pushes my legs apart, over the tops of his thighs, my feet come off the floor. It's awkward, but then he wraps a strong arm around me and begins to play with my nipples, and I decide I wouldn't care if I was upside down.

Biting my bottom lip, I brace myself against him and ease into the pleasure as he lightly rolls my nipples between his fingers. The rise and fall of his chest is steady, his delicious warmth radiating into my back. A soft moan escapes me. I can tell that what he's doing to me is having an effect on him too, judging by his harsh breathing. It only makes me more excited.

His hand slides lower, trailing over my belly, my hips, my underwear. As he cups me between my legs, he runs his hot mouth over the side of my neck.

"Mm," I whimper desperately, pushing myself into his hand.

"You don't come until I say so, do you understand?" he growls in my ear.

"Yes," I pant.

With a low chuckle, he tugs my panties to the side and slips two fingers inside me. I widen my legs even farther, giving him full access. He pumps slowly at first, working his fingers deeper and deeper into me, and then begins thrusting harder and faster. My pulse is racing, my hips jerking as I meet every push of his fingers. It feels so good I stop worrying about the driver and let myself get carried away with my moans.

"That's my good little whore," Rhys whispers.

He cups my breast with one hand while stroking me with the other, and I can feel his hard cock digging into my ass through the fabric of his pants. The mix of sensations quickly has me turning into a gasping, needy mess. As if sensing the orgasm I can feel coming on, Rhys slides his fingers out and switches his attention to my clit.

This man knows exactly what he's doing. Exactly how to roll his fingers around the swollen nub, when to squeeze, when to tap, when to ease off. I roll my hips faster, seeking more pressure, more pleasure. My wetness is all over Rhys's hand, but he doesn't seem to mind. If anything, he seems to be toying with me even more aggressively.

Every part of my body is tingling, on fire. My cries become louder, more guttural. The modest part of my brain knows the driver can hear me, but even though my cheeks heat with shame, I don't do anything to stop what Rhys is doing.

I don't want him to stop.

I'm lost in the feel of his fingers, in the rush of the pleasure. Nothing else matters. Grabbing his wrist, I hold him steady as I work myself against him, my release hovering oh so close but just out of reach. He lets me guide him, lets me rub myself against his hand, pump my hips. His soft moans flutter against the sensitive skin on my neck. I'm so close...so damn close.

And then Rhys pulls his hand away.

With a yelp, I grab for him, my center throbbing. I'm right at the edge, my knees weak. But he laughs and pushes me off him, guiding me onto my knees on the carpeted floor.

"I didn't say you could come, did I?" he says. "But *I* can."

He unzips his pants and pulls out his cock, fat and thick and ready.

"Suck me off, Izabela," he says, pumping himself up and down. "Show me you're grateful for the pleasure."

I move in closer, pulling my braid behind my head and licking my lips in preparation. It doesn't escape me that I'm sitting here at his feet, almost completely naked, while he remains dressed. Just another way he's asserting his power over me. But I have power, too. I've learned to enjoy the way he loses control of himself when I take him in my mouth.

Gripping the base of his cock, I look up at him as my lips hover just over the tip. Passing lights flash into the car and I see the strain and anticipation on his face.

Slipping him between my lips, I take him all the way to the back of my throat, until the fabric of his pants tickles my lips. He groans loudly and I feel a rush of triumph. I'm not the only one the driver might hear. It makes me feel better.

Rhys digs his fingers into my hair and tugs, just enough to make my scalp tingle. It's something I'm coming to love. Does he realize that I like it when he's rough with me? I've noticed that even when he talks to me in that cold, detached way, he still looks satisfied when I get off. He likes using me, but he always makes sure I feel good, too.

He swells in my mouth, his hips thrusting so violently that I know my lips will bruise. I relax my jaw even more and take it all, bobbing my head in time with each thrust. When he releases down my throat, I take that too, swallowing down every last drop as I look up at him, watching his face in the shadows. His eyes are narrowed, his expression impassive. Without a word, he zips himself up and turns away from me.

I pull my dress back on and fold my hands in my lap, silently taking in the view of the city outside the window.

Maybe Rhys thinks he was punishing me by having me suck him off in the back of the car, in nothing but my thong...but the truth is, it was no punishment at all.

Because when it comes to being Rhys McConnell's whore, I can't seem to get enough.

15

IZABELA

"FINALLY, something interesting and mysterious is happening here."

This is the first time I've called my sister in weeks. Normally, we talk on Saturday mornings (evenings for her, since Zamość is seven hours ahead), but ever since the auction, I've been skipping our calls.

It's been easy enough to lie to her in my texts and emails, pretending I've been extra busy with work, but I knew I wouldn't be able to avoid my sister forever. And I also knew that if Eva heard my voice, she'd instantly intuit that something was wrong. Which is why I've been dreading this call. That girl has a knack for squeezing the truth out of me. Even though she's only fourteen, she's always been perceptive and wise beyond her years.

Perhaps it's because she had to grow up so fast after

our parents died, just like I did. Or maybe it was living with a chronic illness that did it. Pain has a way of maturing you either way.

"And what would that be?"

"A man has been standing outside every day, watching the house."

Eva says this with youthful innocence, as if we're discussing which boy she finds cute at school, or how many new lambs were born in our uncle's barn.

But her words make my blood run cold.

"What do you mean *a man has been watching the house*?" I ask, my stomach dropping.

For a moment, static is the only answer. My cell phone doesn't handle international calls well, and a lot of times I'll end up dropping the call and then struggling to get her back on the line. I desperately hope that doesn't happen before I can warn her. She might think this stranger is interesting, but he's *dangerous*.

"...he smokes a lot, and he's old, so this isn't the first chapter of my romance novel. Uncle says he's American, though, so maybe I should see if he has a younger son, just in case."

"No, I don't think you should, Eva. What did the man say when Uncle Julian talked to him? Did he cause any trouble?"

"No. But he was back again this morning, even though Uncle told him to stop coming around. I saw him when I was getting ready for school. Do you think he's going to steal our chickens?"

My heart lurches painfully. If that's the worst thing she can think of him doing, I want to keep it that way. Eva chatters on, but I'm only half-listening. Is this man some kind of insurance policy sent by Zoric to keep me in line and remind me of his threats against my family? As if I could possibly forget.

"Eva, please, whatever you do, stay away from him. Don't talk to him, don't look at him, and if you're out walking by yourself and you see him on the street, run and hide. And make sure you tell Uncle Julian that the man is still hanging around."

"Don't worry, I already did. I think the police might get involved."

Hearing that doesn't comfort me at all. I can only imagine what might happen if Zoric's enforcer is confronted by the police. He'll either lie to them and then return to the farm later, taking care to hide himself better, or he could become violent.

A wave of panic washes over me. All I want to do is race home to my family and try to protect them. But I don't have my passport, I don't have the power to stop one of Zoric's men, and I'm still indebted to Rhys. It doesn't matter what I want. I have no control over my own life. Whatever happens to my family in Poland will happen without my intervention.

I can't keep my sister safe.

Except I can. I just have to obey Zoric. Be a good girl. Keep my mouth shut. At least until I can figure out a way to break my contract.

In the meantime, I can't let on that I think anything is wrong. Eva is under enough stress just dealing with her illness and getting through each day. I miss her so much it makes my chest hurt, and I wish more than anything that I was sitting with her now, in our aunt and uncle's kitchen with its stone walls, the worn planks of the wood floor gleaming from daily scrubbing. The scent of bread permeating the air, lingering long after the morning loaves have been removed from the oven. Wildflowers gathered from the yard in a vase by the window.

"Tell me about school," I say cheerily, wiping tears from my eyes.

Changing the subject will be good for both of us. She chatters on about her classes and her friends and how she had to miss an entire week because she was too tired after starting a new treatment to go to school. She insists she's feeling better now, and I can't tell from her tone if she's lying or not. I'm going to believe that she's telling me the truth because that's easier for me than imagining her in pain. Being this far away, and not being able to help her will slowly kill me if I allow it. I have to remind myself that I'm doing this for her. One of these days, I will bring Eva here and everything will be fine.

"How about your modeling jobs?" she asks. "It sounds like things are picking up!"

The question makes me smile. She was so excited when I told her I was moving to America to be a fashion model like the ones she fawned over in her magazines. Recent issues of *Vogue*, *Vanity Fair*, and *W* are rare commodities in our small Polish town and sell out quickly when they do arrive. When I was Eva's age, I spent hours poring over the glossy pictures too, daydreaming about someday being able to wear such beautiful clothes and expensive jewelry. Little did I know about the chains that come along with such luxuries.

"They are picking up," I tell her, glad that I have some legitimate good news to share. "Big time. In fact, I have my very first national job in a few days. It's for Cate Diamond, the handbag company. If you're lucky, you might even find the ad that I model for in one of the fancy magazines you stockpile in your bedroom."

She shrieks excitedly. "I'll be able to tell all of my friends!"

"I'll send you copies when the advertisement is released. It might be a while, so you'll have to be patient."

"I can be patient. I swear. Ooh, maybe you'll get to be on a billboard!"

It makes me happy that she's so excited. I wish I could feel the same. I used to, before I knew the truth about this industry and the nightmare that many immigrant models get themselves into. I don't let my thoughts wander beyond that, because if I do, I won't be able to keep the bitterness from my voice.

"What else is going on?" she asks. "There must be more. I mean, you've been so busy."

"Just work," I say, panic making my voice pitch higher. "Just a lot of work."

There's a pause, and then, "*Just* work? Are you sure?"

"Of course! You know how it is. I'm trying so hard to make it, I have to be available all the time for whatever comes my way. And the shoots have such long hours and...you know."

"Do you have a boyfriend?" Her innocent voice takes on a singsong quality.

I don't know how to answer that. Rhys is definitely not my boyfriend, but also, I am not telling my teenage sister that I have been purchased by a millionaire for six months. No, Rhys isn't my boyfriend. Right now, he's my owner.

As I think of how to respond, a brilliant fantasy opens up inside my mind. I don't think too much about it as I let the words tumble out of my mouth.

"As a matter of fact, I have met someone. He's been helping me learn more about the modeling industry and even helped me get the job I was telling you about."

"Is he handsome, like Prince Charming?"

Well, there's no need to lie about that answer. "He's handsomer than Prince Charming. The most handsome of any prince you've ever seen. But, not really a prince. Just handsome."

She begins asking a million, rapid-fire questions. "Tell me about him! Did he pick you up in a limo? Did he bring you flowers? Tell me everything," she begs with a happy sigh.

"Eva, slow down." I can't help but laugh.

"Are you going to get married?"

"Not all fairytales end with a wedding, you know. We're still getting to know each other. Right now, we're just going on dates and enjoying each other's company. I don't really want to look beyond that."

The line goes staticy again, and I wait to see if I will lose the call. But then I hear her asking for me to tell her about our last date. I let my mind continue sinking into the fantasy, expanding it and creating it into something that any girl would want. It has to be far, far from the reality I'm in, doesn't it? If my sister knew what was going on, she'd never believe in love. I don't want her to lose that innocence, that hope.

"Well, he had his driver take us to a restaurant, where we had dinner reservations. It was the kind of place where you have to know someone to get them—very tiny and very fancy."

"What did you wear?"

"A sleeveless blue dress and a pearl necklace. And he wore a dark gray suit with a blue tie that matches his eyes. He held my hand while we talked over candlelight, sipping wine. We shared some caviar and toast, and then we ordered dessert before our meals. Cheesecake with raspberries, which he fed to me. It was just like something from a movie."

Of course, none of that happened. Oh, what if it had? What if Rhys had caught my eyes over the table at a fancy restaurant, his flashing sapphire and candlelight as they practically ate me up? What if he'd held my hand so tenderly, and listened intently to what I had to say is if my words actually interested him? What would it be like for Rhys McConnell to actually want me?

She's waiting for me to continue, but I can't. I can't keep this up. It's all a lie. And I don't want her becoming invested, thinking that maybe someday she'll come to America and find that her sister has the perfect Prince Charming waiting to welcome her with open arms. That's never going to happen. I can't stand the thought of breaking her heart.

"I have to go help Aunt Sofia set the table, Izabela. When will you call again?"

I don't want to hang up. But I'm afraid if I don't, I'm going to continue filling her head with fantasies. And because, if I'm honest with myself, there's a stupid, silly, childish part of me that wishes the story I was telling was real, too. "Soon, honey. Very soon. I promise."

Something pops into my mind, and I quickly talk into the phone before she hangs up. "If that man shows up again—"

But she's gone. The line goes dead with an eerie silence rippling with static.

Staring at my phone, it's a few minutes before I can put it in my pocket. I need to get home, to keep her safe from whatever Konstantine Zoric has up his sleeve.

Tears fill my eyes at the hopelessness of my situation. I'm trapped here, like a prisoner. Stuck in this country, in this house, with a man who I just made my sister believe is the perfect boyfriend. A groan rumbles from my throat and dislodges into a loud sob. I've been in my room for a while and I have no idea if Rhys's home or not. Not that I care. Not right now.

I don't hold back the tears as they come with pained, desperate sobs that bubble from my lips. There is a strange man watching my sister, my family, inserting himself into my reality by turning a threat into something very real.

If I'm not careful, there's no telling what might happen to them. And if I'm not very, very careful, I might start believing the lies I told my sister about my very own Prince Charming.

The sound of footsteps outside my door draws my attention. Slapping a hand over my mouth, I get up from the bed and tiptoe to the door to listen. But all is silent.

Wiping my eyes on the hem of my t-shirt, I crack the door open and look out—only to see Rhys's back as he retreats down the hall. On the floor at my feet, there's a tray holding hot tea, a little plate of sugar cookies, and a box of tissues. It takes a moment for me to comprehend what I'm looking at. Is he trying to...comfort me?

Picking up the tray, I carry it inside my room and shut the door as a fresh waterfall of tears floods my cheeks. This time I'm not crying out of fear or longing for what could be. I'm crying because it's too late.

I'm already falling for the story.

16

IZABELA

SLINKY NAVY-BLUE DRESS with spaghetti straps and a side-slit halfway up my thigh. Matching stilettos with gold heels. Hair perfectly curled and hanging in glossy waves around my shoulders. Tinted gloss on my lips, loads of mascara, and gold hoops in my ears.

I know I look good in the only designer dress I own, yet the moment Rhys and I step into the private ballroom, my confidence evaporates. These people ooze wealth, casually gliding across the floor in their piles of sparkling diamond jewelry and their bespoke suits and extravagant, frothy gowns. I'm way out of my league. Guess I'll have to treat this like a shoot, where I exude poise and self-assurance that I don't necessarily always feel. It's the job, right?

But it doesn't help that my emotions have been all over the place since finding the tea and tissues outside my door. Things have been awkward between us since.

Rhys's unexpected gesture opened tender feelings inside me that I can't ignore. And he's different too— gentler, somehow. More solicitous.

I'm not stupid, I know it doesn't mean anything. Probably just a passing kindness. Men are terrified of tears; they'll do anything to avoid more.

Even so, I can't pretend I'm not growing attached to him. That steaming cup of tea warmed something inside me that has been frozen over for months. Ever since I arrived in America, I've had to be completely self-reliant...and while I'm proud of my ability to take care of myself, I had to become a different person in order to survive. Someone tougher, thicker-skinned. Someone who's always in survival mode.

Back in Poland, my aunt and my sister were always available to me when I needed them, ready to cheer me up or baby me when I was sick or help me if I asked. Here in Chicago, I have nobody. My roommates are nice enough, especially Diya, but I've tried to keep my distance from them in order to protect myself. It's not just about being rivals in the same industry, either. I can't risk getting attached to people when I don't know how long I—or they—will be around.

I guess that's why Rhys's kindness was so disarming. I've put up all these walls, and with one simple cup of tea, he knocked them down.

"Stay close to me," Rhys says, his tone cool and detached as he takes my hand and places it in the crook of his arm. He must attend things like this so often, they aren't special. I lift my chin and force a smile onto my face, pretending I'm not overwhelmed.

I am *utterly* overwhelmed.

This party isn't at all what I was anticipating. I was told we'd be attending a 50th wedding anniversary celebration for one of the board members of Rhys's grandfather's company. I expected a dance floor and a cake and a DJ. Not...this.

Yes, I knew it would be fancy, but this is beyond anything I could have imagined. The extravagant ballroom with its glittering chandeliers and gleaming parquet floors, the five-piece orchestra, the professional photographers and the staff in tuxedos who circle with trays of food and champagne. It's impressive enough for royalty.

The only information I got from Rhys was that the board member and Rhys's grandfather are close friends, and that anyone important in the company was invited. Including Rhys's father.

A man approaches us, his hand outstretched as he steps into our bubble.

"So nice to see you, Rhys." He nods in greeting to me. "And Celine, you're—*oh*, my apologies."

I can feel the way his body goes tense beside me. "This is my girlfriend, Izabela. Izabela, this is Mr. Arlington, another member of the board at McConnell Enterprises."

The man doesn't miss a beat as he lightly elbows

Rhys in the shoulder. "They say everyone has a doppel-gänger, huh?"

Rhys smiles tightly. "There's only one Celine, trust me."

"Pleasure to meet you," I interject, in as friendly a manner as I can.

"Believe me, the pleasure is entirely mine," he says, grabbing my hand and raising it to his moist lips for a kiss.

It takes some serious effort not to rip my hand away from his mouth, but I manage. Arlington's eyes rake over me before he's blessedly called away.

Who is Celine? Of course, asking Rhys is out of the question. She must be of some importance because his entire demeanor has morphed into slowly simmering anger.

He suddenly takes my other hand and presses it over the top of his forearm, so both of my arms are wrapped around his.

"Hang on to me, dammit," he says under his breath. "Act like you never want to let go."

Is he serious? Does he really want me clinging to him? Is this a ploy to make this Celine woman jealous? Fine, then. I'll play the starry-eyed, codependent girl-friend if that's what his fragile male ego requires.

Tightening my grip, I match his steps as we work our way through the crowd. People offer us greetings and make small talk, and I'm introduced about a dozen more times. Rhys seems disinterested in the socializing, absently giving everyone the same polite, vague responses, never stopping to truly engage with anyone. Fortunately, there isn't a line at the bar when we get there. Apparently he needs something stronger than the champagne that's circulating on trays.

He orders a scotch and immediately tosses it back, then gets a refill and turns back to the crowd, sipping more slowly.

"Did you want something?" he asks me distractedly.

"A vodka, please."

I take the glass from him gratefully, eager for the cold, sharp taste of celebrations with *my* family to anchor me. The last time I had any was the day I won the contest, when Aunt Sofia pulled a bottle from the freezer and poured drinks for what felt like the entire town.

I open my mouth to share that memory with Rhys and close it again when I see the look on his face.

My hairline tingles. Has he seen Celine? Unsure if I'm allowed to let go of him yet, I'm still clinging to his arm when I spot what he sees, his father coming our way. My hand tightens on Rhys even more, my smile going stiff.

"There you are, son! I should have known to check the bar first, ha!"

"Rupert," Rhys says coolly, giving him a nod.

"We're back to that, are we?" The elder McConnell

pushes past us to flag down the bartender. "Hope the scotch is drinkable, anyway."

"Glenfiddich, and it's excellent," Rhys says.

"It'll do," his dad says, pointedly ignoring me.

Rhys downs the remainder of his scotch and leaves the glass on the bar. He puts his arm around me, intending for us to leave.

Five callous words stop us. "Having fun with your new toy?"

My breath hitches and my pulse picks up. I hate the insinuation in his words. As though I'm not even human. Suddenly feeling embarrassed and small, I look down to my shoes and silently beg Rhys to ignore his dad so we can walk away. As screwed up as my situation is, I'm so very grateful that I didn't end up with Rupert McConnell. He's not a good person.

I'm relieved when Rhys leads me away without engaging further.

"Don't go too far, son," his dad calls after him. "Don't want you to miss the big announcement!"

I barely know the man next to me. It takes time to learn what makes someone tick and how they respond to situations, stress, joy. The weave of family dynamics and their mutual pasts isn't something to be unraveled quickly. Yet, I've witnessed Rhys interact with his father enough to know how he'll respond to that parting shot. His shoulders tense and a spark of fire flashes in his eyes. His lips press into a thin line, parentheses deepening on the sides of his mouth.

Without thinking, I lightly pat the back of his hand and then squeeze as if my unsolicited touch can be of any comfort. He stiffens more and I brace myself to be chastised. I think of the tea and tissues he left outside my door and wish I could reciprocate with something meaningful but surrounded by all these people in such a public place, the only comfort I can offer is subtle.

He looks to where I touch him, then meets my eyes and I feel the tension in his shoulders and arms release even before he snags a champagne flute from a passing server. We weave through the crowd, making our way over to the tables set up at the edge of the room.

"Rhys! Come sit with us!" A middle-aged man in a bespoke blue suit waives us to a table in the back.

His companions are an older woman in a sequined blazer, her dark hair pulled to the top of her head in a tight bun, and a bearded man with a short afro and glasses, who looks like a college professor in his tweed vest. I can't tell if they're a couple, but they appear to be enjoying the people watching from their table. Rhys seems eager to join them. Or maybe he's just glad to have a chance to sit down and take a break.

Pulling a chair out for me first, he introduces me to Ariadne Lyle, another one of the company's board members, and her husband Gordon, who actually is a professor at Northwestern. They quickly immerse themselves in conversation, leaving me to sip my champagne and admire the many designer gowns I see floating by.

"I hear congratulations are in order." Gordon slaps Rhys on the shoulder.

There's a pause that draws my attention.

"For?"

"Celine." Gordon says with a flourish. He pauses, then his brow furrows. He doesn't elaborate as a look of realization and disdain crosses his face. "Oh, wait. I'm sorry. Never mind. I'm mistaken."

Rhys puts one hand on the table. "Too late. Congratulations for what?"

"Gordon! Now you've put your foot in it!" Ariadne scolds.

He looks at both of us, spreads his hands in defeat and lowers his voice.

"I'm sorry, Rhys, I thought you knew. Your dad's been talking about it all night. He's going to make an official announcement, but Jesus, he's already told everyone else."

"I just arrived. Told me what?" Rhys says.

More silence, which quickly becomes even more awkward.

"Gordon, it's not your place..." his wife says warningly.

His brow furrows. "Why don't we just forget I said anything? You'll find out soon enough, anyway."

Rhys leans closer. "No. Tell me. I'd prefer not to be blindsided by another one of my father's big public announcements."

"Oh." Gordon clears his throat, looking as though

he'd rather be anywhere else. "Well, Celine... she's, well, she's expecting. You're going to be a big brother, as odd as that sounds I suppose, at this age."

Rhys tries to school his reaction, but the slow morph of disbelief plays clearly across his handsome face.

"Gentlemen, have room for one more?"

It's Rupert. Was he waiting in the wings for this exact moment? The predatory, satisfied smile on his face suggests that he was. He's enjoying his son's discomfort immensely.

Smoothing his tie, he calmly gets up. "Take my seat. I was just leaving."

Their gazes clash. Rhys has amazing self-control for someone who so openly despises the man in front of him. Furious energy rolls off him as if he's seconds from wrapping his hands around his father's neck. Instead, he gestures for me to get up, pulls my chair back for me and then takes my arm. We head to a smaller bar in the back of the room where he gets another scotch. I know that I should keep my mouth shut, but I can't.

"Are you okay?"

"I'm fine."

Who am I to argue?

"Why don't you go freshen up or something? I need a minute alone."

"But—"

"*Just go*. Please."

His dismissal hits me like a slap. I shouldn't have

181

said anything. I overstepped. My cheeks burn as he walks away.

Quickly losing sight of him in the crowd, I lean my hip against the end of the bar and give myself a minute. Women spare me curious glances as they pass by, probably because I'm doing a poor job of hiding my curiosity over which of them might be the mysterious Celine.

This woman meant something to Rhys. Maybe still does. She's off-limits considering his father got her pregnant. A sinking feeling goes through me. Maybe that's the problem. This woman belongs to someone else... His father, of all people. That would certainly explain the tension between the two of them.

Setting down my champagne flute so I don't drop it, I consider where to go for some air. My chest constricts and it's hard to breathe. All those tender feelings that sprouted with Rhys's kindness yesterday become a tangled briar inside me. Am I falling for a man who's in love with another woman? Falling for him is my first mistake. There's no basis for it. My circumstances are so skewed and messed up. How can I possibly hope to find love in a situation like this? I'm nothing more than a toy as Rupert put it. A plaything on a timeline. I am an expendable woman.

Angry at myself, I make my way through the crowd to the restroom. This is ridiculous. I have no right to get emotional over a man who will never love me and who's made it very clear that I'm to be used and tossed away.

Besides, a man can't give away a heart that belongs to someone else.

Tears sting my eyes as I reach the end of the hallway and find myself outside the restrooms. Luckily, it's empty when I rush inside.

Taking a moment to slow my breathing, I dab any stray mascara from beneath my eyes with my pinkies and smooth down my hair. The familiar movements do little to calm me down. Inside, I'm a mess.

Looking in my handbag for my lip gloss, I don't pay attention when the door opens until someone clips across the marble floor and stops uncomfortably close to me. The cloying smell of heady, white floral perfume nearly takes my breath away.

"*Mon dieu.* For once, the gossip is true," a throaty voice says. "You *do* look like me."

Glancing up, I see the reflection of a woman in the mirror staring openly at me. Startled, I take a step back. It's like I'm looking at myself, but different. Her hair is darker than mine. Her eyes a deeper shade. Her body is rail-thin, and her breasts are much bigger.

But our faces and the structure of our features, are uncanny.

It's the way our faces are arranged, the structure of our features, the cheekbones. The arch of the brows. The same full lips.

I say the name that's been in my mind all evening. "Celine?"

Her Gallic-red lips form a smile that doesn't reach

her eyes. "Has Rhys been talking about me? He's obsessed. It's sad, really, isn't it?"

It takes a beat for my brain to catch up to her French-accented words.

"He's never mentioned you," I say. "Everyone else has, though."

She shrugs. "Because they all know he's still hanging onto hope. It's my fault, really. I need to cut him off completely. It would be best for all of us."

Cut him off? What does that mean? Is Rhys still sleeping with her?

My gaze drops to her abdomen. Her silvery dress hugs every curve of her body, but her belly is as flat as a washboard. It must be too early for her to show...but it is too early to determine paternity? The wicked thought pings between my eyes. Is there a chance that Rhys fathered her child?

Nausea burns the base of my throat.

"I can see why he chose you, of course." She laughs, and then leans closer to the mirror to dab on more lipstick, glancing at me as she does. "It's because you remind him of me. You're the next best thing he can get. The question is, will you stay now that you know the truth? Is a big dick and cold cash enough to forget that he's thinking of me when he fucks you, darling?"

"That's unnecessary."

She pats my bare shoulder with a sharp, cold hand. "It's the truth. We women owe each other that, don't we? You're just a pawn in a rich man's game, darling.

Remember that and things will go easier on you. *Au revoir*." She sprinkles her fingers at me and walks out with her head high and her hand on her stomach.

The room has become stifling, so I leave the restroom and head to the balcony to gulp warm night air before I suffocate.

Rhys told me his business wasn't mine. At the time, I had no choice but to agree.

But now, it seems, everyone knows about *my* business but me.

17

RHYS

My FATHER LIVES for public confrontation in all its forms.

Making a scene is his forte. I'm not sure he's ever gotten through a disagreement without resorting to theatrics and exuberant hand gestures and ending his performance with a dramatic flourish that may as well conclude with "and scene."

That's probably why my grandfather never comes to events like this.

That's also why my father corners me at the bar.

When I tell him I need to find my date and try to walk away, he throws an arm around my shoulder and loudly proclaims that he knew I'd be thrilled about my stepmother's big news. Then he shouts at the bartender to pour us another round to celebrate. All the party guests around us are watching, grinning, nodding at Dad's bullshit display of fatherly spirit.

What he'll never understand is that I'm not upset about the baby.

I feel nothing, and it's deliciously sweet.

At one time, this news would have caused so much friction on my nerves that I would have imploded.

Our drinks are poured, and my father raises his in a toast. I play along, go through the motions, but after our glasses clink, I set mine on the bar without sipping. Dad doesn't seem to notice.

"It's a shame Gordon got to you first, Rhys. I didn't mean for you to find out like that."

"Right, because you were planning for me to find out when you made your big public announcement later tonight," I say. "I'd think if you were so concerned about me finding out, you would've come to me directly *before* spreading it around a room of three hundred people."

Refusing to take the blame for anything, per usual, he spreads his hands innocently and says, "Celine was just so excited that she couldn't help but tell a few people! It's not my fault word spread so fast."

"You could have called and told me when you got the test result back," I point out.

He shrugs. "Truth be told, I figured the news would come as a shock to you. I suppose I didn't want to hurt your feelings any sooner than need be."

"My feelings aren't hurt."

Grinning around the rim of his glass, he downs half

of his scotch and then says, "Come on, kid. I stole your girl right out from under you, married her first, and now I've knocked her up. That's gotta sting a little, eh?"

Ah. So that's what he wants. Confirmation that he's won, that he's gotten under my skin. But he won't get it. Slipping my hands into my pockets, I back away, leaving the drink untouched.

"Honestly?" I say. "The only part of this that stings is knowing that another child is going to have to grow up with you as a father."

I turn on my heel and walk off into the crowd.

"Rhys!"

I keep walking, even as he chases after me.

"Rhys, dammit, look at me!"

His hand clamps on my shoulder and he roughly turns me around to face him. He scowls. "That's it? That's all you have to say? You're not going to congratulate me and Celine? You're going to be a brother, for God's sake."

A brother. It will take a while for that tidbit to sink in.

Here's the thing that's niggling at me about all of this: Celine never wanted children. She worried that pregnancy would change her body too much and ruin her modeling career. So if she's pregnant now, there must have been a very compelling reason for her to change her mind. Maybe she's looking to secure child support payments in the future, or at the very least ensure she produces an heir to my father's fortune. But whatever it is, it's *her* reason. It's not something that concerns me.

"All I'll say is, I sincerely hope fatherhood suits you better the second time around."

Our eyes lock and I can tell he's struggling to deliver a good comeback, something to make him feel like he's got all the power in this situation. My father needs to be the center of everything, all the time. His life is nothing short of a great epic, and he's the hero. Nobody else matters. It's always been that way with him.

As a child, nothing I did could earn his favor or praise. Unless, of course, there was a group of people around to witness his saccharine affections that turned poisonous as soon as they stopped looking.

So right now, I know that all he wants is to "win." To get a big, emotional reaction out of me. He doesn't care if it's a slap on the back and a hearty congrats or some kind of temper tantrum over the fact that he's having a kid with my ex. As long as he succeeds in gaining all the attention and focus he can get from me—and from everyone else at the party tonight—he'll consider the evening a personal triumph.

But that's not how this is going to go.

"Have a good night," I say, turning to go. Of course, he isn't ready to let me.

"You're just pissed that I put a baby in the gorgeous

woman you couldn't hang on to. You think this act makes you seem powerful or indifferent? It doesn't. It just shows how jealous you really are."

Turning calmly back to him, I offer him a reminder. "Powerful? Remember who's going to have all the power in two years when your father retires. And you might also want to remember that you helped make me who I am. Unsentimental, calculating, mercenary. Just like you."

"Don't count on getting the throne, Rhys. I'd hate for you to be disappointed."

"I'd hate for you to be disappointed, too, Dad. You'd better get a paternity test and save yourself some heartache."

He mumbles something under his breath, but I'm already gliding away, practically walking on air. I'm more than ready to collect my "girlfriend" and take her home. She's mine until our contractual time is over and I'll be damned if I give another man a second of her time.

I just have to find her first.

I shouldn't have left her as abruptly as I did. Truthfully, I've been feeling out of sorts since hearing her cry in her bedroom last night. I can't explain why it affected me. It's not the first time a woman has cried in front of me, but it is the first time I've reacted to it. Maybe it's because she'd locked herself behind her bedroom door where she could let out her grief in privacy. She wasn't performing, or reacting. She was being honest—something I'm not used to seeing in my life.

As I cross the ballroom, the orchestra transitions to a livelier arrangement, something from the swing era, and people start to kick up their heels on the dance floor. I still haven't had a chance to rub elbows with the couple for whom this party is being thrown, but I can't bring myself to care.

A stream of guests pour into the room from the balcony and make their way to the dance floor. The full moon is visible outside the glass doors, and suddenly I just *know*. Izabela is outside right now, enjoying the moon and the balmy air. I didn't miss the way she gazed wonderingly at Lake Michigan at my mom's house, and she's mentioned her family's farm in Poland. She's the kind of person who appreciates the world's beauty in all its forms.

When I get out on the balcony, sure enough, I see her looking out at the view of the city. Her hair rustles softly in the breeze and the moonlight makes her skin glow like a pearl. Even with her face turned away from me, I can tell it's her by the way she holds herself, the elegant line of her neck, the curve of those hips outlined by her silk dress. She's simply...radiant. There's no other word for the way she looks tonight.

Maybe in the beginning, there was something in the back of my brain that thought Izabela was the perfect replacement for Celine.

Her face bears more than a passing resemblance, and they both have the tall, angular bodies particular to most models, but now I know that their physicality is where the similarities end.

Izabela is so much more than Celine could ever be.

Unlike Celine's perpetual cool, inscrutable detachment—a trait I once found inexplicably attractive—Izabela is warm, open, and kind. I saw this side of her at my mother's house, and haven't forgotten it since. Celine never would have thought to offer help to my mother at a Sunday dinner; I brought my ex to enough of those dinners that I can say that with certainty.

"There you are," I say softly as I walk up to Izabela.

She glances over her shoulder and then turns to face me. We're completely alone out here, the only two people who aren't inside dancing to Duke Ellington tunes. I can do anything I want to her and there's no one to see. My blood thrums with exhilaration.

Without a word, I cup her face and draw her against me for a searing, hungry kiss. Our first kiss. Her body is tense, but I'm well aware of the effect I have on her. If I suck her tongue long enough, she'll melt in my arms and do anything I say.

I wrap a hand around her neck and guide her back against the railing, keeping my mouth on hers. With my other hand, I skim my knuckles down the front of her dress and then rub them over her mound. A muffled gasp escapes her. I can feel her heat through the fabric.

Seeking more, I dip my hand into the high slit of

her dress and rake my nails up the length of her silken thigh, touching her again when I find her thong. Izabela presses against my fingers with a soft moan, then pulls back as if she can escape my touch.

She's not going anywhere.

Claiming her mouth again, I slip a finger inside her, and she moans as I pump slowly back and forth. God, she's wet. I could easily take her right here, fuck her on the balcony. Listen to the sounds of her trying to keep silent as I force her to come for me. But her body is tense and rigid. That's not like her.

I break the kiss, take her chin, and look into her eyes. Defiance and uncertainty flicker back at me. Maybe this is too public for her. Maybe she's not an exhibitionist. Too bad.

"Izabela, now isn't the time to challenge me. Take off your panties."

She lets out a huff of air, pulls herself to her full height, and pushes against my chest. Lightly grabbing her wrist, I'm about to demand that she tell me what's going on when she raises a hand and slaps me. The sound reverberates in the warm air.

I release her wrist, not hurt by the slap but shocked by her outburst nonetheless.

"We're not fucking again until you wear a condom," she hisses.

And then she storms off, leaving me standing there. I'm not even angry. Just confused.

I can't remember the last time a woman spoke to me like that—but whenever it was, I know this is the first time I've actually cared.

18

IZABELA

I'm TRYING to focus on this shoot, but I can't stop thinking about what Celine said to me at the party last night.

What kind of screwed-up love triangle is Rhys involved in? Celine made it clear that they used to be a couple, and that he never got over her...but now she's married to his father and carrying Rhys's half-sibling. And she very plainly implied that she and Rhys are still being intimate. Not only does the possibility exist that the baby is his, but who knows what kind of diseases he might be exposing himself to?

It's even more infuriating that he made *me* get tested when he himself might be carrying something. What a hypocrite. When it comes to my health, I'm not taking any chances. I'm already fighting the battle of my sister's autoimmune disease.

Still, he was clearly taken aback by the way I spoke

to him. I'm not sorry for standing up for myself, but I shouldn't have snapped at him like I did. Will there be consequences? Will Zoric find out I behaved badly? The thought that I might have jeopardized my position or even put my family in danger turns my stomach. I need to talk to Rhys in person when I get home tonight.

I need to make him see that I know better, that I'll be better.

"Better cheer up," one of the other models teases me. "You've had that sour look on your face since we got here."

We're sitting next to each other in front of a long, well-lit mirror, the makeup artist working on my face while the hairdresser works on the other model. It's 8 AM and we aren't allowed to have coffee, though we can smell the crew's. I'll use that as my excuse. I can't let my mood get me down. The last thing I need is to be known as the model with the bad attitude.

"I'd smile if they gave us cappuccinos."

"You don't need to *smile*," she says. "Perfume advertisements are all about sultry glares and pouty faces."

I laugh along with her, but I'm forcing it.

"I'm Talia, by the way."

"Izabela."

Talia occupies herself with something in her bag and I take the opportunity to grab a bottle of water from the snack table in the back. The snacks, of course, we're not allowed to eat. Just water. Always, only just water. I couldn't eat anyway. My insides are too knotted.

It's our first day on the set of a national campaign to launch a pop star's brand-new perfume, called Idlewild. Every single one of her albums has hit the top of the music charts, so being one of the faces of her perfume is going to propel me to instant recognition. These images will be distributed all over the United States. I'm going to be everywhere.

It's an incredible gig, one I never would have been offered if Rhys hadn't called Zoric to demand higher profile modeling work for me. Thanks to his intervention, I'll be appearing in several short commercials *and* print ads for Idlewild as the brand gears up for its holiday marketing push. This is also the longest shoot I've ever been on—five whole days—and I'm incredibly nervous. The photo part should be fine, but what if I'm no good on video?

I know I should just try to soak everything in and enjoy myself, but I can't. Not just because I'm anxious about the job, but because of what's going on with Rhys. He hasn't spoken to me since we left the party and drove home in silence. I'd foolishly hoped that Rhys might explain his relationship to Celine and what was going on between the two of them and Rhys's father. He didn't, of course. No explanation, no apology, nothing. He probably thinks I don't need to know, since I'm just his Rent-A-Lay.

The cold, calculated way that woman spoke to me in the restroom said it all anyway.

I have a sneaking suspicion that she's still in love with Rhys even though she wears another man's ring. Oh, do I ever get farther and farther from the fairytale I told my sister. I laid in my bed last night waiting for him to come to me. He didn't. He moved around the house so silently that I suspected he'd left, but then I heard him walking downstairs and I was relieved to know he was still home. This morning, he poured himself coffee and was out the door slightly before me.

I can't imagine what he'd need to do at the office at four in the morning, but who am I to ask?

The hairdresser finishes with Talia and bustles off to rub texturizing cream on another girl. In the mirror, I take in my partially finished makeup. The eyeliner is dark and heavy, the shadow is a metallic silver, tapering to a point at the outside corners of my eyes. I look a little wild, which I guess is the idea. Meanwhile, Talia's black hair is teased into a messy cloud, strewn with sparkling rhinestones and clip-in beetles and butterflies.

"We look like sexy fairies," she says. "I wish we were going out after this."

I could drown beneath the wave of despair that crashes over me. This, *this*, is what I thought I won that godforsaken contest for. Dressing up like a depraved rockstar, partying after a great shoot with my new friends. Instead, I've been sold. Ravished. Confused.

Blindsided, and just when I thought maybe Rhys and I could forge new common ground. Just when I thought I could see how to fit into his life.

"I found the glue, don't look so upset," says the makeup artist. I close my eyes so she can apply my lashes.

But in my head, all I can think about is Celine, Celine, Celine. Is he still in love with her? He hasn't touched me since our fight on the balcony. Maybe he's reconsidering our arrangement. God, I hope he doesn't call Zoric.

"All done," the makeup artist says. "Let me go grab a coffee and then I'll start on you next, Talia."

"So," Talia says, raising her brows as she drinks from a bottle of water, "man troubles? I recognize that look."

"I think he's sleeping with his ex," I blurt, and then I'm immediately horrified by my candor. I shouldn't be talking about this to anyone.

But Talia just makes a knowing sound as she shakes her head.

"Poor thing," she says kindly. "Look, I'm guessing you're pretty new at this, so let me give you the best advice I received when I was in your shoes: Don't confuse a client for a boyfriend. The man who bought your way into the shoot today is never going to ride in on a white horse and sweep you off your feet."

My mouth drops open. "How did you—"

"How do you think I got here?" There's no judgment in her tone, just sincerity. "This industry is a bitch, and a lot of us have to hustle on the side to get our foot in the door."

All I can do is nod, grateful for her kindness.

After we're all finished getting made up, an assistant escorts us to the set we'll be using today. The director is this artsy, intimidating indie film auteur, some famous Hollywood producer's nephew, who just won a bunch of awards, and demonstrates it by making us wait for him to have a long, loud phone call with his boyfriend.

It gives me a moment to close my eyes and center myself. Picturing the hills behind my uncle's farm usually helps. It's so green and vibrant in the summer and filled with cows lazily grazing over the rolling acreage. There is a narrow stream that runs through the back property. In the spring, snowmelt from the neighboring hills fills that creek so much it forms small rapids here and there. Pulling a slow, cleansing breath through my nose, I allow the sound of the water gurgling and tinkling over the rocks to fill my mind.

The meditation session is short-lived, but every little bit helps.

We all gather in a circle so our esteemed director can go over his concept for the first day of the shoot and what's expected of us.

"Think snowy evening in Paris, think glamour, seduction, fantasy. The idea is that when someone wears this perfume, it transforms them into a creature of mystery and allure. Every head will turn your way, every door will open, no conquest is out of your reach. Got it?"

I nod along with the other models as the director goes on, glad that nobody is asking for my opinion. The whole thing seems a little silly to me. That doesn't mean the photos won't turn out looking incredible, though.

Once the director is done giving us our pep talk, we're brought to the wardrobe area, where various outfits are tailored to our bodies. Two seamstresses flutter around us to nip and tuck the clothing so everything fits the models perfectly. If you can call our outfits clothing.

The backdrop for the first photo session is a winter night in Paris, yet we're all wearing white bikinis with ostrich feather boas around our necks and armloads of fake diamond bangles. I'm arranged on a pile of fake snow, where I'm told to put on a pensive, mysterious expression while holding a giant globe of Idlewild perfume in one outstretched hand. Then the other girls drape themselves around me, our long limbs tangling so that we probably look like a heavily-scented hydra. An assistant sprinkles more snow on us from above.

No one explains why we're wearing bikinis in the middle of winter. Creative license, I suppose.

Maybe I should give up modeling and become a director. Someone needs to design a scene that makes sense.

The next round of costumes works better. It's the same backdrop, but this time there's more light, warm like a sunrise, and pink roses are peeking through the snow. We're dressed in elk skin skirts and suede halter tops with wide, fur-trimmed hems, elbow-length red gloves, and matching crimson boots. Then we are instructed to frolic in the snow, while also wearing mysterious frowns. Plain water is misted on us from above this time, sparkling in the light and simulating droplets of perfume in the air.

I don't have to understand the director's vision to enjoy the experience. By the time this session is done, clumps of fake snow have gathered in every nook and cranny of my outfit. Talia and I look at each other and try not to laugh.

Maybe I should suggest that my uncle invest in elk herds instead of our standard beef cows. I imagine elk skin outfits might make a furry debut at Fashion Week next year after these photos come out.

But then the pang at missing Rhys's smirk when I describe this all to him reminds me this is just a temporary escape. When I go home—whatever that means—I'll have to face the silence again.

At least Eva is going to love hearing all about it.

WE BREAK FOR A LATE LUNCH. Thai veggie wraps with peanut sauce, tofu satay, steamed edamame, and sliced mango. It's the best meal I've ever had on a photo shoot.

"Who do you work for?" Talia picks the peppers off of her wrap and sets them on the side of her plate.

"KZ Modeling."

Her eyebrows shoot up. "No kidding? There's a lot of shady shit that goes on over there, isn't there?"

My smile is unintentionally tight. She has no idea, nor am I at liberty to talk about it. But I am curious what she's heard. I don't know how to ask her without insinuating I'm open to talking about it.

"I couldn't say."

Her eyebrows shoot up. "No horror stories to share? That's surprising."

"I wouldn't know."

Talia tilts her head, and I can tell she's not buying it.

"Come on," she says. "You belong to someone. I've been through it, I know how it works. The big dogs get a nice kickback for handing out beautiful women like candy. I mean, it's fine if you don't want to talk about it. I get it."

I just shrug.

"What about you?" I ask, hoping she'll let it go. "Who do you work for?"

"The same as you. I was just poking to see if you've heard any recent gossip. So, what are you going to do about that man of yours?" Talia says.

It typically takes me a while to warm up to people

and I never discuss personal issues unless I know someone well and feel comfortable with them. But something about Talia gives me the impression it's okay to talk. Maybe because she's clearly in a similar situation to me, but she's kept her humor, her spark. I could see us being friends if that opportunity ever arose.

"Nothing. I'm not the one with any power in our relationship."

"True, but if you don't do something, you'll be replaced. You don't want that. Jobs like this one don't grow on trees. Did you know we're shooting with *Mario* tomorrow? All of this opportunity could go away." She points to the set behind us. "If it were me, I'd do whatever I could to make him happy again."

She's right. But I don't have the first clue about what would make Rhys truly happy. I don't know if it's even possible. He's the perpetually brooding type.

"How would you do that?" I ask.

"Well, what exactly did you do to upset him?"

I relay the shortened version of how I copped an attitude with Rhys last night after my unpleasant run-in with his ex-girlfriend. I don't mention any names, of course, or give up any details that might hint at the people I'm talking about. When I get to the part about how I rejected his advances on the balcony, Talia shakes her head.

"No wonder he's not talking to you. No man who has paid an exorbitant amount of money for on-call sex wants to be given an ultimatum about using condoms."

"Am I wrong for wanting to protect my health?"

"Of course not. But your man doesn't want his ego bruised, either. So you need to turn things around in your favor. Make the condoms sexy. I don't know, maybe seduce him and roll it on with your mouth or something."

We giggle about it, but I take her advice to heart when I finally get home later. Rhys isn't there when I arrive, so I take a quick shower to wash off the remnants of the day. Then I tiptoe to his room in my towel and duck inside before any of the staff can see me, hanging up the towel in his bathroom and then making my way to his bed.

I slip the condoms I bought under the pillow and pull the covers down, arranging myself face-up in the sheets with my naked body on full display. I tousle my hair and spread it over my shoulders, pulling my arms up over my head. When he walks through that door, he's going to find me ready and waiting for him.

I close my eyes, relishing the feel of his luxurious sheets on my skin and the scent of his cologne. Before I know it, I'm lulled to sleep.

The next thing I know, sunlight is streaming into the room and Mrs. Dunham is pulling the covers off me and barking at me to wake up. Sitting up with a jolt, I realize that I'm alone, and that somebody covered me up last night, complete with a throw blanket over the end of the bed. Was it Rhys? It obviously wasn't Mrs. Dunham. She wouldn't have pulled the comforter over me just to turn around and yell at me to get out of here.

"Up, up, up," she's saying, flapping the blankets at me. "It's morning."

I reach for the throw blanket, attempting to cover my bare chest as I slide off the bed, but Mrs. Dunham isn't having any of it. Shaking her head, she goes into Rhys's closet and returns with a thick Turkish bathrobe, tossing it unceremoniously at me.

"Put that on. You'll bring it down to the laundry once you're dressed," she tells me.

"Yes ma'am," I say, cheeks flaming with embarrassment.

She herds me out the door and into the hallway, waving a finger at me.

"Don't come into this room again without an invitation!"

With that, she throws the packet of condoms at my head and slams the door, leaving me standing there in Rhys's robe, stunned and confused.

19

RHYS

"ARE you aware of what your little girlfriend is up to?" my father says, marching into my office and brandishing his cellphone like it's a weapon.

When I left the house around two a.m., Izabela was cozily tucked into my bed, sleeping like a baby. Shocked isn't quite the word to describe how it felt to find her there last night, naked and half uncovered, like she'd been waiting up for me.

I hesitated at first. I was sorely tempted to fuck out all my frustrations until I was fully spent—in a condom. But it didn't seem right to wake her up just to make myself feel good about feeling bad. Her driver had informed me of the long hours she'd put in on her shoot all day. Clearly, she was exhausted, and not thinking straight. She needed some time to cool off. I did too. So after pulling the blankets over her, I'd grabbed my toiletries and a change of clothes and gone right back to the office—where I'd spent the night.

I guess now, I can actually claim that I live at work.

Which is for the best. Between the endless shifts I've been putting in and the fact that I'm sleeping on my office's leather sofa now, I'm finally getting some extended time away from Izabela. It's clear to me that I need to set some boundaries with her.

Obviously, I've allowed too many lines to be blurred. Let her mistake my kindness for weakness. For guilt. There's nothing for me to be sorry about. I'm not the one behaving like a bad soap opera here. She needs to realize that there's only one person in control of this arrangement, and it sure as hell isn't her.

So no, I'm not aware of what my fake "little girl-friend" is up to, and considering the pile of work on my desk, I don't think I care.

"Please leave," I tell my dad without looking away from my computer screen.

But my father, as usual, won't be ignored. He sets his phone screen-up in front of me, displaying the social media account of something called Idlewild. There are three pictures posted from the set they're currently working on, apparently for perfume. It's very Moulin Rouge, very burlesque style, except it's snowing all over the stage.

I don't get it, but I'm not the target audience, either.

I recognize Izabela immediately, posed beneath a huge sign that says *Idlewild* in blinking lights.

She's wearing a glittery bra and matching G-string made of triangles of fabric that are barely the size of tortilla chips. Her hair is teased to the sky, her makeup dark and bold. She's perched between a muscular, tawny-skinned young man and another woman. Both have their hands all over Izabela.

Each of the photos shows her in a more risqué threesome. The man has his lips on her neck, his hand on her thigh as he pulls her leg over his hip. The woman has her finger slipped under the waistband of Izabela's G-string. Finally, the two women kneel in front of the man, who sits in a furry armchair with his legs spread wide. A muscle in my jaw twitches.

Nope. This is not the job I approved. My father doesn't need to know that, though.

Tossing the phone back to him, I grit my teeth and turn my attention back to my work. He doesn't get the hint to leave.

Flicking him a glare, I say, "This isn't a good time. I have work to do."

"It doesn't bother you that some random man has his hands all over the body you paid for?" he says, his tone smug under the veneer of false outrage.

"No. Because I don't need to control my women to feel like a man."

That's not exactly true, but I'm happy to pretend that I'm the kind of person who takes the high road. That I don't have the strongest urge to race out of here and go pull Izabela from that photo shoot. Toss her over my shoulder and carry her home, while I'm at it.

My dad cocks his head. "Bullshit. If you let her do a gig like this, what will the next job be? *Playboy*? A porno?"

Over my dead body.

But I just shrug like I haven't a care in the world.

"Izabela is free to make her own decisions about her career," I lie. "I'm not the jealous type." Another lie. "I appreciate your concern." The biggest lie of all. "Though I'm surprised you're so bored with Celine and the baby already." Truth.

Dad leaves to take the call rather than dispute the point.

Leaning back in my chair, I replay the images of Izabela in my head. I told her she could model and even got her this gig, but I never authorized something so... intimate. So seductive. So unsettling.

I hadn't planned on going home tonight. I was going to work through the night and sleep in my office again.

The melancholy expression on her face in those photographs nags at me.

Her expression could be coached as part of the aesthetic, but the hollow look in her eyes and narrow set to her lips suggest she's not comfortable. After seeing these photos, I've decided that I'm going to sleep in my own bed tonight. Once I'm finished using my mouth and my hands to erase every touch and embrace that Izabela received during the photo shoot.

It only takes one phone call to find out where the shoot is taking place.

After telling Tamara that I'll be gone for the rest of the day and to reschedule my afternoon meetings, I slip into my jacket and hurry out of the office. What should have been a twenty-minute drive is closer to forty with heavy traffic. By the time I reach the location, I'm tense with righteousness. How many more poses has she been subjected to in the time it took me to get here? How many ways did those other models touch her?

It's not fucking professional, and I should have made certain she had legal counsel on set.

When I stroll into the space—a huge loft in River North—I see that the crew has moved to a different stage. This one is an over-the-top rendition of Versailles, complete with tall, gold-framed baroque mirrors, low-hanging crystal chandeliers and towers of pastel-colored cookies and cakes.

Izabela is dressed in a skimpy, ruffled pink bra with matching panties and a Marie Antoinette wig. The male model is in a curled white wig as well, and is shirt-less. The only thing he wears is a pair of ludicrous baby blue velvet knee pants, unless you count the fake beauty mark on his cheek. He has his arms around her waist, his face pressed into the back of her neck, like he can't get enough of the scent of her.

The other female model is in a lime-green bustier

and ruffled bloomers. She's holding a cupcake with a swirl of pale pink frosting on it, and I watch as the director orders her to dip a finger into the frosting and then hold it out for Izabela to suck.

Slipping out of my jacket, I loosen my tie slightly. My clothes feel too tight. My skin, too hot. An assistant sees me striding toward the set and runs over with an alarmed expression.

"Sir, you can't be in here. Sir? You need to leave. This is a closed set."

"And you clearly have no idea who I am," I say.

Bypassing him, I make my way toward the young guy dressed all in black who just told the other model to feed Izabela the frosting off her cupcake. He has an imperious air, and he's speaking into an earpiece, pointing up at one of the chandeliers and motioning for it to be lowered. I have no doubt that he's the director of all these shenanigans.

"Are you the creative muscle behind...whatever this is?" I ask.

He looks over at me and his expression falters. "And you are?"

"Unhappy."

He frowns. "I don't know why I should answer to—"

"McConnell. Rhys McConnell. Should I get on the phone with Konstantin Zoric and tell him how unprofessional this set is? Because I doubt he'd agree to let his girls work under these conditions without representation."

He glares at me and opens his mouth to argue again, but then an assistant rushes over and whispers something in his ear. Suddenly, he's looking nervous. Good.

"*Rhys?*" Izabela's surprised voice calls out to me.

I don't respond. But I do step closer to the director as she appears at my side. Taking her arm because I need to touch her, I move her a few steps back.

"You said I could work," she whispers. "If you interfere, KZM might not be able to book jobs for me in the future."

"Are you comfortable with all of this?" I ask, gesturing at the set. Then I indicate her lack of clothing, resisting the urge to throw my jacket over her shoulders. "And...this wardrobe? Just because they're paying you doesn't mean they own you. You aren't just a body."

Oh, the irony. Her lips twitch because she recognizes it, too.

The director has moved closer to listen in on whether or not I'm going to demand that his model leave the shoot.

"I'm fine, Rhys," Izabela says. "This is an opportunity for me."

"You ought to remind your face, then," I tell her. "Right now, you don't look happy, and you don't look like you're prepared to tell them."

The director gasps and clutches his clipboard to his chest. The room has gone still, everyone watching us.

Izabela shakes her head. "No. I *want* to do this. Nothing unprofessional is going on. I'm perfectly comfortable." Assessing her body language, I'm not sure that I believe her.

"Right here," I tell her. "Right now. Look me in the eyes. If you like this so much, look me in the eyes and explain to me why you're so happy."

"I wasn't." She stares at me for a moment longer. "But I feel better having you here."

"I'm not going to interfere. Just keep an eye on things. Make sure everyone is observing a professional boundary." I reassure her, but then look over at the director and add, louder, "Unless you have any objections?"

The director spins on one heel as if he's heard all that he needs to. "Set up for the next shot, and someone get Mr. McConnell a chair!"

Izabela leans closer and says, "You don't have to stay. I'll be fine now."

Dragging my hand lightly over her arm, I say, "I want to watch. Because it's hot."

I see that familiar spark of lust in her eye, and then she walks away and resumes her place on the set. The chair the director asked for appears at my side, and I sit and give the director a nod. He hurriedly gets to work repositioning the models, immediately placing the male model's hands back on Izabela's body.

Pulling my lower lip between my teeth, I will myself to relax.

I'm not like my dad. I'm not a possessive, insecure jackass. I'm the kind of boyfriend who's laid back. Supportive. Someone who can watch his woman be touched by another man in a professional capacity without losing his shit. The jealousy I'm feeling is purely a primal thing, but I can ignore it. I won't let it control me.

So why do I feel ready to jump out of my skin?

Riveted to the scene in front of me, I sit back in my chair and take it all in. I'm still not entirely clear on what the concept is, but there's no denying the draw of what the director is creating. I can't tear my eyes away. The tableau is decadent, fantastical, dreamy. Honestly, I want to be a part of it. And maybe that's really all there is to it, because by the end of the shoot, I'm ready to go out and buy the perfume.

Once the Versailles shoot is complete, the models are sent back to makeup and wardrobe to change for the next scene. The director instructs the crew to move to another set and get ready to start shooting video next. A flurry of hectic activity ensues. Lights, cameras, and equipment are arranged and rearranged to the director's liking. I move my chair to the new area.

This set is decorated like a cozy winter cabin in the French Alps. Floor-to-ceiling wood paneling, knit blankets thrown over a brown leather couch, a rough stone fireplace with flickering electric flames. There's a bearskin rug on the floor—faux, of course—and light fixtures made from antlers. Incidentally, Chamonix is one of my favorite places, and when I see Izabela spread out on the couch in plaid flannel short-shorts and a crocheted crop top, it makes me consider taking her there for a weekend and reenacting this scene in real life.

Her hair is in pigtails now, and she's lying on her back with her legs draped over the arm of the couch. The male model is instructed to sit at the other end of the couch and put her head in his lap. Then the director tells the female model to kneel on the floor with her head resting on Izabela's bare midriff, looking up at her longingly while cradling a gaudily oversized bottle of Idlewild perfume.

"Izabela, arch your back," the director calls out, giving me a quick glance to see how I react. "And then cup Talia's chin with your left hand and put your thumb over her lower lip. Talia, you can tuck that free hand between Izabela's legs. A little lower. That's great. Mario, just look over at them. Give me half a smile. Less smile. Little bit less. Perfect."

My cock pulls at the seductive pose. I readjust myself in my seat, but the tension inside me only grows worse with each passing moment, each direction that gets called out.

Izabela is a natural and she looks amazing in every single ridiculous outfit they've put on her. I have no doubt that her face and body alone could sell this perfume. It's impossible to look away.

When the director calls for a meal break, Izabela slips into a silky robe and walks toward me. It's hard to catch my breath when her eyes land on mine.

"So? What do you think?" she asks.

Her eyes are bright, her smile genuine, her shoulders relaxed. It's nice to see her looking so alive after watching her wear the same glazed, fake, orgy-ready expression for the last few hours. She's better at her job than I realized.

"It's looking good," I say quietly, trailing my finger down the front of her robe. "You're very good."

Another female model pauses as she walks by, her eyes darting back and forth between me and Izabela.

"Hm. Maybe I was wrong," she says to Izabela. Then she winks and walks away.

I have no idea what that means...but whatever it was, it made Izabela blush.

20

IZABELA

THE DIRECTOR CALLS wrap around eight p.m. Since we're all returning to set first thing tomorrow, the crew leave most of the equipment where it stands and quickly head out. It sounds like some of them are planning to meet up for a drink at a bar a few blocks away.

Talia gives me a quick hug before going to wardrobe to change into her street clothes, and Mario doesn't even bother putting a shirt on, he just grabs his bag and goes. I don't blame him. It's been another long, grueling shooting day. We're all exhausted, and Mario is running late to meet his boyfriend for dinner.

I realize the room is emptying rapidly, the lights going out in the process. Looking around for Rhys, I finally spot him standing by the door talking to the director. Both of them look my way, and then I hear the director say, "Lock up when you're done."

He follows the last few assistants out, leaving me and Rhys completely alone.

Pulling the sides of my robe tighter, I watch him move purposefully toward me.

"What's going on?" I ask, confused.

"Come."

Rhys places a hand on my lower back and guides me back to the set. The huge industrial loft we're in feels different now that everyone is gone and most of the lights are off. All the frenetic energy has dissipated. It's nice. Relaxing, almost.

Our footsteps echo against the cavernous ceiling, and the set suddenly looks a lot smaller in the yawning room. I was too focused on work to really notice the scale of everything, but now I take in the four separate sets, laid out in different areas of the wide-open space, each designed to transport the viewer to another kind of fantasy. A Paris street at night; a wide-open, grassy field; the Palace of Versailles in its decadent heyday; the tranquil ski cabin.

A lot of detail went into the cabin set. Now that I have the time to really look, it's obvious someone's job was to make it look just like a real cabin, high in the Alps. A backdrop of majestic, snow-covered mountains hangs behind the set, visible through the windows, along with a brown and white sign that says, "Bienvenue à Chamonix Mont-Blanc!"

Rhys stops and I turn to face him, still unsure why we've stayed behind. Reaching for the neckline of my

222

robe, he runs a finger down the front and then pulls it open, revealing my little white halter top. It's crocheted so I'm not wearing a bra underneath, and I know the pink of my nipples is slightly visible. He hisses an appreciative breath and then slides the silken fabric over my shoulders, down my arms. When it hits the floor, a shiver runs through me.

"Have you ever been to Chamonix?" he asks.

"No. I've never been to France," I admit.

"Perhaps I'll take you there when things calm down. To a cabin in the mountains just like this one," he says. "Where no one can hear you come but me."

My mouth goes dry. I gaze up at him, unable to stop the hard beat of my heart, a hot tug pulling at my lower belly as he feasts on me with hungry eyes. What is happening? I waited for him last night, naked and ready, and he never came to bed. Or, if he did, he didn't stay. And now he suddenly wants me?

But why am I questioning it? When it comes to Rhys McConnell, my job is to submit to him, completely. So that's what I'm going to do. Because it's my job.

Not because I want him, too.

Indicating that I should stay where I am, he walks onto the set and looks around until he finds the switch that turns on the fake flames of the electric fireplace. Then he turns off all the other lights in the room. Everything goes dark save for the warm, soothing glow of the fire. It almost looks real.

Rhys comes back toward me, and without a word, he pulls me against his rock-hard body. His hands slide down to cup my ass as he kisses me, hard and bruising. I slide my hands into his hair, and when he lifts me in his arms, I wrap my legs around his waist. He carries me to the set, but I'm barely conscious of it as I get lost in the thrust of his tongue.

Until I realize he's laying me down on the floor in front of the fireplace, the rug plush and soft under the bare skin of my back. Rhys kneels between my legs, breathing hard. That look in his eyes is my undoing, as always. Lust, desire, awe. A heady cocktail of want.

I don't break eye contact with him as I reach up and untie the halter straps behind my neck. I lower my top, letting Rhys take in the sight of my breasts while I work on the second set of ties that are knotted at my waist. Before I can get them fully loosened, Rhys rips the top off me, a groan escaping him just before he drops his mouth over my left nipple, sucking hungrily.

"Ahh," I moan, arching my back.

His lips and hands are everywhere, trailing fire. My breasts, my belly, my neck, my shoulders, the soft spot behind my ears. Unlike when I lied to my sister, this man legitimately can't keep his hands off me. The throb between my legs becomes an urgent pulse, a hot ache that I can't possibly control. I need him. I need to feel him inside me. I reach for his zipper, stroking the bulge beneath, but he bats my hand away.

Hooking his fingers in the sides of my shorts, Rhys

draws them down, taking my underwear with them. Now I'm naked on the rug, the yellow glow of the fireplace dancing over the curves of my body. Rhys is still fully dressed, but he doesn't seem to be in a hurry to change that. Instead, he slowly unbuttons his shirt, tosses it aside, and lowers himself between my thighs. I gasp as he pushes my legs farther apart. A low rumble works from his throat as he looks at my bare pussy. The air is cool against my wetness.

My skin crawls with the need to be touched, tasted. Tense with anticipation, I cry out when his tongue touches my opening, dips inside, and then drags up my slit. All I can do is pant helplessly while he devours me, lapping me up and down until I'm trembling.

"You're too quiet," he growls. "Make noise for me or I'll stop."

Rhys plunges two fingers inside me, and I moan loudly in response.

"Louder, Izabela. I won't tell you again."

He starts pumping, gliding in and out of my soaked pussy.

"Yes," I sigh, lifting my hips to meet the thrust of his fingers.

"Say my name."

"Rhys. Yes. *Rhys*. Mmm."

The passionate sounds spilling from my lips echo around the empty room, growing louder and more desperate by the second.

"That's a good girl." He strokes harder, in and out,

sending sparks of electricity through me. "You're going to pay me back for getting you this job. You owe me."

"Yes. I owe you, Rhys," I pant, fucking his fingers even faster. "Anything you want."

"I want your orgasm, Izabela. It's mine. It's my payment."

He wraps his lips around my clit and starts sucking, his fingers still plunging deep into me as he sucks. It feels incredible, his tongue and his hands working me at the same time. I've never felt anything like this before. I'm on fire.

"Rhys, Rhys, Rhys," I wail, all my inhibitions gone.

I'm thrashing now, the rug creating friction on my lower back and stinging my skin. My head falls back, and I stare into the shifting flames of the fire as I grab his head and grind even harder against him, so his swirling tongue puts extra pressure on my clit every time I thrust.

"*Rhys*," I moan desperately. "I'm going to come."

"Not yet you aren't," he says, pulling back and roughly turning me over onto my belly. "Get on your hands and knees."

I do as he says, ready to let him take what he needs. I can hear the clink of his belt buckle, his zipper, the sound of a condom wrapper tearing open. He listened —*he listened*! But the repercussions of what it means are...I'd rather lose my thoughts in the sensations. It's easy, given how wet I am, so when he enters me from behind, he glides in hard and deep and right. We instantly find a rhythm, perfectly in tune with each other, every stroke drawing moans from both of us in tandem.

"You feel so good," I moan. "So good. So damn good."

In response, I get a slap on the ass. I yelp at the sting, but it only turns me on more.

Outside the cabin's window, I can see the snowy peaks of the French alps, and in the dim light of the fire, I can almost believe we're really there. Just me and Rhys, making love in a romantic, secluded ski cabin. I lean into the fantasy. I let myself believe. Somehow, this feels more real, more intimate, than any of the other times we've had sex at Rhys's actual house. Here, I can pretend I'm not just another member of his paid staff. And that Rhys McConnell is just...Rhys. My Rhys. And we're together because we want to be.

His hand cups the base of my neck and then he trails his nails down my back. Tingles rise in the wake of his touch. He does this again and again, tenderly stroking my back as he rams into me, scratching the hills and valleys of my spine and making my skin sing. My body jerks forward and back, my breasts shaking, my knees aching as I desperately chase my orgasm. I grab the edges of the rug, bunching the fake fur in my hands, doing everything I can to just hang on as Rhys fucks me into sweet oblivion.

"Take that cock. Take it all. Tell me how much you like it."

"I love it." And I do. God, I do.

He grabs a handful of my hair and pulls hard, his thrusts increasing as I cry out in pain. He pulls again, and again, jerking my head back each time. It hurts, but it's the kind of hurt I can't get enough of.

"Rhys, Rhys, Rhys," I chant, feeling my orgasm building fast.

I quicken my pace, riding the high, impaling myself on his dick. I'm determined to make it last, but suddenly his cock swells and he curses softly, a throaty growl escaping him as he starts to spill into me. The sound of him coming, the harsh jackhammer of his final thrusts, it all pushes me right over the edge. It's all I can do to keep up with him as my climax hits, sapping my energy with every hard, crashing wave. For just a second, I look out the little window at the snowy mountain backdrop and let myself believe we really are in the French Alps.

He's slow to pull out of me afterward, and I shudder at his absence. I feel bruised and sore, in the best possible way.

Rhys lifts me easily to my feet and hands me my clothes before even discarding the condom, then starts putting on his own. I just stand there, still weak in the knees from our exertions. Lifting my chin, Rhys kisses me with equal tenderness and possessiveness, and a flash of that hunger again.

"Go change. I'll take you home."

Picking up my discarded robe, I slip into it and then hurry to the wardrobe area.

As I dress, I think back to what he said earlier, when he came rushing in here today. About how I'm not just a body. Strange for him to say so, considering that he literally bought me, yet...he seemed genuinely concerned about my well-being on this shoot. Which doesn't seem to jive with his rules about our relationship. Instead of being indifferent and simply using me, it almost seems like he's starting to actually care about me.

Maybe he's starting to see me. *Really* see me. And maybe...maybe I can start to trust him. Maybe he'd be on my side if he found out the truth: that I'm not the one making money off of this arrangement. That I was forced into this whole thing.

I give my face a quick swipe with a cotton pad soaked in makeup remover, then gather my things. I'm still shaking. Rhys just gave me quite a workout.

"Let's grab takeout on the way home," he says when I join him.

"Okay."

"Do you like Moroccan food?"

"Never had it. But I'm game."

"Lucky you," he says. "You're in for a treat. Trust me."

How I wish that I could. Our entire relationship is based on a power play. We didn't have a meet-cute and go on dates and fall in love. We weren't set up on a blind date, or bump into each other in the street. Rhys bought me for six months. He's using my body and my time. I'm not sure trust is built in what we have.

But what if I *could*? If he knew the truth about how I ended up in this position in the first place, would he believe me? Glancing at him, I quickly look away. But then he takes my hand and opens the door to the takeout counter, as if he knows exactly what I need.

Comfort.

Food.

Love.

Stop it, Izabela.

Hunger is making me delusional.

At least, that's what I'm telling myself. I try to hide my grin. He doesn't take my hand, but we walk close enough that our bodies touch, all the way to the waiting car.

21

IZABELA

I'VE NEVER BEEN to the opera before.

At first, I was incredibly excited about the whole thing. When Rhys called me on his way home from work to tell me that some executives from McConnell Enterprises were hosting a bunch of clients from out of town tonight, and that we had tickets to attend, my heart soared. This would be the kind of performance I'd be talking about for the rest of my life.

...and then I realized I didn't have anything to wear.

Which is why, for the past forty minutes, I've been frantically trying on of every piece of evening wear I have, trying to accessorize my way into looking as elegant and classy as possible.

So far, I'm failing.

I scowl at my reflection in the walk-in closet's dressing mirror. My hair is in a sophisticated knot and my makeup looks good, but this outfit is a disaster. I'm in a black strapless dress, satin, with an A-line and a mid-calf length. It's not bad, but it's definitely more appropriate for a cocktail party or a night out than an opera house. I tried to dress it up with a black crocheted shawl and my gold cross necklace, but the effect just isn't formal enough.

A knock at my bedroom door startles me from my despair.

"Izabela."

At the sound of Rhys's voice, my stomach drops. It's time.

"I'm ready!" I call out in a panic.

When I fling open the door, I find him standing in the hallway in a tux, and *my God*. The man could have a modeling career himself if he wanted to. And his cologne is different than what he usually wears. This one is smokier, with something caramel-sweet underneath. I practically have to dab the drool off my chin.

"You're not wearing that, are you?" he says, instantly crushing that urge.

"This—this is the nicest thing I have," I sputter. "Unless you want me to wear the navy dress again? I thought we'd be seeing some of the same people, so I didn't think it would do—"

"It won't do. But never mind." He checks his watch. "Get your shoes on and let's go."

I grab my heels and clutch and follow him down the hall. I feel so stupid. I should have known I wouldn't have anything nice enough for this event. And if I had told Rhys sooner, maybe he could have invited someone else to be his date tonight.

The thought sends a bolt of jealousy through me. Jealousy I have no right to feel. I repeat that to myself as I follow him out of the house and into the waiting car. The second we slide into the back seat, he takes out his phone and starts texting.

We don't speak as his driver takes us downtown to the address Rhys gave. He's tense, and so am I. We're not even at the venue yet, and I feel like I ruined the entire night already. The last thing I want to do is embarrass him.

Suddenly, the car whips into an alleyway, making the tires squeal. At first I think it must be a shortcut, but then the driver pulls to a stop and parks.

I turn to Rhys, confused. "This is...the Lyric Opera House?"

"This is a boutique. The stylist knows my taste well and will dress you appropriately."

We get out of the car and Rhys leads me to one of the nondescript doors on the backside of the huge brick building. He's just about to ring the bell when a silver-haired woman pulls open the door and smiles at us.

"Rhys!" she croons, leaning in to kiss him on each cheek, her voice rich and melodic. "It's been too long. I'm so glad you reached out. Come, come."

I'm awed as I follow Rhys into the shop, my footsteps slowing as the huge space opens all around us. Exquisite clothes are hanging left and right, so gorgeous that I can't help staring. Tiered skirts of pleated chiffon, silk bustier tops that look like folded origami, jewel-toned gowns with beaded straps or necklines that plunge to the waist. The air smells like rosewater and there's nothing but marble and gold as far as the eye can see. Eva would be in heaven here.

As for me, I'm mostly just intimidated. Everything in here must cost a fortune.

The woman turns to me, and I notice the measuring tape around her neck and the huge diamond earrings hanging from her ears—the only accessories to her impeccably tailored gray suit, which has a 1940's look to it and which is fabulous.

"I don't believe we've met, *mademoiselle*. I'm Nicolette. Welcome."

Rhys says, "This is Izabela. We're on our way to see *Eurydice* at the Lyric, and I don't want her to look like the rest. So anything she needs, just put it on my tab. Sky's the limit."

"I see." Nicolette smiles. "I have some ideas already."

"Good. Work your magic. I'll be back in half an hour."

Rhys doesn't look back as he strides away. Nicolette taps her chin twice and then asks me to walk in front of her. So I do.

"Ah, you're a model," she says, nodding. "Come with me."

I trail behind her as she darts here and there,

pulling dresses off racks one by one, lifting a few up to see if the fabric complements my coloring and then putting them back or draping them over her arm. I wonder how she knew my sizes just from looking at me. It's true that I look like Celine. Rhys probably brought her here for fittings, too, which explains why the stylist knows him so well.

Once we have about half a dozen options, she leads me to a fitting room, smiling at me as she hangs the dresses on a wardrobe rack.

"I'll find you a purse and shoes after we decide on a dress. Now strip, please."

I do, quickly. Once I'm standing in my underwear, Nicolette turns me to the mirror and stands behind me, then holds one garment after another in front of my body, assessing what she sees in the mirror each time before moving on to the next dress.

"Am I...going to try any of those on?" I ask, confused.

"No need," she says crisply. "The right one will sing."

She vetoes several dresses before finally lifting one off the rack with a happy little sigh. It's a blue-gray silk chiffon, sleeveless, with a high neckline that's twisted and gathered in a way that will draw attention to my shoulders. Nicolette removes the dress from the hanger, then slips it over my head and smooths it down over my body.

A gasp slips out of me. The design is simple, yet

stunningly elegant; the tiers of fabric are layered like ocean waves lapping at a shore. I look like a statue of a goddess, almost. And the open back plunges so low, it shows off the dimples over my rear end. I love it.

"It's incredible," I murmur.

"If you're going to take a trip to the underworld, you might as well look like a million on your way down."

My brow knits at the reference. Nicolette catches my expression in the mirror. "The opera is about a woman who is killed on her wedding night and descends to the underworld... do you not know the story of Eurydice?"

"No."

Taking my arm, she leads me to a make up counter and helps me sit, and covers me with a drape. She tells me about the opera as she lightly styles my hair into a half-up bun. Then she does my makeup with the deftness of a well skilled artist. My skin is pale and shimmery, my eyes big and lips bold when she's done. Not only do I look incredible, but I also now fully understand about the show I'm to watch. I feel... less uncultured than I did before coming here.

We go back out to the sales floor and she grabs a pair of heels and a clutch as we make our way to the cash register. Somehow, she managed to choose my exact shoe size. I slip into the silver heels as she tallies up the purchases on a tablet. When I glance over and see the price of the dress—$12,000—I feel my stomach drop.

"Um. Are we sure this is really the right dress?" I ask, even though I'm sure everything else in this store is just as expensive.

"*Absolument*. Besides, we are out of time. Here is a bag for your personal items," she says, handing it to me for my discarded clothes. Then she steps back to judge her work.

"Good?" I ask nervously. Rhys is going to be back any second now.

"Mm. One more thing."

She hurries off and returns with a cream-colored wrap, which she arranges around my upper arms. She's still fussing with it when I hear footsteps and look up to see Rhys striding into the boutique. He gives me an approving nod, but doesn't say anything about my makeover as he thanks Nicolette. Then we dash to the waiting car. I feel a little bit like Cinderella.

When we arrive at the Lyric, we're instantly surrounded by posh couples, the women in colorful designer gowns, many of them outlandish statement pieces. Some women side-eye me, while the men stare more openly.

"Rhys, darling!" a woman calls out, swishing over in a voluminous black-and-white gown with a geometric pattern that hurts my eyes.

She's beautiful, with glossy black hair, deep red lips, and tight, glassy-smooth skin. The kind of woman who actually looks like she's in Rhys's league. Unlike me.

After kissing him lingeringly on the cheek, she tries to talk him into getting a drink with her at the upstairs bar, fawning over him all the while. It's obvious she's attracted to him, the way she can't stop touching him. As they ignore me, I shrink further and further into myself. I don't fit in.

And then Rhys peels her off his arm and turns to me. "Izabela, this is one of our board members, Corinne Markarian. Corinne, this is my date, Izabela."

"Your date? I see. Izabela. Well. Lovely to meet you," the woman says to me, though her tone is anything but friendly. "Is this your first time at the opera, dear?"

She's talking to me like I'm twelve years old, but I ignore my humiliation since I want to reflect well on Rhys. "Yes. I'm very excited to be here."

"It certainly shows," Corinne says disdainfully.

"It does, doesn't it?" Rhys says. "I think it's refreshing. Everyone else here looks like they're going to fall asleep during the first act. Izabela will enjoy every second, I'm sure."

"I hope I will," I say, buoyed by Rhys's words coming to my defense.

Corinne clears her throat. "And that dress. It's certainly...understated. I'm not sure it's entirely appropriate for the opera, but I suppose this isn't exactly your milieu."

My cheeks go hot. Is it possible Nicolette chose wrong? Judging by the way this Corinne woman is smirking at me, it's obvious I don't look like I belong here.

"I think it suits her perfectly," Rhys cuts in again. "After all, true beauty needs no adornment. Though that would clearly be news to this room full of peacocks. Or should I say peahens? It's as if they've forgotten we're here to experience the opera, rather than swan around while getting intoxicated. Speaking of, is that your husband over there?"

Rhys tilts his head and I look over to the other end of the lobby, where I spot a man in a hideous black-and-white patterned tux that matches Corinne's dress. I have to work hard to keep the smile off my face. For a moment, Corinne seems too stunned at the subtle insult to speak.

"Yes," she finally chokes out. "If you'll excuse me."

With that, she sashays away.

Rhys pulls me close to him, his hand skating down the length of my back. When he reaches the dip in the fabric right over the cleft of my ass, he trails his fingers underneath the dress, tracing the waistband of my thong. Tingles race through me from head to toe.

"You are, without a doubt, the most exquisite woman here," he whispers, his hand sliding lower, those electric fingertips skimming the curve of my ass possessively.

I shiver, but then he's pulling his hand away and

guiding me into the theatre to find our seats. The lights are dim, the plush velvet seats mostly filled already. I lean into Rhys, gripping his arm like a lifeline as we weave through the crowd of beautiful people.

Once we're seated, I can't help looking around with wide eyes. I hear snippets of conversation floating around us, people discussing past operas and commenting on arias and librettos, things I know nothing about. I look over and glance anxiously at Rhys, but suddenly the room darkens so I sink back into my chair, pulse pounding. It's starting.

There are no words to describe the feeling that blooms inside me as the orchestra music swells, as the voices of the singers rise all the way into the rafters, rolling across the audience in hypnotic waves, like powerful incantations. I'm transported first to a beach, then to a wedding, then down into the Underworld. I'm crestfallen as amnesic rain falls on Eurydice inside the elevator car. My heart tugs painfully in my chest at the stark imagery of the woman losing all her earthly memories, for reasons I can't quite explain. The loss is somehow incredibly visceral.

Halfway through, Rhys taps my shoulder and passes me a tissue, and I realize that I have tears rolling down my cheeks. By the time the curtain falls, Rhys is holding my hand tightly. I don't remember reaching for him, or him reaching for me, but it's magical all the same.

"Did you enjoy it?" he asks softly as the lights brighten.

"I...loved it," I tell him.

"Really? It's such a tragic story," he says.

"That's one way of looking at it. On the other hand, the Underworld is pretty interesting."

His lips twitch, but he stops just short of a smile and then we're both applauding as the cast comes out to take their bows.

As we ride home in the back of the car, Rhys slowly lifts the hem of my dress up my legs, higher and higher, and then traces lazy circles over my knees with his fingertips. I wait for him to slip his hand between my thighs, or start issuing commands, but he doesn't.

"Tell me what you liked," he says. "About the opera. Was it the music? The story?"

"Both," I answer easily. "The emotions in the singing, but also the love story."

"But Orpheus and Eurydice didn't end up together," he points out. "Which just proves that love, even what is supposed to be the truest, purest love, is no guarantee of happiness. It doesn't prevail against all. You can lose somebody and never get them back, no matter how much you want them, no matter how hard you try. Sometimes I wonder if the story isn't actually a dark comedy. Young lovers are idiots, you know. Love makes fools of us all."

"You're so cynical!" I say, slapping his arm playfully. "But I didn't get that from it. In fact, I think it's saying the opposite. I think it's saying...something quite beautiful."

"And what's that?" he asks, leaning closer, placing his hot palm flat on my knee.

I suddenly feel self-conscious, like maybe my reading of the story is all wrong, but I take a deep breath and answer, "I think it's saying that you can't look back. In life and in love. Otherwise you'll never move forward. All Orpheus had to do was put one foot in front of the other, right? Just keep walking, one step at a time, until he stepped into the light with his love. But he failed. Not because fate is cruel or because love makes you a fool, but...because he didn't have faith in what lay ahead. He looked behind him. He didn't trust the future."

"Even if he did, fate would have intervened again. He would have lost Eurydice again."

"Maybe," I say. "But it's defeatist to think of it that way. If you follow that line of thinking, why bother with love at all?"

"Now you see my point," he teases.

I laugh. "I see your point but I disagree. Because love is...it's the most beautiful thing about the human experience. We're here to live and to love. With open arms. To eat the cake, to run in the cow field in the spring thaw, to dance and sing and...and go to the opera."

"And what else?" he asks.

"And this," I say, grabbing his lapels and crushing

my mouth to his, feeling emboldened by my passionate speech.

He kisses me back like he means it, like he's hungry for me, like he needs this connection just as much as I do.

"I appreciate your perspective," he says breathlessly when we finally break apart. "Why don't you share some more of it?"

I climb into his lap and we kiss the entire drive home. Once we're through the front door, he takes my hand and leads me upstairs to his bedroom.

In the middle of the night, I wake up in his bed to find that he's spooning me, his arm wrapped around my waist. His breath is warm against the back of my neck, and I feel a peacefulness inside myself like nothing I've ever known. And that's when some part of me starts to wonder...if maybe there's a chance we could actually work together after all.

22

RHYS

"You CAN'T CONTINUE to add money to your expense accounts without clearing it first with the CFO."

My father scoffs and rolls his eyes. Our roles have been reversed many times over the years, me acting as the parent instead of the son, but this is the first time it's happened at work. Or, in front of my grandfather.

I'm not the only one who considers my father to be a self-indulgent, compulsive over-spender. My grandfather doesn't trust his own son to manage, well, anything and do it well so he's reduced him to nothing more than a glorified secretary just to keep him on the payroll. Yet, somehow, my father managed to not only give himself an expense account, but a business credit card, too. I'm sure he sent the paperwork through with my grandfather's forged signature on it, knowing full well the CFO wouldn't ask too many questions.

"If the CFO had concerns about my spending, he would have approached me about it."

"He approached me, Rupert." My grandfather's voice trembles slightly with age. "After you bought yourself twenty-thousand dollars' worth of office furniture that you certainly didn't need."

"Oh, I did need it. Celine wanted my old desk to turn into a changing table for the baby. Something she saw online."

"That *old desk* was a turn of the century British antique, a gift from a descendant of Queen Victoria!"

My grandfather's face turns red, the color shocking against the white of his beard and thinning crown of hair. My father nods nonchalantly. "Yes, that's why Celine wanted it."

"Do you think money grows on trees, Rupert?"

"Obviously not, which is why it's sheer foolishness that we're not building new factories in India right now!" my father is saying as he paces my grandfather's massive office. "Everyone else is doing it! It's the cheapest manufacturing hub in the *world*. What about this isn't making good business sense to you, Dad? Are you going senile?"

I clench my jaw, squeezing the armrests of my leather chair, suppressing the urge to tackle my father to the ground. It wouldn't be a good look for the Vice President to tackle the Senior Vice President in the office of the President and CEO, would it?

Not to mention, my grandfather Reginald might be

in his eighties, but the man can fight his own battles—and he prefers to do so. Me intervening on his behalf wouldn't be seen as heroic, but emasculating. A lesson I learned years ago and have taken care to remember.

Leaning forward over his mahogany desk, Grandpa (whom I address as "Reg" when we're around our colleagues; my father always calls him "Dad" which I personally think demeans both him and Reg in professional situations, but that's just my two cents) clears his throat and dryly says, "I'm sorry to disappoint you, but my medical records don't support that accusation. My mind is fit as a fiddle."

"Really? When's the last time you got a checkup? These things can creep up out of nowhere, and you're not getting any younger. You know, I worry about you. Maybe you should get reevaluated soon," Dad says. "I can make you an appointment with my own doctor."

Grandpa would actually have to be senile to agree to that. There's no way he's going to let my dad's personal physician decide whether he's mentally fit enough to serve as CEO of McConnell Enterprises. He might as well hand the throne over to my dad on a silver platter with a bow on top.

"Though it's clearly of little true concern to you," Reg says evenly, "I am assessed both physically and mentally by a team of professionals every three months, after which I meet with my lawyer to confirm the details of my legacy. I'm of sound mind and body, rest assured."

I already know about my grandfather's regular health assessments. My father, however, looks absolutely crestfallen. If he had big plans to get Reg fired by the board due to mental incapacity, those plans just went right out the window.

"Just give me one good, solid reason why we shouldn't be making these components for less," Dad wheedles, refusing to drop the subject. "Cheaper manufacturing costs means higher profits, which is the whole point of a successful business, is it not? That's all I care about. It's what I live for! The continued success of this company, of your legacy…"

He doesn't seem to realize that his bullshitting is getting him nowhere.

Reg rises from his chair, broad shouldered and a few inches taller than my father and still quite imposing in his old age. "Sit. *Down.*"

Dad sits.

"Rhys," Reg says, glancing my way, "if you'd be so kind as to explain to the Senior Vice President why we will not be building factories in Tamil Nadu."

I don't even need to think about my answer. The topic is one about which I am passionate. My grandfather knows this. We've discussed it at length in the past.

"McConnell Enterprises is not in the business of selling the cheapest-made goods for the highest markup," I begin. "We've built a reputation for high quality and consistency, and we're proud of that reputation. It's why we're so successful, beyond maintaining a strong global network of satisfied partners and customers. People come to us because they know our goods are the best in the industry, that we're reliable, and that we care about everyone we work with."

"There are other considerations—" Dad tries to interrupt, but I don't let him.

"Now I won't get into the garbage ethics of paying people pennies per day to work for us in poor factory conditions overseas," I continue, "but it is worth mentioning that when we manufacture in places close to us, like Mexico and here in the U.S., we have the ability to liaise with management directly, in person, on a same-day basis. That means we have better oversight of production and working conditions and that we can course-correct as needed. India is a fourteen-hour flight."

"So what? We can just...set up a satellite office," Dad interjects.

Ignoring him, I go on, "Perhaps you've also forgotten how unpredictable and financially unfeasible that is. The reason we moved all of our manufacturing out of China a few years ago was that many of our components were delivered with a clear lack of quality control, not to mention the supply chain and transportation delays. Having all our factories exclusively overseas was a mistake; one this company won't make again." I look to my grandfather.

"Reg? Does that about cover it, sir?"

I'm usually not such a blatant brown-noser, but I

know it irritates my father to no end to see me in the role of my grandfather's pet, and I'm frankly enjoying the moment.

Reg nods. "Well stated. Thank you."

My father opens his mouth but then seems to think better of arguing. In his most reasonable tone, he says, "Fine, then. I've said my piece about the matter. Perhaps the board will feel differently at the next quarterly meeting."

"Perhaps they will," Reg says, in a tone that implies how unbothered he is by Dad's thinly-veiled threat. "Dismissed."

Clenching his fists, Dad turns to storm out the door.

"Oh, and Rupert?" my grandfather calls after him. "You need to stop charging up your expense accounts at those cabarets."

Cabarets? Dad spins back around, and the guilty expression on his face says it all. That's when I realize that Grandpa's referring to strip clubs. It's difficult to keep from smirking.

"They're not cabarets," Dad protests. "They're *dinner clubs*. I'm entertaining clients. It's a perfectly acceptable business expense."

"Which clients?" Reg asks, clearly not buying it.

"Potential clients! And...and colleagues," Dad sputters.

Raising a brow, Reg flips open a file on his desk,

looks it over, and says, "And who did you take to... Delilah's Den on the seventeenth?"

My father hesitates and then blurts, "The Dubaians."

"Rhys closed that deal a week prior to the charge," Reg says. "No Delilah necessary."

"It was celebratory," Dad insists.

"Then you can celebrate on your own tab," Reg says humorlessly. "This last foray of yours cost the company over thirty-thousand dollars. And don't for a second think that I don't know what 'champagne service' means at these types of establishments. The CFO is watching you, and I've capped your AmEx limit at 10k per month. For the foreseeable future."

This confrontation about my dad's spending is a surprise to me. For years, he's been spending company money in ways that would get anyone else fired, if not arrested for embezzlement. I always assumed my grandfather was fully aware, and tolerated it because the company can afford to foot the bills. Maybe not.

I'm not sure how it finally caught the attention of our financial department, but I can only surmise that it means my father has spent far more than he usually does.

"Don't act like I haven't contributed to the success of this company over the last four decades," Dad says. "If I want to spend some piddly little portion of our many billions, who cares? You have to spend money to earn money. I'm trying to maintain client relations!"

"We'll need the receipts for everything you've purchased with business dollars in the past year, all your expense reports, and your balance sheets," Reg says. "Rhys will handle it."

I nod. My father looks like he's about to explode.

"Get out. You will turn over all of the financial documentation I have asked for to Rhys within one business week. All of it."

Ignoring the command, my father says, "Let's resume this discussion later. In the meantime, here are your invitations for Friday."

Reaching inside his jacket, he pulls out two golden envelopes. Tension pulls the insides of my chest as he holds out one of the envelopes to me.

I don't take it. His left eye twitches as he thrusts it into my hand, then quickly sets the other on my grandfather's desk.

"Feel free to bring a plus-one, or plus-twos if you happen to be that lucky!"

Smiling like he's made the best joke, my dad strides out of the office.

The door slams behind him.

Without opening the invite, I tear it in two and feed it to the paper shredder.

23

IZABELA

Mrs. Dunham and I have formed something like a truce since the day she dragged me out of Rhys's bed. I stay out of her way, and she barely acknowledges me. When we do speak to each other, we're polite but cool. It works for us.

I'm not sure why she comes every day. The house is meticulous, always. Rhys is certainly never home enough to make a mess and I hardly leave my room. I wonder if they've formed a sort of comfortable, symbiotic relationship over the years. She's become accustomed to coming to this house and Rhys enjoys having her around. She is quiet and unobtrusive, gently filling the space as she putters around. There has to be some comfort for him in that.

When I was younger, I secretly enjoyed the sounds my aunt would make as she cleaned the house. The sound of the duster whisking over the counters and windowsills. The soft tap of her shoes on the wooden floor. I especially liked the sound her broken spray bottle made whenever she depressed the lever. It made a quiet snick, snick, snick sound that made my scalp tingle every time I heard it.

I wonder if Rhys experiences something similar by having her around?

Ms. Dunham arrives at the house this morning later than usual, while I'm still eating the breakfast of yogurt and fruit that I made myself. I give her a smile when she peeks into the dining room. She looks a bit harried. Maybe she slept through her alarm clock or got stuck in traffic.

Imagining she's only human might be unrealistic, but it's fun.

"I apologize for my lateness, Miss Jasinski. Most irregular. Would you like me to have the cook prepare you something more substantial? Some eggs, perhaps?"

"Oh, no, I'm good with this. Don't worry about it. Thank you, though."

I receive a brisk nod in return, and then she hesitates before asking, "Did Mr. McConnell go in to work today?"

"He left at seven, just like he always does," I answer. "Did you need to speak to him?"

"No, I...well." Helga looks away, then back, pointedly. "Tiptoe carefully around him today," she tells me.

"It would be better to stay out of his way until tomorrow."

The warning makes the back of my neck prickle. I'm about to ask her why, but she's already busily dusting, humming loudly to herself as if to deflect any questions.

"Okay," I say, utterly bewildered. "I'll try."

She bustles away before I can attempt to get any more details, and I hear the sound of the vacuum upstairs a few minutes later. She always starts cleaning up there first, in my room at the end of the hallway, and then works her way toward the front of the house before coming downstairs. Her last tidying area is the front foyer, and then she gets to walk out the door and go home. I have to say, it's an efficient method. Efficient and smart, just like Mrs. Dunham.

Since I feel awkward going up to my room while she's straightening it, I drop off my dishes in the kitchen and then bring my tea into the den. I'll sit and watch the news until Mrs. Dunham moves on to another room. But before I can curl up on the couch and get comfortable, I notice a sprawl of papers and Rhys's laptop on the coffee table.

That's odd. It's not like him to leave his things laying around. He must have been up late working—he definitely didn't knock on my door before I fell asleep like he usually does, so he must have been down here long after midnight. I figure it can't hurt to help Mrs.

Dunham out a little bit since she's so frazzled, so I gather up Rhys's things and bring them into his office.

The room isn't explicitly forbidden to me, although I was never told I could come and go as I please, either. Still, I have no intention of lingering. I briskly open the door, go over to the L-shaped desk, and then deposit the computer and paperwork on top.

I'm turning to leave when something on the desk catches my eye. A turquoise box, very obviously Tiffany blue. My pulse picks up as I instinctively reach for it. But I stop myself. I shouldn't. It's not mine. *Or is it?* No, that's just another dumb fantasy. Rhys wouldn't buy me designer jewelry. But...what if he did? What if he's planning to surprise me?

He's not, I argue with myself. He's made it clear that he isn't interested in anything beyond our temporary arrangement. There's no reason he'd lavish such a luxurious gift on me. What we have is simply a business transaction, no more and no less.

I take two steps away from the desk before I freeze, my curiosity getting the better of me. Glancing nervously at the door, I wet my lips, and despite my better judgment, I tiptoe back over. Quickly, I grab the blue box and open it, then crack open the smaller velvet jewelry box inside. Sitting there, wedged into a bed of satin, is a stunning engagement ring. It's so beautiful, it actually takes my breath away.

The band is made of rose gold, embedded with tiny

diamonds all around, and the center diamond solitaire is huge. I don't know much about fancy jewelry, but I imagine that this had to have cost hundreds of thousands of dollars.

Why is it sitting here on his desk?

My pulse thumps in my ears as I pause to listen for any sounds outside the office. I can't have Mrs. Dunham walking in on me snooping, or God forbid, Rhys himself. But the pieces are starting to fall into place, and I can't just drop everything and run away from the truth, no matter how upsetting it is. No matter how ugly.

I carefully pull the ring out of the box and study it. Something is engraved on the inside of the band. Holding it up, I make out the cursive letters: *Celine, mon coeur*, it says, and then today's date, except three years ago. *Mon coeur.*

My heart.

Tears prick my eyes as I'm overwhelmed with sadness and grief. I can't make sense of it, but I know I feel sorry for myself.

Swallowing down a lump in my throat, I allow my eyes to scan the top of his desk. There are three envelopes there, the kind you send an invitation or card inside of. One is open with the tip of a card peeking out. I've come this far, why stop now? Listening once again for any sound outside, I pulled the card out.

It's a birthday card. Inside, someone had written,

'*Enjoy your day on the fifth. Wishing you many more happy birthdays.*'

Oh, no.

Oh, please, no.

The fifth is today. The ring was engraved with today's date but from three years earlier. Is it... Rhys's birthday today? I connect the dots as a flood of emotion goes through me. He was going to propose to Celine on his birthday, but considering they are definitely not married something happened. She left him on his birthday?

How cruel.

No wonder he can't stand this day.

There are so many pieces to this puzzle.

I'm holding an engagement ring that Rhys apparently intended to give to Celine. Celine, who Rhys clearly has never completely gotten over. Celine, who married Rhys's father.

Slipping the ring back into the box, I set it back down on top of the torn invitation, exactly the way I found it. Then I leave the office and run up to my room, quickly breezing by Mrs. Dunham in the upstairs hallway so she won't see the tears spilling down my cheeks.

Locking the door behind me, I grab my laptop and climb onto my bed. I've done very little internet research on Rhys or his family since our arrangement began. Looks like I'm about to make up for lost time.

Ten minutes later, the reasons behind Rhys's tragic

heartbreak are crystal clear. Society gossip websites were all over the story when it broke. Three years ago today, Rupert McConnell threw himself a lavish birthday party—for the birthday he shares with his only son—and invited everyone worth inviting in Chicago.

There was no indication that Rhys was involved in this party beyond simply showing up as a guest. What kind of father has an extravagant birthday party without including the child with whom he shares the date? But it gets worse. Because Rhys found out that night, at that party, very much in public, that his father had married Celine behind his back. The two had eloped in secret.

I think—I'm *sure*—that Rhys had intended to propose *that night*. With the ring I had just held in my hand downstairs.

Instead, his whole world must have come crashing down.

The comments Rhys made at the opera the other night suddenly make perfect sense.

I'm so angry and hurt for him. Celine never deserved him. What kind of woman does something like that? Yes, I knew she'd ended up with Rupert, but I had no idea that it had played out like this. It turns my stomach to think about it. Of course Rhys hates his birthdays.

I want to do something for him. Give him a better birthday, a do-over. Maybe if I can make some happy new memories for him, it will ease the pain of the old ones still haunting him.

There have been many birthdays and holidays that my sister was too sick to fully celebrate or enjoy herself. My uncle and I would always do something special to try to make her smile. No child should be too sick to enjoy their own birthday. And no man should be blind-sided by his double-crossing girlfriend and douchebag of a father. I mull over what I can do to make this day special for him. I understand now that Helga warned me to tiptoe around him today because he probably hates this day and is reminded once a year how terrible his family is.

IMMEDIATELY, I start to perk up, my mind full of ideas. I can make festive decorations out of colored paper and string, I can whip up a cake, I can sing in Polish.

I'm giddy just thinking about it. This will be good for me, too. I've been going crazy lately just sitting around the house all day when I'm not working.

After taking a quick shower, I put on a light blue taffeta dress with a nipped waist, a puffy skirt, and colored dots all over it that remind me of the rainbow sprinkles on nonpareils. Then I spend a few minutes on my makeup—minimal, just BB cream and mascara and pink lip gloss—and go look for Mrs. Dunham. She's polishing the wood balustrade of the staircase.

"Mrs. Dunham," I ask timidly, suddenly feeling nervous. "Would it be okay if I did some baking? I'll clean everything up when I'm done."

"The kitchen is none of my affair," she tells me, "but as long as you don't get in the cook's way, I'm sure it will be fine."

"Thank you."

Practically skipping down the stairs, I'm relieved to find the kitchen empty. I start opening cabinets and taking inventory of the huge walk-in pantry, gathering the tools and ingredients I'll need.

I have no idea what kind of cake Rhys likes, so I decide to make him a favorite from my homeland. *karpatka* cake is like two giant cream puffs with the most decadent and rich cream sandwiched in between. The top is dusted with powdered sugar and it's so delicious it's hard to only have one slice.

Plus, he's probably never had it, so there's no chance of it bringing up bad memories.

I use a delivery app on my phone to get the ingredients ordered. Since I have at least thirty or forty minutes to wait, I sneak back into Rhys's office and find paper, scissors, a hole puncher, and colored markers. The paper is actually a pack of manila file folders, but I'll make do. The string I need is harder to find, but I dig through all the drawers in the kitchen until I locate some cotton twine.

Everything goes onto the dining room table, and I start cutting triangles out of the thick manila paper, one flag for each letter of "Happy Birthday Rhys!" But they don't look quite fancy enough, so I decide to cut scallops into their edges. It'll take twice as long to get my bunting put together, but I think the extra effort will pay off in the end. If this was for Eva, I'd have to douse the letters in glitter, but I think Rhys will appreciate more subtlety. I alternate the markers I use so that each letter is a different color, and add a border to each triangle flag. Perfect.

My phone buzzes with a notification that my order has been delivered, and I run outside to collect the bag that's waiting outside the gate. I carry it into the kitchen triumphantly, even though the actual baking hasn't begun yet. I've got this.

After I tie on an apron, I grab the mixer and get to work. It takes some time to make the choux pastry for the creampuff layers, but I've made this dessert so many times before that it comes naturally to me. I don't even consult a recipe at this point. The kitchen smells amazing by the time I'm done baking the pieces. Then I get back to work on the birthday bunting while they cool.

My art project gets put on hold when I get a call from Diya. We've texted a bit over the last few weeks, but I've been pretty tight-lipped about the details of my arrangement with Rhys. All she knows is that a hot young businessman is renting me for the next six months, that I'm shockingly enjoying the sex, and that he's covering my rent while I'm with him. Diya has been cautiously optimistic, but she's still concerned for me, hence the frequent check-ins.

"You're making a special cake for him? Girl, you've got it bad."

"I do not," I lie. "It's his birthday."

"You do," she insists. "This is not *Pretty Woman.*"

Just then, the oven timer goes off. I hang up with Diya to make the filling for my now-cool creampuffs. The filling turns out perfect. Thick, luxuriously creamy, and so very rich. My final step is assembling the whole thing, but I have to finish hanging the bunting first.

An hour later, I've finished sprinkling the *karpatka* with powdered sugar and moved onto arranging blue and silver birthday candles on top when I hear footsteps coming down the hallway.

"Mrs. Dunham?" I call out, setting the cake down.

She doesn't answer.

"Rhys?" I try again.

My heart is pounding as I suddenly start to second-guess myself. I don't want Rhys to feel overwhelmed, or that I've overstepped on his private day.

I just want him to know that someone cares.

Like he did for me when he heard me crying. He shouldn't have to erase himself from the day that his father and ex-girlfriend hijacked to break his heart.

When he steps through the doorway, both of us freeze. His eyes dart to the cake, then up to the banner, then to me.

I gesture at the cake and say, "*Sto lat!*"

His face goes pale, all the color draining from it.

"Mrs. Dunham did this?" he asks.

My stomach drops. I can tell that he's not pleased.

"No," I say quietly. "I did."

Without another word, he storms out of the room.

I've ruined everything.

24

RHYS

It takes a moment to fully process what Izabela has done for me.

Shrugging out of my jacket, I throw it over the arm of the couch and run a hand over my face. She'd looked pretty shocked when I left the dining room. I hadn't meant to stomp out like that, but she caught me off guard with the cake and the sign. It was a knee-jerk reaction.

Mrs. Dunham had made me a birthday cake once, shortly after I hired her. The cake was tall and layered, with pristine white buttercream. It had instantly reminded me of a wedding cake. Needless to say, I'd never touched it. She seemed to understand that it upset me, because she never made the attempt again.

Aside from that, it's been a very long time since I've had a special treat on my birthday. Ever since the night Celine crushed my heart, even my own mother has known that it's best to tread lightly on this day. In fact, she goes out of her way to plan a weekend brunch for us each year that specifically does *not* fall on the actual date of my birth. Which is partly why I'm so floored by Izabela's gesture. Nobody else has dared. I'm genuinely...touched.

Not to mention, that cake looked damn good. The smells of sugar and butter crisped into golden pastry that has permeated the house has me practically drooling. I can't remember the last time I had a homemade cake, baked from scratch, rather than some overpriced, fussy confection from a bakery that's all style and no substance.

When I go back into the dining room, Izabela is gone. I study the banner that's hanging over the sideboard, attached to the wall with blue painter's tape. It says Happy Birthday Rhys, of course, each word on its own curved swag, but what's remarkable about the thing is the obvious care that went into each carefully shaped letter, each triangle of paper that's been cut with decorative edges. This must have taken her hours to make. I look over at the table and realize that the cake is gone. But I can hear water running from the kitchen, so I go in there next.

Izabela is doing dishes when I enter. Her back is to me, and she doesn't turn around, even as I pull out a stool and sit at the island. I know she hears me, but she's probably worried about my reaction considering how I walked out on her a few minutes ago. Taking a deep breath, I look at the cake sitting on the island, the candles on top still waiting to be lit. She deserves an explanation. And an apology.

"My father and I share a birthday," I begin.

I hear the water turn off, and Izabela turns around and wipes her wet hands on the too-big apron that she must have borrowed from my cook. It looks cute on her, all oversized like it is, but I don't tell her that. Instead, I gesture to the stool across from me. She reluctantly sits down.

"If my dad was any other dad, it would be safe to assume that we've always celebrated the day together," I go on, "but...he's not really the sharing type. He likes everybody to make a big fuss over him, so as a kid, I tended to get overlooked on our birthday. Eventually, I just stopped thinking of it as my day at all. Even when my mom would get excited and try to plan parties for me, I'd talk her out of it. I never wanted anyone to treat it like a big deal. It was my dad's thing, you know?"

She nods, her eyes down. "I understand. I'm sorry for presuming—"

"No. Don't apologize. I'm glad you presumed."

Reaching across the table, her warm hand slips over mine. I almost pull away, but the feel of her touching me is so good that I can't make myself break the contact.

"I've spent so much time avoiding this day that I forgot how nice it can be to just...stop."

"I'm sorry for everything you've been through with

your father, Rhys. He doesn't deserve a son like you. I hope you know that."

Our gazes catch. It feels like she's looking right into my soul.

Obviously, there's more I'm not telling her. The gory details of the night three years ago when I lost Celine forever. But looking back, I realize that the real heartbreak of that birthday wasn't getting dumped by my girlfriend. It was the irrefutable evidence that my father didn't love me. In his eyes, I was just another competitor. Not a son.

"Well," I say, taking back my hand. "Thank you. Truly. For the banner, and...I don't think I've ever seen a cake like this. What kind is it? It looks delicious."

"It's a Polish recipe. A *karpatka*. It's actually my sister's favorite. I thought—" she glances shyly at me from beneath her lashes. "I thought, I want to give you something happy from my family, because we have enough to share."

My chest feels warm as she continues, glossing over the magnitude of the gift she's just given me. "Anyways, I have to make it for my sister every year or she throws a fit. No other cake will do. When she's having a bad day, I bring it to her in bed."

Her smile falters and she drops her gaze again.

"A bad day?"

"Juvenile rheumatoid arthritis. It's better and then it's worse. And when it's worse, it *hurts*." It hurts her too, I can hear it in her voice. To see her sister in pain, and to be far away.

"You miss her," I say. "Her name is Eva, right?"

"Yes," she whispers. "Eva. I miss her very much."

"I remember you talking about her at my mom's. Is that who you were..." I hesitate, not wanting to over-step, but then ask anyway because the question has been nagging at me. "Who you were on the phone with, that day you were so upset?"

She looks back up at me, and I see the tears starting to gather in her eyes.

"I'm sorry. I shouldn't have brought it up—"

"No, it's fine," she says, forcing a smile. "And yes, to your question. I was on the phone with her that day. Eva loves getting updates about my 'glamorous' life here in America." Her voice is bitter. "I told her I will bring her here as soon as I can, but I didn't know it would be like this."

Hell. It is completely unfair that her job modeling at shitty bridal boutiques left her feeling like escorting was the only option. I'm fiercely thankful that my ego managed to convince Konstantin to give her the jobs she needs. The ones she deserves. And fuck him for putting her in that position in the first place. I hadn't realized what a rigged game he had going. But I don't want to lose my temper and ruin the evening. I want to hear about Izabela's sister, and her life back home on the farm.

"And when you bring her cake, do you say what

you said when I walked in?" I ask, gently steering the conversation away from the topic that's making her sad and me furious. "Happy birthday in Polish?"

"Oh! *Sto lat*, yes," she says, her cheeks turning pink. "I didn't even think, it just popped out. It's sort of a catch-all we use for good wishes. It means 'one hundred years.'"

"*Sto lat*. Like when we say 'Many happy returns,'" I suggest.

She brightens, gives me a teasing smile. "Yes. We wouldn't want to limit your happiness to only one year."

I think I might have done that all by myself when I signed a six-month contract with Konstantin Zoric.

"So should we eat it now?" I ask. "Or wait until after dinner?"

"It's your cake. You can do as you please."

I get a knife from the drawer and grab us two plates. Izabela watches me cut two slices and plate them. Handing her a fork, I hold her gaze for a moment before sliding her cake over.

"Thanks again for this."

"You're welcome," she says. "I'm glad to bring a bit of my home here."

Shrugging like it's no big deal, I take a bite of cake. And then another. And one more, just to be sure that I'm tasting what I think I am. The pastry is shatteringly crisp on the outside, giving way to a thick layer of pastry cream, delicate and rich at the same time. It's like eating a crunchy cloud.

"Mmm," I half moan.

"Good?" she asks around a mouthful, looking pleased.

"Amazing. Best thing I've tasted in a long time."

"I should have lit the candles for you."

She takes a candle from the top of the cake and sets it into the small bit of cake I still have left on my plate.

"Drawer to the left of the stove," I tell her, and she fetches the barbecue lighter to light the candle for me.

I blow it out, breathing in the distinct scent of hot melted wax, burned wick, the puff of smoke. It brings me back to my childhood, when I actually used to look forward to having a birthday cake each year. I remember being young and very eager to lick the frosting off the bottom of each candle.

"Did you make a wish?" Izabela asks softly.

I didn't, but she looks so eager that I can't tell her that. "Of course."

She smiles. "What did you wish for?"

"If I tell you, it won't come true. Or maybe that's just an American superstition."

"I never understood that," she says, shaking her head. "You have to give a voice to what you want most before it will come true."

"Maybe."

I pluck the candle from my cake and hold it out, my

gaze hot on hers. Right now, I know exactly what I want most.

"Go ahead," I say. It's not a request, but a command.

She leans forward, not breaking eye contact, and opens her mouth. I slide the candle between her lips and watch as she sucks the cream filling off the end. My cock is instantly hard.

Dropping the candle, I grab her chin and slip my thumb into her mouth, stroking her tongue in little circles. With a low moan, she closes her lips and darts her tongue around my thumb, then starts to suck on it. Soft first, then harder. My eyelids flutter.

I'm off my stool and around the island in half a heartbeat. After I scoop Izabela up, I carry her into the sitting room and set her on the white sofa. She looks up at me, flushed, eyes dilated. She wants this as much as I do.

"Take off all your clothes," I tell her.

As she fumbles to untie her apron, I go to the pocket door and slide it closed, then flick the latch. Nobody will come in here with the door locked. Even if they did, it wouldn't stop me.

Izabela's dress slides to the floor on top of the apron, her strapless bra along with it, but I'm too impatient to wait for her little black thong to come off. I hook a finger around the crotch and pull, feeling the wetness that's soaked into the fabric. She's more than willing in my arms as I drop onto the sofa, lean back, and pull her onto my lap.

I kiss her neck, tracing the curve of her back with my fingertips. I grab her hips, pushing and pulling her over the hard bulge between my legs. She shivers under my hands, moaning, tugging at my belt, but I'm not in a hurry. This isn't how I want this to go.

"Lie back," I say.

She stretches out on the couch, her head pillowed on the sofa's arm, looking up at me. Her nipples are tight pink rosebuds, her breaths fast.

"Open your legs."

She drops her foot to the floor and hooks the other over the back of the sofa. Spread wide, her pussy wet and ripe for the taking. Beautiful.

"You're a work of art, Izabela."

I strip quickly and climb over her, covering her with my body. She's shivering, goosebumps on her arms. I kiss her again, slowly, letting my warmth seep into her skin. For the first time since I met her, I don't feel the need to fuck her brains out. Instead, I want to explore her one inch at a time.

Kissing behind her ear, nipping softly at her neck, I run my hands over her narrow shoulders, her smooth biceps. Her skin is soft and supple, her breasts a perfect fit for my palms. She arches her back, pressing her nipples into my hands. I thumb them gently as I kiss my way down her neck. Her pussy is so wet I catch the scent of ripe peaches. It makes my head spin.

I trail my lips over the ridge of her collarbone, the hollow at the base of her throat. My hands skim the ridges of her ribs, the curve of her waist, the crest of her hips. Her body is becoming familiar to me, yet I learn something new every time I touch her.

She watches me with heavy-lidded eyes as I move down her body, slowly kissing across her chest and the soft rise of her breasts. When I suck her nipples into my mouth she cries out, as if the pleasure is almost painful. My cock is throbbing, but still I take my time, drawing increasingly breathless moans out of her as I suck, lick, nibble.

Soon, she's writhing against me, desperate for more contact, flaming my urge to bury myself deep inside her. Knowing how easy it is for me to get her off only turns me on more. I don't even care about myself; I just want her to enjoy every second of this.

Moving my fingers down between her hot thighs, I part her pussy lips and dip inside. She's literally dripping wet, and the evidence of her arousal drives me insane. The head of my cock pulses against her thigh, but I force myself to exercise restraint. She gasps my name as I release her nipple from my mouth and cover her lips with mine.

Now I'm sucking her tongue, thrusting my fingers into her faster and deeper, teasing her to the brink of orgasm before I've even put my dick inside her. Izabela meets my kiss with abandon, fucking my hand, her nails clawing down my back, each frantic touch making it harder for me to stay in control.

"Rhys," she pants. "I'm going to come."

I want to come with her.

Pulling back, I say, "Get up."

Moving off her, I sit up on the sofa and then pull her onto my lap so she's facing me. Then I wrap a hand around my shaft and trace her opening with the tip, dragging myself through her wetness, up and down, up and down, until both of us are groaning with anticipation.

I can't wait any longer, but I force myself to pause and wait for her nod that means I don't have to run upstairs to find a condom. She gives it immediately.

Cupping her face in my hands, I draw her down for a kiss and plunge inside her. Hot, tight, heavenly.

"Fuck," I murmur.

"Fuck," she whispers back.

I ease into a rhythm, never rushing, thrilling in the sweet glide. My muscles tense. I can feel the pressure building with each thrust. I've never fucked this slow in my life, yet it's nothing short of incredible. Every inch of me inside her, filling her, completing her. Izabela starts rocking harder against me, faster, moaning inside my mouth.

The sounds spilling from her throat—Jesus, I can't hold back.

Grabbing her hips, I pump up into her, slamming her down on my cock.

"Rhys," she moans.

And then she's coming, gushing, her pussy contracting around my shaft. I climax with her, exploding into her so hard that blackness edges my vision. Her arms encircle me and for a while we just stay as we are, her head tucked under my chin, both of us catching our breath as the sweat on our bodies begins to cool. When she finally eases off me, she stands there naked and perfect, gazing down at me with a smile.

"What?" I say, unable to keep from smiling back.

"I think I need to bake you cakes more often," she says.

RHYS

MY FATHER's deadline is up, and I've seen neither hide nor hair of the receipts that my grandfather requested from him. It's not surprising in the least, but it does mean that I'll have to go chasing the financial documentation down, which I'm not looking forward to. I wouldn't be surprised if Dad hasn't even started gathering up all the paperwork we need.

I'm nothing if not fair, so I give him until after the lunch hour. By two p.m., any last shred of optimism I had about those receipts materializing on my desk has disappeared.

Knowing that he probably has a laundry list of excuses prepared, I don't bother dialing his extension to ask his assistant, Kaia, if Dad is busy right now. Instead, I just walk down the hall, give Kaia a polite nod, and push open the heavy glass door of Dad's office.

He's hunched over his desk, eyes glued to his

computer screen, but his head pops up instantly when I walk inside.

"You can't just barge in here—"

"Where are the receipts and expense reports that Reginald asked for?" I interrupt. "It's been a week."

"Those were due *today*?" he says innocently, as if I can't see through his bullshit.

"I'm not leaving this office until you turn everything over. I don't care how long it takes."

"Rhys, come on. The old man wasn't serious about all that," Dad scoffs. "He was just playing the hard-ass to try to get me in line. Besides, I'm sure he's forgotten all about it by now. He's practically senile."

"He's not, and if you don't comply, there will be consequences."

"God, you turned out to be a suck-up," he says, shaking his head. "The way you grovel and kiss his ass. It's pathetic."

"If you can't get the documents together, I can have security keep you company while I go through your files myself. We've got records of all the charges from AmEx, so I'll call every number of every vendor on that list if I have to. They'll be more than happy to provide itemized receipts to us if they're threatened with a charge dispute."

Something calculating flashes in his eyes. He's up to something.

He gets up from his desk, gestures me toward a chair, and then closes the door.

"Look, Rhys. You've gotta let this go. It'll blow over, kiddo. Trust me."

I bristle at the nickname he knows I can't stand. "The documents," I say flatly. "Now."

"I'm sorry you missed the party, by the way. Wasn't the same without you there."

Is he seriously trying to distract me by changing the subject to his damn birthday party? While, per usual, completely ignoring the fact that it was my birthday as well? My irritation doubles by the second, and I let myself get sidetracked.

"You knew damn well I wasn't going."

He sighs and sinks back into his desk chair. "I was really looking forward to seeing your little friend again. I assume she made sure you were taken care of for your special day?"

The lewd undertone in his words inflames my anger.

Pulling out my phone and scrolling through my contacts until I find the direct line for building security, I say, "Should I wait while you get that documentation sorted, or do you want to do this the hard way? I've got security right here in my contacts."

He laughs. "No need."

Pulling open the bottom drawer of his desk, he takes out a leather portfolio and unsnaps it. He withdraws a few sheets of paper and several receipts, some photographs, and other paperwork that I can't ascertain from my vantage point.

"I was trying to protect you," he's saying as he continues digging around.

My scalp tingles. "Protect me from what?"

"The thing is," he says, "my father has given you so much freedom within the company that he doesn't bother looking over your shoulder. Because you're Mr. Perfect, aren't you?"

"I'm not—"

"No. You're not. Everyone just *thinks* you are," he says, an edge to his voice.

He finally seems to find what he's looking for—a small black rectangle with a silver plug on one end, which I recognize as a USB drive—and holds it up with a grin.

"But they won't think that for long. You see, kiddo, this video I've got here is pretty damning. Your expense account is 10 times the amount of mine and no one ever asks you to justify your expenditures, do they? Not even when you buy yourself a woman."

I can feel my blood pressure spiking as he plugs the drive into his laptop, double-clicks something, and then turns the screen to face me. There's a small window playing a digital video file. Inside a lavish office, an older man in a flashy suit with gray streaks in his dark hair sits behind a desk, his fingers steepled. It's Konstantin Zoric.

Across from him, a young woman perches stiffly on a chair. Izabela. I'd know the set of her shoulders anywhere. She's clearly uncomfortable being alone with this gentleman. The urge to pull her out of that chair and away from that man courses through me. My chest hitches as an ominous sensation presses down on me.

"What the hell is this?"

"Just a little insurance policy that I spent quite a pretty penny obtaining a copy of," Dad says with a pleased lilt to his voice.

The dread presses harder down on me as my father turns up the volume.

"I'm sorry, can you repeat that?" Izabela is saying, sounding panicked.

"Are you a virgin," Zoric says, his tone deadly. *"Yes or no? Have you engaged in sexual intercourse or not? It's a simple question."*

My stomach churns as the video plays on.

"Is this...relevant to a modeling job, Mr. Zoric?"

"You didn't read the fine print on your contract before signing. Ah, well, that's your fault, not mine. It clearly states that you are legally bound to provide any and all relevant information about your body, including height, weight, medical history, and health status, and therefore you are required to answer the question. Are you a virgin or not? Because the men who are going to bid on you at the auction tomorrow night will want to know. So. Yes or no?"

It hits me like a ton of bricks. Konstantine Zoric is trafficking women through his modeling agency and auctioning them off to wealthy assholes. Like my father.

"Enough," I thunder, slapping the laptop shut, my blood gone cold with horror.

Because instinctively, I know what must unfold next on that video. Konstantin Zoric forcing Izabela into agreeing to be sold at that auction. Something she never chose to do. Never *wanted* to do. So much makes sense now. Her lack of experience, her virginity, her flashes of attitude.

My dad gestures to the chair across from him. "Have a seat. Let's chat because, I promise you, your life's about to change."

I absolutely won't sit down, nor will I allow myself to get closer. My hands already itch to wrap around his neck. A sickening burn chars my throat. "What did you do?"

"As you well know, Reginald McConnell, your doting grandfather, has always prided himself on having impeccable ethics. In fact, he claims that's the foundation for the success of this company. Now, I'll admit, I was surprised when he named you as his successor and not me. But at the same time, I understood. He believes that my actions at times can be...less than complementary to the company's reputation. Not good optics."

"PR nightmare is more like it."

"Beside the point," he says, waving my comment away. "If he thinks my actions are inexcusable, imagine how he's going to feel when he finds out his golden boy likes to fuck hookers? There's no denying it, either.

You've been seen out with her countless times. I have photographic evidence."

"I'll tell him I didn't know."

"Doesn't matter if you did or didn't know about it. Either way, this is going to be, what did you just call it? A 'PR nightmare.' The damage has already been done. Once the tabloids get wind of this scandal, there will be a media frenzy. Like sharks to chum. Your grandfather will be humiliated, shamed, not to mention furious at how you've conducted yourself."

His words sink in hard. But something else hits me even harder: if Zoric did this to Izabela, who else has he done it to? He's obviously got his methods down to a fine art. How long has the man been trafficking young women through his modeling agency? The thought turns my stomach.

"Why are you doing this? Hurting the company hurts you, too." I seethe.

"I won't have to hurt anybody if you do the right thing and walk away now." My father shrugs. "It's a means to an end, kiddo. Don't take it personally. Working out this deal with you is the most efficient way to put that promotion back in my hands. The *right hands*. You know damn well your grandfather won't stand for this. You can kiss that CEO's chair goodbye."

"I'm not going to let you get away with this. You're the one who purchased her to begin with! What if I tell Reg that?"

"And yet, somehow that charge found its way onto

your company card. You should really be more careful about your personal information, son."

There's a throbbing at my temples. This fucker's got me and he knows it. I'm not innocent in all of this. I did purchase six months of Izabela's life. But if I'd known that she was forced or coerced, I would have never. I had no idea that Zoric had forced her into service. Why didn't Izabela ever say anything to me?

Then again, why would she? She probably thought that I knew. I can't imagine what Izabela must think of me deep down inside. She probably hates me, and she'd have every reason to.

Dammit, what the hell have I gotten myself into?

"This is going to cost you your job," he gloats. "Unless you walk away first."

I look up, staring daggers at my father. He's right. Fuck.

And that's not even the worst part of this entire situation. No, the worst part is that I've played a role in Izabela's trafficking. I had a hand in ruining her life. Everything she's done for me, all of her kindness, and all of the understanding she's extended to me, and I'm sure all of it was done out of fear.

I'm no better than my father.

Fuck, I'm no better than Konstantin Zoric.

"No need to drag it out, son. These are your options," Dad says. "You can either resign, and I'll keep all of this under wraps...at least, until you give me a reason to use it against you. Or you can refuse to step aside, in which case I'll blow the lid off this thing so fast it'll make your goddamn head spin. Choice is yours. I'll give you a few days to think it over."

He looks at his watch, pulls the USB drive out of his laptop, and shoves it back into the leather portfolio, which he puts back in its drawer before locking it. Then he stands.

"I'm late for a meeting, so I've got to go. Oh, and I'd start polishing up the old resume if I were you. See if you can put that business degree to use elsewhere."

With a self-satisfied grin, he slaps me on the shoulder and walks out.

My rational brain begins to creep in. Maybe there's a way to fix this. Not just for me, but for Izabela, too. Hell, I'll call Konstantin Zoric directly if I have to. Work out some kind of deal.

As for my grandfather...I guess I'll just have to let my dad go ahead and reveal how I met Izabela. Conveniently leaving out the part he played, of course. I won't try to lie to Grandpa about paying for her, but maybe I can convince him to see this as more of a mail-order bride type of situation, minus the wedding. Or really expensive dating.

Yes, I could always ask Izabela to explain that my dad was the original buyer, that I paid for six months with her to keep her away from him, but I don't want to retraumatize her like that. Besides, my dad will just insist that she's lying about his role in the whole thing.

And I doubt my grandfather will care how I came to buy Izabela, just that I did.

There's no way out of this: my father will stop at nothing to destroy my reputation. But I'll just have to cross that bridge when I come to it. And you know what I say? Screw PR, screw the tabloids, screw public opinion. The most important thing is making this right for Izabela.

If I get fired from McConnell Enterprises in the process, then so be it.

I am going to burn Konstantin Zoric to the ground right along with me.

26

IZABELA

WHEN I HEAR Rhys yell my name from downstairs, I panic. It's midafternoon, way too early for him to be home from work. Unless something bad happened. Or unless...am I in trouble?

Heart pounding, I pause the yoga video I've been doing on YouTube and dab the sweat at my temples with the back of my hand. I was not prepared to see Rhys for hours, so I'm barely presentable in my workout pants and a cropped tank top, but—

"Izabela!"

His fist hammers at my door, and I cross the room and open it, breathing hard from a combination of physical exertion and panic.

"What is it? What's going on?" I blurt.

Did he find out that I snooped around in his office and found Celine's engagement ring? It's the only thing I can think of.

He holds my gaze, working his jaw, and finally says, "There's something urgent we need to discuss. Are you comfortable speaking in here, or is my office better?"

My adrenaline is through the roof. And yet...he doesn't seem angry. If anything, he looks apologetic. But also stressed out. Maybe he's breaking off our arrangement early. Please, no. Let it be anything but that, even if he is upset with me.

"This is fine," I say, glancing around the room. It's huge, but there's not really anywhere for us to sit and talk together. The floor, maybe.

But Rhys gestures for me to take a seat on the bed, then pulls over the chair from the vanity for himself. He rubs his temples for a moment, seeming to gather his thoughts.

"Why didn't you tell me you were trafficked by Zoric?" he says.

"*What?*"

"I found out today," he says. "I saw a...I saw evidence." He moves to the windows and stares outside with his hands on his hips.

My legs suddenly go weak and I'm glad I'm already sitting. I didn't realize that he didn't know about that. I figured, since he was buying my time, that he understood the arrangement I had with my employer. Realizing that this is new information for him—I need to process that. But he's already moving on.

"It's just, this situation is going to cause a lot of problems for me," he says. It's not a complaint, just a fact. He's in damage-control mode. "So we need to figure out how to fix it."

I frown. My being forced into sex work by a man holding all the power is a problem for *Rhys*? "In case you didn't realize it, the situation has *already* caused a lot of problems for me," I say. "So, yes, let's find a solution that serves you."

I don't hold back the bitterness from my voice. Throughout this whole arrangement, I've played my role as ably as possible, keeping the majority of my feelings and opinions to myself. I've done every single thing these men have asked of me in order to protect my sister—her health, her safety, her future—and my family.

And despite being played like a puppet, I found myself fully entwined around Rhys McConnell. Emotionally, physically. I've fallen for him, and though I don't fully understand it, my tenderness towards him grows every day.

Maybe he didn't know about my arrangement with Mr. Zoric, but I swear to God, if he tries to make me feel guilty about it, I'll—

"Izabela, that came out wrong—"

"You think?" We're both quiet for a moment, staring at each other across the chasm of what we didn't know about each other. "Just, whatever solution you come up with, it can't compromise my family. Zoric has people on the ground, *everywhere*. Don't do anything to anger him. *Please*."

Realization lights his face. "Your family. Of course. He's been holding them over your head to ensure that you comply, hasn't he?"

Looking at the floor, I nod. "He also has my passport. I couldn't run if I wanted to."

"I listened to part of your interview with Zoric, the interview in which you found out about the auction. He... Wanted to sell your virginity to the highest bidder."

"Oh, I am very aware of what happened to me, Rhys. You don't have to spell it out for me."

He holds up a placating hand. "I'm sorry. I'm just trying to work this out in my head. I can't begin to understand what that must've been like for you. And had I known about all of this when I made the offer to buy six months of your time, I would have paid for your total freedom instead."

Standing, I go to him and grip his bicep, forcing him to continue looking at me. "What?"

"I'm not perfect, Izabela. You know this. I've done things that I'm not proud of. Probably too many things if I really think about it. But I would never participate in holding a woman prisoner. What he forced you into is deplorable and unforgivable. But what's done is done, and I need to change the narrative here or everything I've worked for is going to implode."

I'm torn. I hear a lot of selfishness in his words, but I also saw a deep regret in his eyes when he spoke about what happened to me. His voice is thick with apology, almost pleading as if I need to forgive him. He has a lot at stake. I'm sure if it comes to light that he purchased me from Konstantine Zoric, who's been sex trafficking women for who knows how long, it will shine very badly on his company. What would it be like to have my name leaked in all of this? To have my name and face thrown into the press? My modeling career would be over before it even got started.

Then again, Rhys isn't in a position to confront Zoric about this, either. Then it will become a tit-for-tat media game, with each of them dragging the other through the mud. I don't know him well, but I get the impression that Mr. Zoric is a very powerful man. There's no telling how much damage he could do to Rhys's business.

Pulling away from him, I return to my seat on the bed.

It all comes rushing back.

The helplessness and the hopelessness and the un-believability that something this bad could really be happening to *me*.

It made me feel small then and it does so now as I sit on this huge, luxurious bed and relive it.

Rhys seems determined to lay it all out. He's trying to be sensitive about it, I think, but it doesn't make it easier for me.

"Has he threatened you?"

"When I spoke to Eva the other day she told me that an American man has begun watching the house.

That my uncle told him to leave, but he came back. I would call that a threat, yes. Zoric knows all my money goes to them, that they are the most important thing to me. That's why I can't step out of line."

Emotion makes my voice crack. Rhys leans forward and takes one of my hands in his, squeezing gently.

"Jesus, I'm sorry, Izabela. What Zoric forced you into is deplorable, indecent, not to mention illegal. He needs to be punished."

"He needs to be stopped," I interrupt.

"Yes."

"I wish we could just go to the police and get Zoric thrown behind bars, but I know it isn't that simple," I say, thinking out loud, my hand still warm in his. "We would need evidence, and the testimony of other trafficked girls. The kind of proof that Zoric's lawyers couldn't find a way to shoot down in court."

"That's all assuming the case ever *got* to court. Zoric has the kind of money to make sure that never happens," Rhys says. "He's an evil man. I have no doubt that if I went to him with the information I have, he'd destroy McConnell Enterprises. Or just have me killed."

Pulling away from him, I hug my knees to my chest. "It's not worth the risk, Rhys. You won't be able to scare him into backing down. You can't threaten men like him. And there are other KZM models who have disappeared, and nobody knows what happened to them. That can't happen to me. Or anyone else."

He shakes his head. "Okay. Let's just think this through. Tell me everything. From the beginning, from your first interaction with KZM, up to now. I need all the details."

"First, tell me how you found out," I say. "Your father must have said something, right? There's no way Zoric told you any of this."

"It was my dad," Rhys confirms. "At work today, he showed me a recording of you and Zoric talking in an office, about you participating in the auction. It was awful."

My cheeks go hot with shame recalling the details of that conversation with Zoric, but Rhys doesn't seem to notice my shame.

"Dad's trying to use that video to blackmail me out of my promotion," he goes on. "I'm supposed to resign, leave the CEO position to him, otherwise he'll take this to the media and destroy my reputation in the process. The company's reputation too. But before I can try to fix any of this, I need to know what we're dealing with. So tell me your side of the story. Please."

"I can do that." I close my eyes, take a deep breath, and begin. "It all started with the modeling competition in Poland last year. KZM was the sponsor. I didn't really think I'd win, but the grand prize was five thousand dollars and a contract with KZ Modeling in America. My sister encouraged me to at least try. And...I wanted it."

I remember every single thing about it. How it felt

to be chosen out of thousands of hopeful girls. I was desperate and so, so naïve that I'd believed them.

The thrill of the check from KZM that I didn't believe was real until it cleared at the bank and I brought the money—in cash—to my aunt and uncle, giving it to them to take care of Eva so I could go to the U.S. to chase my dreams of a modeling career. How I'd promised them that I would soon be making so much money that I could bring my sister to America to get her the very best treatment.

How much they believed in me.

The whirlwind of moving into the shared apartment with Diya and the others in the city of Chicago, the excitement of my first gigs, how motivating it was to get updates from Eva and share my small victories.

And then the night my dreams came crashing down in that office. How it felt to sit across from Mr. Zoric while he coldly revealed the truth of my fate with his modeling company.

Rhys listens, not interrupting, his hand warm on my knee. It doesn't make the telling any easier for me. I've worked so hard not to relive what's happened to me and how it's made me feel. Focusing instead on moving forward. Looking ahead is the only thing that's gotten me through, as if each day is a step closer to bringing my sister to me. Deep down, I know that that may never be a possibility. I could up and disappear like other models have before me.

It's taken all of my strength to block out this night-mare and just keep going.

"I'm sorry," he finally says. "I know it's not the answer to your problems, but my God. I'm so sorry. For all of it. And your sister, and everything you've been through."

"Thank you." For all his faults and gruffness and indifference, Rhys is a small light in this darkness. Because when we connect, the stars seem to align, and everything falls into place. There's something within him that I recognize and can commiserate with. As cliché as it might sound, I do think that Rhys and I crossed paths for a reason.

"You know that you did nothing wrong, don't you?" he says, his voice getting more vehement. "None of this is on you, Izabela. None of this is your fault. It's Zoric. That piece of shit is wholly responsible for this, and I swear to God, I will find a way to make him pay."

"But how? How does this get fixed? You have a reputation to protect, and my contract still stands."

"Not if someone else buys it out," he muses.

"What do you mean?" I ask, my heart stirring with hope. "How would that work?"

"As cold as it sounds, what Zoric is doing—illegal or not—is business. And in matters of business, money talks. So what if I make Zoric an offer he can't refuse, to buy out your contract in its entirety?" He nods to himself. "I'm sure there's a number that'd get him to warm up and give me whatever I ask for. I'm not sure how much he planned to make off of you during the term of your contract, but I'd top that, double or even triple it. How long *is* your contract?"

"Two years. Less, now. I've been working for KZM for about four months."

He seems so certain and confident when he looks at me. "That's it, then. I'm going to buy your freedom. And then we'll present our relationship as nothing more than what people expect it to be. You will be my very pampered, very spoiled, very beautiful girlfriend. You won't have to engage in sex work ever again. You can switch agencies and keep modeling if you want, keep sending money home, but you don't have to. I can take care of you, and help with your family's needs, too."

My heart sinks.

"So...I will be a kept woman. And you're my, what? My sugar daddy?"

"Sure. At least, that's our cover story. If news of this should ever come to the attention of the press, they'll see our relationship as an unremarkable arrangement that's typical for powerful men. Nobody will question it. There's no reason to dig deeper."

"What about your father's blackmail? He threatened you with the video," I point out.

"I think he was bluffing," Rhys says. "I didn't think that at first, but...he has to know that if he leaks the video, Zoric will retaliate. Or worse. My dad doesn't have a death wish. He just wanted to scare me. Push me out of the company."

"What if he's not bluffing and the video goes public?"

"Then I'll do damage control. Spin a story about how I rescued you from an unfortunate situation, but then I fell for you and decided to keep you around. People will love that."

"How nice it must be, when your lies make you look like a hero."

"Izabela, please. I'm just trying to make the best of this. For everyone involved."

"I understand," I say, but I shift further away from him. "Let's say your plan works, and Zoric lets you buy my freedom, and your father does nothing. Does that mean Zoric is out of my life for good? Will I get my passport back? Will his men stop threatening my family?"

"Hopefully yes, I'll be able to work all of that out. All I can say is, I'm going to do everything I can to give you your life back. That's a promise. I'm going to get that contract from Zoric, and you will have all of your rights again. I will not own you. Nobody will. And as soon as it makes sense for you to leave, you can fly home to Poland. Go back to your family and put this all behind you, try to move on as best you can."

On the outside I'm calm, but inside, my heart is shattering even as it lifts. Yes, I want to go home, but it hurts me how obviously Rhys can't wait to get rid of me. Why did I ever believe that I could actually mean more to him than a bit of entertainment, or a public relations playing card? How foolish to think that he might want something real with me. Something more.

At the end of the day I'm just the person that could cause the downfall of everything he's worked for.

"How long will I have to pay back the cost of purchasing my freedom from Zoric?" I ask. "Can I set up some kind of monthly remittance, or maybe every other month—"

"You won't owe me anything. You'll be able to walk away, no strings attached."

"There's no such thing as no strings attached," I tell him. "But we can figure out the details later. And then...if I stay with you...in this fake relationship. What will that look like?"

"The same as it does now," he says. "Same parameters. But only as long as you want it."

I nod. "Okay. I'll need some time to think about your offer."

His brows arch. I've surprised him. "Sure. Of course."

"I need to be alone now."

He collects his things and looks down at me for a moment. Then he presses the barest of a kiss to the top of my head and leaves.

I stay on the bed, curling into a ball around my pillow. As the tears fall, I try to remind myself that the most important thing is that I have survived. I try not to think about losing Rhys.

Why can't he acknowledge that he feels something for me? I can't be imagining the tenderness in his touch or the small ways he makes me feel important. There must be a reason why he won't give himself over to what's been slowly happening between us.

It will be very difficult to continue living with a man who can't love me.

27

IZABELA

ONCE I'VE PULLED myself together, I go into the bathroom and splash my face with cool water, then change into jeans and a sweater. My first instinct is to call my sister, but she doesn't know the truth about my life in America and I don't want to say anything that will cause concern. Obviously, I can't tell her that I will no longer be owned by my employer because my john is buying out my contract. In the end, I put my phone down. There's nobody I can talk to.

It's hard to believe how much naïveté was woven into my aspirations for coming to this country. I've grown up a lot in the time that I've been here. Now I know that fairy tales are just that, and if something sounds too good to be true, then it most definitely is. Which is why I'm wary of Rhys's proposal for me to remain here as a kept woman.

Not only that, but when I asked him what our new

"relationship" would be like, he said it would be the same as it is now. Meaning his life is his own, no business of mine, and that he can see any woman he wants, while I'm reserved exclusively for him. It's not enough for me.

Despite everything that I've been through, my dreams of having true love and family haven't died. I know to be smarter about things now, but I still want that for myself.

If I lock myself in with Rhys, I'll never have it. Maybe in time, he would come to acknowledge his feelings towards me. Or, maybe with time I would begin to understand that I'm only seeing what I want to see, and he really doesn't feel any affection towards me. That Diya was right, and I thought it was *Pretty Woman*. How much more of myself do I give while I wait to find out? How much more time do I allow him to consume?

All this speculation isn't helping. It's making me less and less certain of what I should do. I need certainties, not hopes and dreams. I need to talk to Rhys. I'll tell him exactly what I want—what I need—if we're going to move forward as a new fake couple. I'll set some boundaries. It's time I laid down some "parameters" of my own. He can take them or leave them. But if he does refuse to give me what I'm asking, then that will be an answer in and of itself.

If he says no, so do I.

My mind is made up. I'll ask Rhys for what I need, and I'll tell him that these things are nonnegotiable,

100% firm. He can decide if he's willing to meet me halfway.

First of all, we are equals in this partnership. He might be saving me, but I'm saving him, too. We treat each other with mutual respect, kindness, and consideration. And while we should both have personal, professional, and social freedom, this is not an open relationship, meaning no outside entanglements. No cheating, no sneaking around, no hooking up with ex-girlfriends.

Once I've settled on my requirements and they're firmly planted in my mind, I go downstairs to find Rhys. I assume he'll be in his office, working. That's usually where he is when he's home during the day.

My adrenaline spikes as I give a light knock on the door. He doesn't answer. I debate going back upstairs and waiting until later to talk to him, but this is urgent. I'm ready to figure this out now. Figure out our possible future together. I knock again, and then gently push the door open. He's not here.

But there's a coffee cup on his desk, still steaming, and his laptop is open. Papers are spread out everywhere. I'm sure he'll be back any second.

I feel confident about this. More certain of myself than I have in months. Regardless of the circumstances that initially threw me into Rhys's life, I know he's come to care for me. Even if he's reticent to admit his feelings. I've seen it in the way he looks at me, the way he holds me when we're in bed together. And those unguarded moments we've shared...at his mom's house or when he had me try Moroccan food for the first time, or at the opera...these experiences have been nothing short of magical.

I'm about to sit in one of the chairs by Rhys's desk when I see a bunch of papers lying messily on the floor. They must have fallen when he got up. Kneeling to gather them, I glance at the top few sheets so I can try to order them properly when I see the name Celine Lefevre.

A sick feeling unfurls in my gut. I skim the rest of the page and realize it's a lease agreement. For a penthouse in the city. Why would Rhys have a copy of this?

And then I see the signature line at the bottom. Celine Lefevre. Rhys McConnell. Side by side. They *cosigned* this. And Rhys paid a $5000 deposit. The date is from last week.

The papers tremble in my hands. I think I'm going to be sick.

How could I be so stupid? *Again?* I knew Rhys still had feelings for her, despite the fact that she'd married his father, and yet I didn't think he had some kind of arrangement in place? The man who thinks any problem can be solved with enough money? What if she's just one more of his "kept" women? There could be others I don't even know about.

It makes sense now. This is why he keeps himself closed off from me, why he won't acknowledge any feelings. All this time, he's been wanting a woman that was technically out of his reach. Something's changed and she's back now he's paid a large amount of money to set her up and luxury. For what purpose? So she's accessible to him anytime he pleases?

I think back to the rules he set down after he first bought me, and now I realize that they were all designed to enable this.

There's something my aunt always used to say, and it has never rung more true: When someone tells you who they are, believe them.

Any happiness that I had over my impending freedom comes crashing down.

Slowly rising, I set the pages of the lease on top of the desk and walk toward the office door, in a daze. It feels like I'm floating.

But then the door opens, and Rhys's smile drops as he takes in the look on my face.

"Izabela? What happened?"

I don't immediately respond. A part of me wants to handle this carefully, yet another part of me wants to tell him to go fuck himself.

Narrowing my eyes, I say, "I found the contract for the penthouse you and Celine are leasing."

I wait for him to say more, but he doesn't. Just like that the conversation is apparently over. He's not going to explain and maybe he shouldn't. He's not obligated to tell me anything. I mean about the same to him as a piece of furniture or pretty object to be sat on a shelf—

looked at, commented on now and then, used when the mood strikes, and then forgotten.

"Are you waiting for me to explain?" He finally says. "Is that why you're not saying anything?"

The slight accusation in his voice hurts me. If the roles were reversed, wouldn't he want me to explain? In fact the dynamics of our relationship demand that I would have to. That's it. It's becoming glaringly obvious that I cannot be in any kind of relationship with the power dynamic like this. It's just not right.

"Yes, I am. I was blindsided to find that you had secured a penthouse for your ex-lover. A woman you claim to have no feelings for anymore. Though, it's none of my business, right?"

"*Stop.* That lease, it's—it's not what it looks like."

A cruel laugh spills out of me. "Right. Just tell me one thing, and this time, don't lie. Are you really going to buy out my contract?"

He pauses, and I wonder if he's trying to come up with excuses, thinking of how to appease me. Instead, he says, "I'm already working on it. It should be finalized by the end of the day."

"Thank you. And I'll pay you back. I'll give you money every month. The last thing I want is to be in your debt. But a business deal is all that this is now. I guess it's all it ever was."

With that, I lift my chin and brush past him. But he grabs my arm and gently turns me to face him.

"Wait. Stop. Please." His voice drops. "Celine is

leaving my father, but he doesn't know it yet. I said I'd help her get settled. The apartment is temporary. It's just so she has a place to stay during the divorce, until she's able to take her share of their assets, that's all."

I pull my arm away from him, indignant. "How kind of you. And how convenient for her. But why would you go out of your way to help her if you don't still love her? If you don't want her back? This isn't a temporary apartment, it's your...your love nest."

He scoffs but there's no volume behind it. "She's pregnant with my *sibling*. It's my duty to help her for the sake of my brother or sister. I'm sure you understand loyalty to a sibling."

"How *dare you*," I seethe, my voice dangerously cold. "You don't have the first clue what I've been through for my sister, and you never will."

His expression turns stricken. "You're right. I shouldn't have said that. I'm sorry—"

"I'm done with this conversation. I don't have to listen to you anymore," I say, my body vibrating with anger and hurt. "You know what the hardest thing about all of this has been? The fact that you can't see me as an equal. You want me to be the pretty thing on your arm, to cater to your desires, your whims. To be your plaything. But that's all I'll ever be to you. You've never had a meaningful conversation with me about anything that's happening in your life."

"Maybe you don't love Celine, and maybe you are helping her for the sake of your sibling. But even if that's true, I can't trust any of the words coming out of your mouth, because you never breathed a word of this to me. You don't think enough of me to let me in on pieces of your life that will also affect mine."

"Izabela, wait—"

"No! I'm not going to wait. You don't get it, do you? For some unexplainable reason, I've fallen in love with you. I know you told me that if that were to ever happen that I'm required to keep it to myself. But I'm telling you just this one time so you fully understand why I refuse to be one of your Celines."

He's quiet again, but I hear his breathing go ragged.

"You're not one of my Celines. I don't have other women, Izabela. It's just you."

It hits me that I'm not the least bit interested in whatever he has to say next. I have reached a level of doneness that completely consumes me, strengthens my spine, and gives me the confidence I need to make a change. They always say when a woman is done, she's done.

"You're a bad liar," I hiss. "Once I walk out that door, I don't ever want to see you again."

My body courses with the feeling of a healing bruise that's been poked too many times. It hurts but it feels good. As I hurry to my bedroom and toss my minor things into a duffel bag, it heals a little more. Clothes, makeup. I have money in my purse.

Everything I truly need to get by is in the bag slung over my shoulder.

The one thing I don't need and wish more than anything that I could leave behind is the weight of my love for Rhys pressing down on me.

I hurry down the road and out of the estate; my body tense and my brain hyper aware as I expect someone to grab me and force me into a car and back to Rhys's townhouse. Worse, I wonder if Zoric will somehow know that I'm attempting to escape and have someone force me back into his clutches.

An hour or so later, I've powerwalked myself to near exhaustion. I'm at least three miles from Rhys's house, maybe more. I find the nearest cheap motel I can and check myself into a room. It isn't until I slide the chain lock on the door that it hits me: I'm free. No one bangs on my door. No one attempts to kick it in. No one calls my phone and threatens me to go back where I belong.

As darkness falls outside and my body becomes stiff from sitting tensely on the edge of the bed, waiting for something bad to happen, I finally begin to relax. I shower, change into sweatpants, order takeout delivery, which I eat in front of the TV news.

Rhys doesn't text or call. He actually let me go.

Double-checking the lock on the door, I decide I feel safe enough to curl up under the covers and close my eyes.

Tomorrow will be the first morning of the first day that I finally become my own woman.

I really am free.

28

RHYS

When I hear Izabela stomp down the stairs and walk out the door, walk right out of my life, I don't make a move to stop her. I just...let her go. It's better this way.

Who does she think she is, to confront me about Celine's apartment? As if it's any business of hers. She has no right. The terms of our agreement have been crystal clear since day one. I do what I want, take what I want, cosign leases with whomever I choose, and at the end of the day, I answer to no one. How dare Izabela snoop around in my office, then have the balls to question me about the private papers she found. And yet.

I can't deny the fact that everything she said about me was true.

No, I don't treat Izabela as an equal. Because honestly, no, I've never thought of her that way. She's a woman under my thumb who also somehow got under my skin. But considering how devastated I feel sitting here in the silence of this empty house, maybe it's time to admit to myself that she's also worked her way into my heart. That's the hardest pill to swallow.

So much has happened in the span of half a fucking day, starting with my father's attempt to blackmail me with the video of Izabela in Zoric's office, and the weight of it all is sitting squarely on my chest. It would be nice to take a breather and figure out my next move, but I don't have that luxury. Konstantin Zoric is still considering my offer to buy Izabela's freedom. Without a concrete answer from him, I can't feel settled or confident that things will turn out the way they need to. He could very well deny my offer and keep her prisoner. And then what?

As much as I'd love to threaten Zoric to get what I want, I know better than to try. It won't get me any closer to saving Izabela. The man is a criminal—a successful one. He got that way by being smart, ruthless, and showing no mercy. If I attempt to expose him or take him down, he'll destroy me and take my family's business down with him. All he has to do is throw my name to the media in the middle of this bloody mess and it will be game over for me.

And quite possibly for Izabela, too.

As if she hasn't lived through enough of a nightmare already.

How is it possible that even amidst Zoric's abuse, after surviving that goddamn illegal auction, all the while dealing with my bullshit to boot, she managed to find the strength to fight for her career, keep supporting her sister, and, against all reason, develop feelings for me?

She said that *she loves me*. That she's fallen in love with me.

I have never been knocked so far off-center as I was when she said those words. I still can't process them. Did she mean it, sincerely? Or is she just conflating appreciation with love? My offer to rescue her from Zoric could easily have confused her emotionally, made her think that she has feelings for me when in fact she really doesn't. It's probably just some passing infatuation. There's no way she really does love me. It's not possible.

But what if it is? What if she meant it, and I let her walk away?

No. I can't afford to think that way. She's just young, and inexperienced. She's over romanticized the situation. It would be foolish of both of us to pretend otherwise.

I grab the lease for Celine's apartment off my desk and run my fingers over it. Who'd have thought that a few sheets of paper could cause so much trouble? When Celine first approached me to ask for help escaping my father, my knee-jerk reaction was to tell her to go to hell. After everything that woman put me through, the absolute last thing I wanted to do was offer her a lifeline. But she begged. Not for herself, either. But for her unborn child.

"I just want what's best for this baby. Please. This is your little brother or sister, Rhys, please don't turn me away," she'd said, and I could hear the genuine tears in her voice coming over the cellphone connection.

Although I told her I'd have to think about it, my mind was already made up. That same night, I wrote a check for the deposit. The next day, I met her at a café downtown, gave her the check, and agreed to cosign on a place for a six-month term, until she got on her feet.

It never once crossed my mind to discuss any of it with Izabela. It might've made all the difference if I had.

Pushing away from my desk, I go down the hall and upstairs to her bedroom. She's gone, of course, but I feel her absence deeply. It's like a hollow in the middle of my chest.

The bed is made, and everything is neat and tidy. A few cardboard boxes sit in the closet, filled with clothes and shoes that she must have abandoned. Her laptop is gone, as well as her toiletries, all the necessary things. Everything she's left here is nothing that she needs now.

Including me.

Cursing softly, I sit on the edge of her bed. She's gone. She's really gone. I chased her away with my indifference and my disrespect, my utter lack of regard for her wants and needs. I treated her like nothing more than a plaything, an object I purchased for my own pleasure and refused to see as anything but. So yes, of course she left. And now I'll never see her again, unless it's on a billboard or in a magazine. I've lost her forever. And it's all my fault.

Panic constricts my chest.

I need her back. I need her here so I can function, and breathe, and my heart can beat properly. I need her here because...oh, fuck.

Because I love her, too.

Except she'd never believe me if I tried to tell her that. I have to prove myself first. I have to become the man she thought I was. The man who deserves her. And that's going to take time.

But I can start now, can't I?

Bursting from the bed, I run downstairs, dialing my driver as I go.

My grandfather never stays at work past six p.m., so I'm sweating bullets as my car weaves through traffic on its way to the McConnell Enterprises building. All I can think is, there's only one way to keep Reginald McConnell and his legacy out of this mess. I just have to hope I can pull this off and not bring down everything my grandfather has worked for.

When I rush into his office, his rheumy eyes go wide with surprise. It's 5:57 p.m.

"Rhys. What's the matter? Has something happened?"

I close the door and try to force the desperation

from my voice, even as I try to catch my breath. "Consider this my formal resignation, sir. I'm stepping down, effective immediately."

His expression doesn't change. He calmly gestures me to a chair, but I don't take it. Fixing my tie and smoothing my hair, I search the strong, deeply lined face I know so well. He's aged a lot in the last couple of years, getting incrementally slower and more easily tired as he inches his way toward retirement. Even so, he's been reluctant to give up his position as CEO, and I don't blame him. Perhaps he's afraid that once he steps down, his whole life will stop. His entire existence will be meaningless, reduced to long, empty days doing not much of anything.

It's exactly how I feel when I think about living my life without Izabela.

My grandfather holds out his hands placatingly. "Just slow down. Let's take a deep breath and talk this through. What's this all about?"

Spilling everything might be more distressing for him than it's worth. I'm afraid of how he'll look at me if I tell him the truth. And I'm ashamed to admit that I bought a woman for the sole purpose of having her at the beck and call of my dick, regardless of the feelings I may have developed for her along the way.

It's not that I think my grandpa is a prude about the ways in which men find their sexual pleasure, but this isn't one of his old cronies or work colleagues admitting to some kind of personal failure. I'm the Vice President, and his future heir. My actions have put McConnell Enterprises at risk.

And how can he not be disappointed in me? All these years, he's groomed me to take over his place in this company. I'm far from perfect, but the good parts of me are because of him. I couldn't bear the weight of his disapproval on top of losing Izabela.

"I've fallen in love," I say neutrally.

"So? That's no reason to walk away from your career," Reg says sensibly.

"It is, though." I sink into the chair he offered, struggling to come up with the best explanation for what's going on. "This woman...she's been trafficked. By her employer, who promised her a career and a future here in America. That career turned into sex work, which she entered into unwillingly. I didn't know all of this when I met her, but now that I do know, I can't, no, I *won't* back out. I intend to buy her freedom."

He stares at me for a moment, his eyebrows arching as he slowly leans back in his chair. "You are in a precarious situation."

"No, *we* are in a precarious situation," I say firmly. "All thanks to my father. He didn't mention the...extenuating circumstances...when he introduced me to this woman, even though he knew. Now, he's dangling a video recording over my head and threatening to take it to the press if I don't resign. And he's going to tell you that my relationship is going to ruin this company, and yes, that might very well be true. But Izabela has been my salvation, and I won't give her up. Not for the business, not for money, not for you, not for anything."

"I see."

"I'm ready and willing to resign," I say, meeting his gaze. "But not because I'm afraid of my father destroying me in the media. I'm not even sure he really will leak the video, to be honest. But if this whole thing does go public, I don't want to risk taking down McConnell Enterprises with me."

He doesn't say anything, his fingers steepled in front of him on the desk.

"Grandpa, I am so sorry that my actions have put you—put all of us—in this impossible situation. But I want you to know that I will do everything I can to protect you and the family legacy. That starts with distancing myself from the company, so the fallout will only hurt me."

Still nothing. A beat of silence passes. My pulse is pounding in my ears, my stomach clenching with nerves. Finally, he shakes his head and draws in a long breath. Here it comes.

"Rhys, dear boy. Did I ever tell you that my hair began turning gray the day after your grandmother died?"

His change of topic throws me. "Ah. No, sir."

"She was the only thing that kept me on a good path, when I could have taken so many other avenues. In some ways, she's more responsible for the success of

McConnell Enterprises than I am. Are you following, Rhys? True love is always salvation. I'd very much like to meet the woman who has captured your heart."

"I'm not sure you understand—"

"I do not accept your resignation; however, I would very much like to meet this woman who has captured your heart. You see, I chose you as my predecessor precisely *because* you always do the right thing, not the easy thing. And because you won't be influenced by profit alone. When I dream about the future of the company, I dream of you at the helm, maintaining our values even as you modernize our goals. So. If there is fallout, we'll handle it together."

My knees suddenly feel weak. "You're not serious. Grandpa—"

"I believe in you, my boy. I always have. Now, what would you say to us having dinner tomorrow night so I can meet this young lady?"

"Tomorrow...won't work," I say, faltering. "I'd love for you to meet her, eventually, of course, but...I need some time. See, the thing is, I've decided to—"

The office door pops open, and my father bustles into the room.

"Dad, we need to talk about...oh, Rhys! Goodness. I didn't mean to interrupt."

His eyes light up as he drinks in my disheveled appearance, the grave look on my grandfather's face. The tension in the room is palpable, but I'm sure he's interpreting it in all the wrong ways.

"Shall I just...step outside and let you finish quitting your job, son?" he gloats.

"No need." My grandfather gets up and comes around his desk, patting my shoulder as he passes me. "I've decided to promote Rhys to CEO, effective immediately."

"What?" Dad gasps, his face going pale. "But you can't do that! He's involved in a sex scandal! He's been dating a prostitute, a common whore!"

"How dare you," I thunder, rising from my chair.

My father goes on, "Jesus, Dad, I came here to warn you that shit is about to hit the fan! We have to call the lawyers, hire a PR firm, figure out how we're going to spin this! There's still time to do damage control, get a head start on—"

"Rhys and I have discussed the situation in full, and I have no interest in your thoughts on the matter," my grandpa says coldly. "Furthermore, I suggest you go pack up your office at once. Security will be here to escort you out momentarily."

"Me? What? Why?" Dad sputters.

"Because I'm finally doing something I should have done ages ago. You, Rupert, are officially fired."

IZABELA

It's been six weeks since I left Rhys. Nine weeks since he texted to inform me that Zoric had agreed to sell my contract, for an amount not specified. Nine weeks since I started my life over.

Thankfully, I've been so busy that I haven't had time to dwell on what I lost. Well, not during the day anyway. Nights are a different story altogether.

As soon as my passport was delivered to the motel where I was staying initially, I was able to check out and secure a long-term room rate at a nicer hotel in the theater district for less than it would cost to rent a studio apartment in this city. Since I pay weekly, it will be easy to pick up and move when an opportunity presents itself. For the moment, I'm happy enough with my new job, working for a boutique (aka fledgling) modeling agency as an event organizer.

One of their agents offered to represent me soon

after I started the organizing job, and I agreed—but I refused to sign any contracts. Thankfully, Mariella was amenable to a handshake agreement, whereby either of us can terminate our working relationship verbally, at any time, for any reason. It was the only kind of "contract" I felt comfortable with.

So far I've been offered a handful of bookings, but I had Mariella decline on my behalf each time. I told her it's not that I don't want to model ever again, but the dust is still settling around me after leaving KZM and I'm not quite ready to put my face back out there. As a former model herself, who left the industry to start a family, Mariella understands. I *really* like her.

Konstantin Zoric hasn't reached out to me, and Eva hasn't seen the mysterious man lurking around the house the last few weeks, but it would be foolish to assume that I'm completely free of Zoric and his influence. I try not to think about it, but at night, when the room is quiet, my mind conjures up all types of worries and what ifs. That's also when I think about Rhys.

"Izabela?" my walkie-talkie crackles. "They need you in the back."

I unclip the walkie off my belt and answer, "Thanks. I'm on my way."

A rush of adrenaline floods through me. It's almost showtime.

This isn't some glamorous, high-profile gig featuring yours truly, however. Instead, it's a tiny little runway show at the Oakbrook mall—the second biggest mall in Chicago—that I've spent the last month organizing, for a local designer whose spring collection will be featured in one of the department stores. It's low-level, sure, but I'm proud of the work I've done. My new agency knew that I didn't have experience producing runway shows, but I convinced them I could handle it, and I pulled from my experience as a model to design the set. Now, looking around at the basic black curtains and plywood stage and bright lights, I get a thrill knowing that I made all of this happen. And I did it on my own.

Before I duck backstage, I adjust the big urns of flowers that are set up on either side of the stage entrance. The models will walk over a long runner in between rows of chairs and then advance to the T-shaped stage, where they'll showcase their outfits. The stage faces the department store, of course, and the designer's name is printed on a glittery banner that hangs over the store's entryway. It was the best I could do with my budget.

As for my paychecks, the money isn't anywhere near what I made on the Idlewild campaign, but that's fine by me. What's important is that I don't have to fly back to Poland in disgrace, and I can still send most of my paychecks home to Eva. Plus, I'm doing what I want to do, and on my own terms. And I have an agent now, one who won't ever abuse me.

My freedom is worth the compromises I've had to make, and my current situation is just temporary anyway. Something bigger will come along. I just know it.

I've got my optimism back.

Two large offices in a utility hallway have been converted into dressing rooms for the models. The rooms are a flurry of chaos when I go there to check on everyone's progress. The show starts in less than an hour and some of the models are still in chairs getting their hair done. I smile at them, remembering myself chatting and gossiping there in the recent past.

It wasn't all bad.

And the next time I'm backstage with Diya, or Talia, or any of the other countless women I've walked next to, I hope we'll all be free.

A stage assistant hurries over. "Miss Jasinski! We're running behind schedule."

"No we're not," I say. "Not yet, anyway. What's left to do?"

I help models into their dresses, I touch up lipstick, I reset bobby pins supporting elaborate hairstyles. Spray hairspray, slick on glittery body oil, and find someone's left shoe. I lose myself in the busyness of it all, exhilarated more than stressed. This comes easy to me. It's different, being on the other side. I'm used to being handed off like a relay race baton between hairdressers, makeup artists, and wardrobe, but today I'm playing all three.

The models line up for a series of social media photos ten minutes before curtain call. I pull out my phone and snap a few pictures of my own, then send the best ones to my sister. I've tried calling her a couple of times the past few days but haven't gotten ahold of her—my uncle said she's been studying with friends, preparing for final exams. I know Eva will be excited about these photos when she sees them. She loves everything to do with beauty and glamour. I'm hit with nostalgia as I remember scouring stacks of women's fashion magazines with her.

One day, I'll bring her along to a show.

When I haven't gotten a response from her a few minutes later, I take a chance and dial her number. I'm not surprised when she doesn't pick up. I leave a message.

"Hey baby sis, it's me. I just sent you some pics. My very first show is about to kick off! Wish you were here. I'll send more photos soon. Love you and miss you so much. Bye."

I'm still fussing with last-minute details when the show begins. The seats fill up, the overhead lights dim, and curious passersby stop to watch. The designer goes onstage and gives her little introductory speech, and then the stage lights go up and the music begins to thump.

One by one, my models start to walk the runway. The crowd is quiet at first, but as the third model makes her debut, people begin to cheer. The sound shocks me. I can't say I've ever done a show to a cheering crowd, but apparently mall spectators take their fashion a bit less seriously than the audiences at Paris fashion week.

Clipboard in hand, I hover at the side of the stage. I'm hiding behind some giant potted plants, quietly monitoring my schedule as each of the girls takes her turn showing off her outfit. The designer presents each piece with a brief description and the crowd seems enthusiastic.

I let myself get caught up in the moment, riveted to each model, each outfit change, my pen making little check marks on my clipboard. It's all going off without a hitch, and I'm so proud of my whole crew. I'm peripherally aware as someone comes close and then stops to stand beside me. I don't look over my shoulder, though. I can't tear my eyes away from the show.

Finally, the last model makes her exit. The crowd begins to clap, and the designer comes back out and takes a bow with all the models who are lined up on the stage, then begins to read her acknowledgments and the closing credits off a sheet of paper.

"You're too good to be a department store model," a voice says.

The clipboard slips from my hands and clatters to the ground. I spin around, heat flushing my cheeks as my pulse jumps.

"What are you doing here, Rhys?" I ask.

He stands there in one of his perfectly tailored suits, looking cool and cocky and devastatingly hot. We take each other in for a second before he answers.

"Checking to see what kind of business my main model has gotten herself into."

Crossing my arms over my chest, I narrow my eyes, refusing to let his flirting affect me. "I'm not *your* model, and you don't have any say in my business."

"Not even for one night?" he asks, his voice dropping lower.

Jesus, my heart is beating fast. I wondered what it would feel like to see him again after all this time. Would I be happy, pissed off, a complete emotional mess? Yes, yes, and yes. And I don't even want to acknowledge the things that his voice is doing to me below the belt.

"No," I say coldly. "You can't buy me for a night anymore."

He moves closer. "I was hoping you might give it to me for free."

I give an incredulous laugh. "Wow, that takes nerve. Why the hell would I do that? Especially after all this time? It's been weeks since I heard from you."

Completely unmoved by my anger, he steps into me even more. The cut of his suit, the scent of his cologne, the confident smirk on his face... God, he's a walking orgasm and he knows it. He knows just how to get to me, and it's working.

"You needed time to miss me, Izabela."

"Bullshit."

He laughs, and it's infuriating how much I've missed the sound.

"I have a surprise for you," he says.

He turns toward the crowd. Most of the chairs are still filled as people continue watching the end of the show. I follow his line of vision. And suddenly I see... Rhys's mom. And sitting beside her is a dapper elderly gentleman who bears more than a passing resemblance to Rhys, and on her other side...it almost looks like...it can't be.

But it is.

Dark blonde hair, pulled high into a ponytail with a braid wrapped around the band. The periwinkle blue cardigan I gave her for Christmas last year.

It's my sister.

It can't be.

It really is.

Rhys waves my sister over and she stands up as my jaw drops in disbelief.

"Eva? How?"

Grinning from ear to ear, she hurries through the crowd and over to me. We dive into a hug, my sister squealing softly and bouncing up and down.

"I saw the whole show, Izzy! It was amazing!"

Taking her face between my hands, I stare down at her as if she can't possibly be real. My eyes sting with tears. "I can't believe you're here."

She nods excitedly. She looks happy, healthy, her eyes glowing. She's still thin, but not quite as much as when I left home.

"Rhys, did you tell her about the clinic?" she asks.

"No," he says. "But you can."

Confused, overwhelmed, and blinking back tears, I look between them. Rhys smiles and Eva hurries on. "Rhys got me an appointment with the best rheumatologist at Lurie Children's next week. It's one of the top ten pediatric cancer clinics in the U.S. People come from all over the world to see this doctor—she's incredible."

"Oh my God. Oh my God!"

I pull her into my arms again and squeeze as hard as I can. Locking eyes with Rhys over the top of my sister's head, I mouth, *thank you*.

"And Rhys said we can live at his house," she goes on, "at least for now, until you..."

Just then, the designer calls my name from up on the stage.

"Let's give a big hand for Izabela Jasinski, our producer and event coordinator!"

Eva pushes me toward the stairs and I make my way into the glare of the lights, still in a daze. The designer kisses my cheek and hands me a bouquet of flowers, then retreats behind the curtains. I step up to the microphone, preparing to say a few words of thanks, when suddenly Rhys runs up onto the stage, a mischievous glint in his eyes.

"Um. Hi?" I say, right into the mic.

The audience laughs. So does Rhys, and then he pulls something from behind his back. It looks like...a cupcake? With a candle in it? Eva hisses his name, motions him to the end of the stage, and lights the candle for him, eliciting more laughter. Then Rhys turns back to me.

One eyebrow arches in amusement when he sees the question on my face.

"It's my birthday candle. I want to make another wish," he says.

I laugh. "But—your birthday was months ago."

"The universe doesn't care, does it? Is there a time limit on wishes, or—"

"No! Make your wish."

He grins as he captures my gaze. "I wish for the woman I love—who I love more than anything—to come home."

He blows out the candle and then eases down on one knee, setting the cupcake aside. From his jacket, he pulls out a black velvet box. All the breath goes out of me.

Rhys cracks the box open, lifting it toward me so I can see the sparkling diamond ring inside. Not that I could have possibly mistaken it for anything else. The stone is huge, oval shaped, and flanked by two pale pink baguette-shaped side stones. It's the most beautiful ring I've ever seen.

"I know I've been out of touch the last couple months," Rhys says, "but the truth of it is, I spent that whole time working to make sure that all your dreams would come true. Because you deserve nothing less. That doesn't excuse all the mistakes I've made, and

God knows I should have treated you better, but if you'll give me the chance, I'd like to spend the rest of our lives making it up to you. Izabela Jasinski, of Zamość, Poland—will you marry me?"

I'm not sure if I say yes as I throw myself into his arms, but the ring slips onto my finger and the gathered crowd erupts in applause, cheers, and whistles. I think Rhys's mom cheers the loudest of all. Rhys lifts me up in his arms, spins me around, and then kisses me softly, searchingly, his lips searing hot on mine, my heart expanding like a rose in full bloom.

Maybe there's such a thing as happy endings, after all.

IZABELA

"She's going to want to get a dog, you know."

Softly closing the door to the guest room where Eva is sleeping, I smile as Rhys slips an arm around my shoulders and leads me down the long upstairs hallway, toward his room.

"Then we'll get a dog," Rhys says easily, like it's the simplest thing in the world. "Who doesn't love a new puppy?"

"Who *are* you?" I tease.

He kisses my temple. "A man in love."

Warmth surges through me. "Remember to tell Mrs. Dunham that when she has to help clean up after all the messes."

"I'll be glad to, *moja miłość*," he says. *My love.*

"What? Are you learning Polish now?" I gasp.

"A little. But only so I can woo you," he says with a smile.

"Keep going. It's working."

Walking into his room—our room—he closes the door and urges me forward, kissing the back of my neck as we unhurriedly make our way toward the bed.

It's been a long day. After the show at Oakbrook, we took Eva on a spontaneous tour of the city, had dinner at an adorable Polish restaurant called Staropolska in Logan Square so Eva could get her pierogi fix, then stopped at a bakery for cinnamon rolls and lattes. Then we strolled the Riverwalk, and Eva relayed how hard Rhys had worked to convince Uncle Julian to allow Eva to make the trip to the U.S. Despite Eva showing him the McConnell Enterprises *and* Rhys's personal Wikipedia pages, he refused to believe this wasn't some sort of elaborate plot to trick him until Rhys flew out and brought him aboard the private jet.

He and Aunt Sofia will be flying on it to visit next month.

I can't wait.

It feels good to be back in this house with Rhys... good, but different. Probably because I'm walking into it as a new woman. A free woman. One who has made the choice to be here with the man who loves me.

Maybe fairy tales do exist.

Rhys dims the lights and cups my face, looking into my eyes for a moment before kissing me. It's slow and deep, the kind of kiss that makes me tingle all over. Losing myself in the feel of his lips, the stroke of his tongue, I sigh happily as he unzips my dress, which falls to the floor in a whisper of silk. It's been too long since we've been together, and this is something I never thought I'd have again.

Giving in to my hunger, I kiss him harder, digging my fingers into his hair. He matches my pace as he unclasps my bra, which I pull off with trembling hands while he kisses his way over my throat, my collarbone, across my chest. His hands slide down my back, hot on my ass, pulling me against him so we're hip to hip. I can practically feel the throb of his cock through his pants, and I stroke my palm over the bulge in the fabric, making him groan.

"Izabela," he whispers over and over again between kisses, lighting tiny fires beneath my skin with every utterance.

I'm panting by the time he lowers me onto the bed in nothing but my thong, the crotch already soaked through.

"Why are you still dressed?" I ask, pouting out my lower lip.

"I won't be for long," he says, already unbuttoning his shirt.

In seconds, he's climbing over me on the bed, naked and perfect, closing his mouth over mine. Lost in the kiss, I run my hands over every inch of skin, every muscle and curve. Biceps, shoulders, jaw, pecs, ass. When I wrap my hand around his thick cock, both of us moan. God, I've missed this so much.

I start to pull off my underwear, but Rhys stops me with his hand.

"Lie back and relax," he says, rolling over to grab something from the nightstand.

Following his movements, I realize there's a cupcake sitting there and I laugh.

"Is that *dessert?*"

"You're the dessert," he says. "But I'll let you have a taste."

Picking up the cupcake, he licks a little frosting off the top and then kisses me again. A sweet, sugary bloom of pure vanilla fills my mouth.

"It's good," I tell him. "Give me more."

Instead of giving me a bite, Rhys turns the cupcake and swipes the frosting against my neck. Yelping in surprise, I laugh as he dips his head and licks away the sweetness, but when he starts sucking on my skin, my laughs quickly turn to moans. He frosts me again, this time on my collarbone. By the time he's done cleaning me up there, I'm a moaning mess, the pulse between my legs turning into a hot, demanding throb.

"Enough. I need you," I say, reaching for his cock again.

"Not yet. This is fun."

Dipping his finger into the icing, he swirls it over my left nipple and then covers the hard peak with his lips, his tongue, tugging gently with his teeth, making me writhe on the bed. When he's done, I lock eyes with him and tap my right nipple, letting him know I want more.

"Good girl," he murmurs.

Dabbing my skin with the frosting and following it with his hot mouth, Rhys works his way down to my lower belly. When he finally peels off my thong and pushes my thighs wide, I drag my own finger into the last bit of frosting left, and then swirl it over my clit. Gazing up at him, I relish the way his eyes darken with lust, with need, but also with...something more.

After setting the cupcake back on the nightstand, he dives between my legs. As he licks the frosting off me with long, slow laps of his tongue, drawing wails of pleasure out of me, he strokes his cock, the precum glistening on the tip. I'm mesmerized by the sight, even as I dig my fingers into his hair, grinding my pussy against his mouth. Watching him get off on getting me off proves to be too much.

"Rhys," I moan, and then I'm coming hard and fast, in blissful waves, his determined tongue thrusting deep into my hole, sending me higher and higher. "Rhys, fuck, yes, *yes*."

The euphoria takes my breath away, and I ride out the orgasm until it finally starts to fade, letting Rhys lick and suck every last drop of juice he can get out of me.

"I missed this," I sigh, scratching my nails against his scalp just the way he likes. "I missed you."

Crawling back up my body, he takes my lips for a

heated kiss. "Not as much as I missed you. Don't ever leave my bed again."

I wrap my legs around his waist, feeling his cock nudge against me, and then he slides right in, all the way to the hilt, until it feels like I can't take anymore. He stops right where he is, buried inside me. When my inner walls give him a squeeze, we both shudder.

"You know how good it feels for me when you come," he says. "Do it again."

He starts to thrust, the pattern of his breathing changing as my body tightens around him. I nuzzle his neck, my palms skating down his back, and then I grab his ass so I can control the pace, urging him even deeper inside me, faster, harder.

When our eyes lock, I see the love there before he even gives it voice.

"I love you, Izabela."

"Say it again," I whisper.

"I love you, I love you, I love you," he repeats, thrusting harder with every declaration, driving me right to the edge.

"I love you too, Rhys."

He drops his mouth onto mine, and I close my eyes, reveling in the feel of him stroking into me with everything he has, filling me completely. When we come, we come together. Looking into each other's eyes. Holding each other tightly. I could swear our souls connect.

Afterward, Rhys turns onto his side and pulls me back against him, curling his body protectively around mine. We lay there for a long time. His breathing evens out as if he's fallen asleep, but my mind is racing too much to do the same. Glancing down at my ring, I hold it against my heart and sigh contentedly.

"What's wrong?" his sleepy voice murmurs over my shoulder.

"Nothing. Just thinking about wedding planning. We have so much to do."

He groans.

"We have to choose a venue. Decide how many guests to invite. I have to pick a dress, and shoes. Eva needs a dress, too. Oh, and what about flowers? We'll need to find a catering company, of course, and choose a cake—"

"Can't forget the cake," he says. "That's the most important part."

Turning in his arms, I tap the tip of his nose. "What's your favorite kind of cake?"

"The one you made. Are you up for making a three-foot tall version?"

I laugh and he kisses me. Then his expression goes serious.

"We could elope. Go anywhere you want, anywhere in the world. No fuss, no drama. Just us, on the beach. Or in the mountains, or in the woods."

"And Eva, and the dog," I jest. "Don't forget the dog."

Rhys rolls over on top of me. He's hard again

already. "You owe me a few more orgasms if you think we're getting that dog."

"Sounds like a deal I'll have no problem closing," I say.

"Then you'd better get started."

Looping my arms around his neck, I smile up at him and sink into my fairy tale.

EPILOGUE

RHYS

"The intel you provided was very helpful, Mr. McConnell. We've opened a formal investigation into Zoric personally, as well as his agency."

Having a phone call with the FBI wasn't on our wedding planning list for today, but when the feds call, you answer.

Izabela, Eva, and the wedding planner are discussing the pros and cons of a table full of bite-sized cake samples across the room. Nobody batted an eye when I apologized and stepped away to take the call, and now I'm relieved that Izabela didn't try to follow me. I don't want anything to disrupt the fun she's been having with her sister trying to pull this wedding together.

Incidentally, the venue Izabela chose is the Lyric Opera House. I agreed immediately, of course. It's a stunning space, and I'm sure the wedding will be beautiful, but the truth is, I don't actually care where we get married. I just want to make her mine.

"That's good to hear, Agent Chase," I say, turning my thoughts back to the call. I appreciate you looking into this."

"Don't thank me yet," he says. "Given how slow the criminal justice system in this country moves, it'll be a while before the ball starts rolling. Not to mention, this kind of case won't come together overnight. It needs to be built, brick by incriminating brick. Hell, it'll probably be years before we bring this guy down."

He's right. But the thought of Zoric behind bars someday is reward enough for now.

"Let me know if there's anything else I can do," I tell him.

"Will do. Believe me, I'm making this thing a priority. This is the kind of case that makes a career, and all personal ambitions aside, I don't sleep well knowing there's scum like this operating without consequence."

"You and me both."

Izabela looks over and tilts her head questioningly. I force a reassuring smile and hold up one finger, signaling that my call is almost over.

"...we'll be busting our asses to gather all the appropriate hard evidence so he can't weasel out of the charges in court," Agent Chase is saying. "We've got to be strategic. Which is why I'm asking you to use utmost discretion going forward. You mention any of this to anybody, the other side could get wind of this, which could give Zoric time to clean up after himself."

"You can trust me. I won't do anything to compromise the investigation."

"Appreciate that."

We hang up, and for a moment I just watch Izabela and her sister chatter excitedly over the cake samples. I can't quite make out what they're saying—though I can tell it's in Polish—but I can guess that Eva is trying to prepare my future wife for the classic wedding cake-feeding ritual as she holds out a forkful of cake to Izabela and then smears the frosting on her cheek instead. Izabela shrieks with delight and I find myself laughing along with them.

Since Eva's medical issues are being treated at the hospital here in Chicago, Izabela's family thought it would be best if she got a student visa and moved here more permanently. She'll be living with Izabela and me for the next few years, with her college plans still undecided. Everyone is thrilled with the arrangement, including their aunt and uncle, who have been supportive ever since I first reached out to them.

I love seeing my fiancée light up every time her sister walks into the room. Ever since Eva arrived, I've gotten to see a whole new side of Izabela. She's not just happier, she's more playful, more at ease. I'll do anything I can to help keep her that way.

As I walk back over to the table, I lock eyes with Izabela. Judging by the way her cheeks flush, I'd bet my life that we're both thinking of the same thing: the last time she had frosting all over her body.

"How's the tasting coming along?" I ask. "Any top contenders?"

"I don't think we've narrowed it down at all," Eva says with a giggle.

"Definitely not," Izabela agrees. "They're all good. Great, in fact."

"They can also create something custom," the wedding planner adds.

"In that case, let's see if they can whip up something that looks like the Carpathian mountains," I say.

Eva gasps and play-swats her sister's arm. "You made him *karpatka*? That's *my* favorite cake!"

"It's everyone's favorite cake," Izabela says.

"It was the best cake I've ever eaten," I say. "Not sure this bakery can hold a candle to Izabela's skills, but I'd be interested to find out."

"Let me go talk to the manager and see how long it will take the bakery to prepare a custom selection for you. Hopefully within the next few days? If you'll excuse me for a moment," the wedding planner says.

Eva pops out of her seat. "I'll go with you. I need to make sure they know exactly how the Jasinskis make that cake," she says, and they both bustle away.

I drop back into my chair and take a few bites of cake, catching up to where Izabela and Eva left off in their sampling efforts. Each slice has a card next to it that details the ingredients, with a few blank lines at the bottom for comments. I see a lot of hearts and happy faces from the girls so far. I don't add anything to the cards myself.

"Well?" Izabela says. "Any top contenders?"

"Nope. I'm holding out for the *karpatka*. You've ruined me for all other cakes."

With that, I pull her into my lap to kiss her.

"Do you believe in fairy tales?" I ask.

"Honestly? I really do."

She smiles, and I can feel my whole chest expand.

"Good." I look into her eyes and then kiss her again. "Because we're about to live happily ever after."

Ready for a world of delicious alphas, arranged marriages, marriages of convenience, friends-to-lovers, second chances with high angst, steam, and untraditional love stories? Meet the Zorics, a trio of siblings, who are trying to cut ties to the mob and rebuild the family business.

The saga begins with **The Deal**.

On my eighteenth birthday my father, the senator, gives me the gift he thinks every little girl dreams of.

The man of my dreams, and the wedding to match.

Stefan Zoric is heir to an elite worldwide modeling agency.
Practically a prince.

My arrangement is simple, as far as sham marriages go.

I give him my virginity, behave as the perfect wife and he'll pay for the college degree my father found irrelevant.

But I don't want to be the perfect wife.

I want him to want me the way I want him.

I want him to confide in me.

But Stefan has secrets that he holds close, dangerous secrets.

And soon I'm wondering what kind of devil have I made a deal with?

————

Get **The Deal**!

PAIGE PRESS

Paige Press isn't just Laurelin Paige anymore...

Laurelin Paige has expanded her publishing company to bring readers even more hot romances.

Sign up for our newsletter to get the latest news about our releases and receive a free book from one of our amazing authors:

Laurelin Paige
Stella Gray
CD Reiss
Jenna Scott
Raven Jayne
JD Hawkins
Poppy Dunne

Lia Hunt
Sadie Black

ALSO BY STELLA GRAY

The Charade Series: Books 1-3

The Bellanti Brothers

Unwilling Bride: A Bellanti Brothers Novella

Dante - Broken Series

Broken Bride

Broken Vow

Broken Trust

Marco - Forbidden Series

Forbidden Bride

Forbidden War

Forbidden Love

Armani - Captive Series

Captive Bride

Captive Rival

Captive Heart

ABOUT THE AUTHOR

Stella Gray is an emerging author of contemporary romance. When she is not writing, Stella loves to read, hike, knit and cuddle with her greyhound.

75076351R00215